# TRAVELLERS

## Books by Roger Taylor

*The Call of the Sword*
*The Fall of Fyorlund*
*The Waking of Orthlund*
*Into Narsindal*
*Dream Finder*
*Farnor*
*Valderen*
*Whistler*
*Ibryen*
*Arash-Felloren*
*Caddoran*
*The Return of the Sword*
*The Keep*
*Travellers*
*Newman*
*Aikido–more than a martial art*

# TRAVELLERS

Roger Taylor

*Published by*
**Bladud Books**

First published in Great Britain in 2020 by Bladud Books

This paperback edition published in 2020 by Bladud Books, an imprint of Mushroom Publishing, Bath, BA1 4EB, United Kingdom

www.bladudbooks.com

ISBN 978-1-84319-967-0

# Chapter 1

Poor old tub, thought Taithur, gently placing a hand on the emergency patch that had been fastened to the hull amid screaming and turmoil, so long ago, in the early days of their journey. The metal plate with its scars and indentations was so familiar that he tended not to notice it. But now, in the quiet artificial shipnight, with most of the systems on automatic, and most of the travellers asleep, he found himself reflective.

You belong to both ends of the journey, don't you? he thought. It's fitting you should remind me what pains we had at the beginning, now we're nearing our destination.

The image of Konrad returned sharply. Konrad, hurling children and crew members out of the connecting passage and activating the emergency doors as air screamed out into space through the Irm hole. Konrad struggling alone with the patching rig, a two-man job at the best of times and never intended for use in these circumstances—ships were meant to be Irm-free when they left port, weren't they? And finally, Konrad dying as the weldcutter slipped and slashed through his emsuit releasing its small quantity of oxygen into the freezing near vacuum.

Taithur screwed up his face at the bitter ironies of Konrad's death. Many a young tech had brought Konrad's anger down on himself by working in an emsuit.

"I know they're easier to put on and easier to move in."

Pause, and a heavenward glance as if for patience to deal with such foolish souls, then a crescendo.

"They're also easier to die in. No autoseal, no atmos backup. And they're made of fabric as tenuous as that which you laughingly refer to as your intelligence." Tap on the head. "You'll have seconds after you stick your little pinkie through that glove, and the most amazing things will happen to you." Then, finally, nose to cringing nose, a blow by blow account of the process of cleaning out an exploded corpse from an emsuit. The usually green-faced offender would then be sent to the kitchens for a span, with orders to the cook that he work in full deep-space kit.

The combination of Konrad's ferocity, the Cook's surly contempt at having, "This walking junk pile," clumping about his kitchens, and the mirth of his peers usually had the desired effect, and offences were rarely repeated.

But Konrad did not heed his own teachings when the Irm had taken flight—he had sealed himself into the corridor, thrown on an emsuit and tackled the hole single-handedly, as if he were dealing with just another prayer-meet brawler—"Lock the doors behind them, and we'll see how brave they are then."

Taithur wondered, as he had many times before, why Konrad had been so reckless. Had he in fact decided, unconsciously, to die rather than face the unknowns into which they were travelling? It didn't seem likely. Konrad was impulsive but not irresponsible, and he certainly wasn't without courage; all kinds of courage, as he had often demonstrated in the many trials they had faced as they battled for the right to practice their religion and to make this voyage.

Taithur patted the patch and turned away. No point pursuing the matter. It could never be answered. And even if it could, it would tell him little. But the thought niggled, refusing to leave him. It was probably no more than a misjudgement. A flutter of panic and desperation brought on by the presence of the children passing on their way from class, when the Irm entered that last, explosive phase of its life and departed the ship propelled by its own gases and the escaping atmosphere.

They had found six more Irm in the subsequent sweep, almost all of them situated where catastrophe could have followed their leaving.

Debate theology how you will, thought Taithur. If there was a devil, the Irm was his invention.

He paused for a moment opposite a viewport and stared out at the uncaring darkness.

Great God, this is an awful place.

The phrase came to him from his own inner darkness and rang in

2

his head. It was both strange and familiar, like some old memory, and it had a poignancy that disturbed him deeply. For a moment it seemed to him that it was one of the brief snatches of coherence decoded by the analysers as they monitored the ceaseless electromagnetic jabber from their destination planet. Odd, disjointed phrases like that burst out occasionally as the machines identified some pattern.

He dismissed the thought as he looked again at the galaxy. So far away. Just a white gauze strewn negligently across the blackness.

An awful place.

So few stars here!

Even though he could see it, he found it hard to grasp such emptiness, such barrenness.

What were they heading for?

What was he leading them to?

Would it all end in bitter failure, with their slow dying on an alien and hostile rock, an interminable distance from home and any form of succour?

He rested his forehead on the cold viewport and let the gloomy forebodings pass through his mind and return to his inner darkness.

A soft, bell-like reverberation sounded through the corridor, coinciding with his own diagnosis. Midwatch. He smiled. Everything at its lowest ebb. That's the time when all the doubts could venture out to torment him.

"Don't fear your doubts, Taithur. Have faith," his father used to tell him. "The Lord gives them to you so that you can test yourself... make yourself strong. Try to crush them at your peril." Then he would pause and chuckle. "Mind you. Don't encourage them just for the sake of a fight."

No need to encourage doubts here though. They were ever-present. But it made no difference. Doubts now were the lingering shadows of earlier debates. Whatever happened, there was only one decision that could be made.

Move forward.

There was no retreat. Not only was it physically impossible in this ship, but their own kind had set their face against them. Perhaps, sometime in the future, a new order might prevail, and they, or their descendants, could return to live their lives and practice their religion in peace. But now...

He twisted his fingers together and stretched his arms in front of him until his fingers glowed in protest. Move forward, he thought. It had a comforting inexorability to it. It cut through speculation ruthlessly, honing it down to various forms of contingency planning.

Moving out of the short passageway he gingerly negotiated the shaky steps down into the main perimeter corridor. To his right, the corridor was sealed, closing off an entire segment of the ship that had been damaged by radiation from an irregularity in the main gravity silo grid.

Like the patch, the jury-rigged sealing with its ominous warning signs was another reminder of the quality of their vessel.

Poor old tub, he thought again. It's not your fault is it? You were old when we bought you. Entitled to a leisurely retirement, not wild hops across the Darvod-hunt contours into the uncharted reaches of the Galaxy.

He pulled a wry face. Thinking about the ship always brought conflicting emotions to the surface. Sadness at the ignorance and intolerance that had forced them to flee their homes. Bitterness at the price they had had to pay for the Rithid because of their beleaguered circumstances. But worst of all, a deep abiding anger at the callous indifference of the Service's Ship Factors who had covered up the Irm trace and blithely falsified the gravity silo certificate, knowing that either could imperil the ship without warning.

Taithur had a strong sympathy for some of the tenets of older religions, particularly those about vengeance, and it galled him that he would not be able to return and confront those individuals forcefully with their perfidy. Strangely, it had been Konrad—Konrad the fighter—who had dissuaded him from sending back a biting message of intent after their first problem with the silo.

"Leave it, Taith. Leave it. Let go. Better they think we're dead or lost in Darvod-hunt. We're still well within range of the Fleet, and it won't make life easier for those we've left behind."

It was sound advice, and Taithur had taken it, albeit with not too good a grace.

But with these thoughts came those that told him it was the very condition of the ship that had brought the travellers into a closer communion with one another. The need to pull together and fight against a common peril had broken down most of the remaining hierarchical restraints that kept each to his own niche in the ordering of all their affairs.

The Way is beyond our understanding, he reminded himself. The great bureaucratic tyranny that had formed their very thinking since birth had, in its last act of malevolence, brought to many of them an inner understanding of their own faith that no amount of debating and discussing could have achieved. The thought tempered his anger, though he still fantasized about appropriate destinies for the Factors from time to time.

Bending down he picked up a small ball and put it in his pocket. Kids!

"Taith." A soft voice echoed round the corridor. Taithur recognized it as the Captain's despite the clipped distortion of the individual frequency transmission. He smiled. It was strange the way people spoke quietly when using the IFT at night even though it could only be heard by the intended recipient no matter how loudly the sender spoke. We carry ancient courtesies with us, he thought.

"Captain," he acknowledged, equally softly.

"Taith, I saw you on the prowl. If you've the time, I'd like to talk. I think we've got problems ahead that I'd rather go through quietly before we come to Council."

"Anything new from the monitoring?" asked Taithur.

There was a pause, then an uncertain, "Yes and no. It's... Come on up, we need to talk."

Taithur turned the child's ball over in his pocket.

"Where are you?" he said. "I'll come immediately."

# Chapter 2

Captain Trasant Ersand removed the monitoring visor and laid it gently on the console in front of him. After-images still lingered and he rubbed his eyes to dispel them. His hands felt cool against his face which was flushed through contact with the visor and, covering his face entirely, he leaned back and relaxed into his chair, feeling its stress relievers adjust automatically to ease the tension in his stiff frame.

Well, at least something still works around here, he thought ruefully, and almost involuntarily he opened one eye and looked across at the damage control screen. The burden of its content weighed heavily on him and, hearing his chair's stress relief circuits starting to whirr anxiously, he stood up. No point gratuitously overloading the thing, it does its best, and the repair gangs had taken no small effort to keep it in good order for him, even though there were more important things to be dealt with.

Far more important things, he reflected, as he looked again at the damage control screen. It was a constant reminder of their condition. He had had it enlarged and left on permanent full display after they had survived the last Darvod-hunt incline.

"There'll be no returning that way," a grim-faced Matthew had told him. "All the Rithid's fit for now is planet hopping—perhaps nursery slopes to local systems—but no more."

"It is the nature of the Way," Taithur had said when Ersand told him. There were times then when Taithur's faith irritated the Captain, and it was with some difficulty that he kept his temper.

"We're effectively stranded Taith," he said angrily to the younger man. "Stranded in the Wastes. Farther out than anyone else has ever been, as

7

far as we know. I'd value a little less fatalism. Everything's going to be one continuous fight now, more even than before. We're going to need every personal and technical resource we can muster, and I don't want anyone sitting back waiting for his problems to be sorted out by divine intervention. If you must invoke the Way, then you can pray that rock we're heading towards is habitable."

Taithur bridled at this response, but Ersand met his stern gaze squarely and pointed towards a viewport. Through it could be seen the thin scattering of stars that was so typical of this bare, empty region. Taithur followed the extended arm and then, turning back, lowered his gaze and, unusually, raised his hands in a placatory gesture.

"I will, Ersand." he said softly. "I will."

At the next prayer-meet he had delivered a thoughtful sermon on the great gift of free will, and how it was the duty of each person to travel the Way with awareness and to make the very best of whatever befell him.

The memory of the incident made Ersand smile as he turned away from the damage control screen. Taithur's integrity, with its blend of sincere faith and hard-nosed pragmatism, made him irresistible.

A soft, two-note hum signalled the opening and closing of the door into the ship's control centre. Ersand turned towards the sound.

"Think of the devil," he said.

Taithur cocked his head on one side and raised an eyebrow in mild reproach.

Ersand's smile broadened and he indicated his chair. It was an old ritual between them. Taithur never took the Captain's seat, for all the comfort it offered, and for all his status as head of the expedition. He sat, as usual, in the daywatchman's chair. A chair with negative stress relievers that were activated if the concentration of the occupant wavered unacceptably.

"Where do we start?" he asked bluntly after a moment. Ersand settled back down into his own chair and made a vague gesture.

"I don't know," he said. "But we have to talk. A few gentle D-h hops and we'll be in the system. There'll be too much activity then for prolonged debate."

Taithur nodded. "We can't make any detailed plans—landing sites, settlement areas—we're too far away…"

"And we haven't the equipment for a proper survey anyway." Ersand finished the sentence. It had been a minor source of irritation between the two men from the beginning, that equipment had been pared down too much for the sake of squeezing in more travellers.

Taithur waved the remark aside. "We've been through that," he said. "That's not what's bothering you. Has something developed out of the monitoring?"

Ersand shook his head unconvincingly. "No," he said. "Nothing specific."

Taithur stared at him narrowly.

They had left their home system in a welter of relief and blind faith and their trajectory had been determined as much by folk history as by calculation.

"In the outer reaches of that sector of the galaxy there are countless planets waiting to be discovered. Rich and bountiful planets where people can live free and unburdened, where people can determine their own destinies." So went the tales persistently through the years, dismissed by scientists and ignored by politicians and bureaucrats.

Blatantly, the travellers had cited this idea in their negotiations with the Service, and equally blatantly the Service had affected serious consideration of it before allowing them their Exploration Charter. What the Service really thought, no-one knew.

One piece of equipment that had not been pared to the minimum was that used for long-range scanning. In fact it was the most sophisticated then available and had cost them dear. Once well away from their system, the travellers had linked this to the navigation data fields and given the Rithid its head. It had been a genuine act of faith that had carried them well beyond the inner systems of the galaxy.

Working from a basic premise that as much distance as possible was to be put between the travellers and their old homes, the Rithid had nosed out into the unmarked areas of the galaxy like a hunting dog after a faint scent. However, it had proved to be a testing time as target after target had been located, approached for a little while, and then rejected. Taithur's faith in the Way had barely wavered, nor had Ersand's in Taithur, but it was only the steadfastness of these two men that held the group together through the long bleak light years of their journey.

Eventually, when it seemed that even Taithur must be plunged into uncertainty, the Rithid located and confirmed a star with a suitable planet.

"It's so far away," said Taithur's wife fearfully. But Taithur had reached and passed his lowest ebb.

"No, Malva," he said. "It's a beacon in a lonely wilderness. We're travelling home now. This is where we have to go. This is where we'll build a free world for our children, away from all the intolerance and oppression."

And now they were nearly there. The star was actually visible, and since their last Darvod-hunt hop they had been receiving electromagnetic radiation from the system. A jangle of transmissions which were obviously artificial, but which seemed to be wildly incoherent.

"If there's nothing specific," continued Taithur, "then what is bothering you in general?" He laid a mocking emphasis on the last two words and Ersand was obliged to smile. Spit it out, was what Taithur was telling him, spit it out.

"I'm sorry, Taith," he said. "I'm not normally so vague, but I've an unhappy feeling about this place."

Taithur's face showed a mixture of sympathy and impatience, and Ersand turned away from it.

"There's some kind of civilization in this system, Taith. The analysers are beginning to put together the bones of what seems to be a dominant language, and…" He paused.

Taithur waited. "And?" he offered after an uncomfortable pause.

Ersand cleared his throat. "And, insofar as it makes any sense at all, it's looking bad. It's mainly a gut reaction on my part, but I feel this system is a dangerous place."

Taithur looked at the Captain thoughtfully. "We're still a long way away, Ers. The signals are very weak and distorted. And, as you're so fond of pointing out, our equipment is rather… er… basic, isn't it? Is it really a time for coming to that kind of conclusion?"

Ersand placed his elbows on the arms of his chair and rested his chin on his interlinked fingers. "It's not a conclusion, Taith," he said. "It's nothing that solid. You're quite right. There isn't enough data to form even a preliminary conjecture—the computer keeps telling me that. But I've travelled too many space miles not to listen to my instinct when it plays up like this."

"Why are you telling me this now?" asked Taithur. "You're the expert. There's nothing I can help with. We'll just have to wait and see."

Ersand sighed and looked slightly embarrassed. "I'm telling you now because I'm following my instinct, and it said—discuss it—discuss it with Taithur."

Taithur accepted his friend's unease. Ersand's need to talk was apparent, and at worst it was a simple act of kindness to allow him to do so. Then, of course, the Way was strange. Who knew what hidden guidance might make itself felt.

"All right." he said. "Let's talk. Let's conjecture. Let's assume this system is inhabited—and inhabited by some dangerous species. We'll have their language worked out fully by the time we arrive, so we can tell them we don't mean them any harm, can't we? They can only be some primitive sub-culture. What else could have developed in a wilderness like this?"

Ersand looked uncertain. A light came into Taithur's eyes and he poked a finger forward. "Good grief. We've survived persecutions and treachery. We've survived Irm blows, gravity silo leaks, D-h distortion fevers… all manner of hazards—mental and physical." He waved his hand extravagantly, then the light in his eyes darkened. "And if the worst comes to the worst. How can they harm us? How can some fringe galactic primitives harm us? We're not Adjustment Troops and the Rithid's no Fleet ship, but we have enough weapons to defend ourselves if provoked, haven't we? Though God forbid we should need to."

Ersand nodded. "That's true enough. And if there'd been a civilization of any worth in the system, they'd have spotted us long ago and been out to greet us, one way or the other."

"Exactly," said Taithur. "Primitives. I'm sure we'll be able to deal peaceably with them. I'm sure we haven't come all this way just to slaughter innocents. Who knows, maybe all our trials and suffering have been just to bring us here, to bring a light to this corner of the galaxy."

Ersand smiled and dropped his hands onto the arms of his chair. The younger man's enthusiasm was infectious, and the shadow of discontent that seemed to have grown round him of late, faded. "You're right Taith," he said. "Too many hours looking out into this emptiness. It's probably incipient agoraphobia. Either that or I'm turning into an old woman."

Unexpectedly, Taithur leaned forward, his face serious. "No, no,

11

Ersand." he said intently. "Never. Only a fool doesn't listen to his inner voices. I trust yours more perhaps than you do. They've helped you keep us safe through some fearsome dangers. Keep listening to those transmissions, and keep the analysers busy on them."

He stood up, his face thoughtful, as if he had just felt the shadow that had left Ersand.

Ersand caught the change in mood. "What's the matter?" he asked, also standing.

Taithur kept his gaze down as he replied. "Konrad always used to say 'Put your faith in the Way, but keep your weapon hand free.'" He moved over to the main viewport. "And he armed us accordingly. I really didn't find out what he'd done until it was too late—as you know." He gazed out at the few points of light ahead. "Don't doubt your heart, Ers. Just by our brief talk, we've raised a spectre that we couldn't afford to have come on unawares. I must think—and pray for guidance."

"I don't understand," said Ersand. "Don't let my worries bother you, they're just an old space-hand's fidgets. You've got enough to do. I wouldn't have spoken if I'd known it was going to distress you."

Taithur smiled. "I'm not distressed, Ers, but our future options are limited. We can't go back. The long-range scanners are keeping us moving towards this system, and they haven't found anything new since we first detected it. We go forward no matter what we find. Forward, Ersand, if we're to survive. Forward into armed conflict if we have to." He paused for a long moment. "It never once occurred to me that that might happen. Konrad armed us secretly for protection against our own kind, but I don't think even he had considered having to fight for our new home." He breathed out noisily. "I'll have to think. We have to determine how we'll conduct ourselves if that eventuality arises. We must guard against becoming like those we're fleeing from, mustn't we?"

# Chapter 3

The final approach to the planet was slow and cautious. Ersand insisted that the Rithid be on status four Battle Alert, although no-one seriously expected an assault from the natives of the bright little disc that dominated all the viewing screens throughout the ship.

The monitoring of transmissions made it obvious that they had not been seen, and from what could be deduced about the primitive technology of the planet it was unlikely that they would be.

Battle alert under these circumstances ironically made everyone feel easier. Everyone had a specific task requiring their full attention, and the tensions caused by the debates and discussions of the last few weeks lay dormant in the face of simple necessity. The atmosphere on the ship was predominantly one of anticipation.

"It might be in a desolate place, but it's a beautiful system," someone had said as the Rithid nosed quietly past the large outer planets. "And almost perfect for us."

"An oasis in the wilderness," Taithur had replied. "Our finding it is a vindication of our faith."

The remark returned to Taithur's mind as he stood by Ersand in front of the control centre's main viewport. It took him back into the arguments that had flowed to and fro across the Council meetings.

Although it had been greatly reduced during the voyage, there still persisted among the travellers a deep-seated tendency for each to scoop out an individual niche and defend it, regardless of wider considerations. At times it had angered Taithur profoundly, and during a recent Council meeting he had said so volubly, unashamedly using the esteem he was held in to dominate the others.

"No," he roared, slamming his fist down on the table and then, equally abruptly, cancelling the image floating above the table.

"For heaven's sake. Why are we here? What in God's name are we doing here, at the fringes of the galaxy?" He looked round the table. There was no reply. One or two looked rather indignant, and one or two looked relieved at this welcome interruption, but the majority avoided his gaze.

"We're here because we wanted to be free. Free of a tyranny that spread across thousands of systems. Free of a mindless, uncontrollable bureaucracy so massive and powerful that it reduced elected Governments to mere cyphers centuries ago. We must all serve the Service. The Service knows all. The Service works for the greater good. Remember all those handy little slogans we used to use instead of actually thinking—and the corruption we needed to get from day to day—and the injustice…" His mouth twisted angrily, and he paused for a moment to compose his features. "And now we're bringing it with us. That rigidity. That blind following of rule and rote." His voice rose again, and he stood up. "That same asinine stupidity."

There was an awkward silence around the table. No-one was anxious to risk speaking until they were certain that Taithur's passion was well and truly spent.

He sat down wearily and put his hands to his face.

"I'm sorry," he said, though his voice lacked even a hint of regret. "But we carry many of our old ways with us, and we must beware of them."

"Old habits die hard, Taith," said Matten, one of the older travellers. "We've all been brought up in the way of the Service, and even when we learned better we had to live that way to survive." He looked down and idly picked at a callous on the edge of his finger. "And our freedom's brought unexpected burdens with it, hasn't it?"

A contemptuous snort forestalled Taithur's reply. Matten looked up angrily. "Proktor…" he began.

"Leave it Matten," Taithur interrupted quickly, catching the older man's eye with a look of reassurance. Then, sternly, to the offender. "Proktor. You've used your gifts well so far, and you've a great deal to offer in the future. But your intolerance will make you as bigoted and narrow as the meanest Service Hewer…"

Proktor's eyes blazed, but he could not outface Taithur.

14

"You're ten years my junior, Proktor. If you'll take some advice I suggest you learn to listen to what people are really saying. Matten's right—he usually is. He's not as talkative as some but what he says is usually worth more." One or two round the table cleared their throats. "We've won our freedom, but we've lost the shelter of Service, claustrophobic though it was, and that's presented problems for some of us more than others. We've all found that freedom has its own constraints, not the least being responsibility."

Proktor opened his mouth, but Taithur waved him down. "No Proktor, I'm not debating with you. Not now. We've more urgent matters to deal with. I just want to remind you that your planet was a minor agricultural outpost and well off-centre, and yet the Service there was bad enough to make you want to risk this venture. You've no idea what it was like on the inner systems. You've no idea what it did to people. What they had to do to survive. The telling of it doesn't put it into your stomach. Just accept that and think before you lay into someone with that quick tongue of yours."

Taithur softened his tone for the last few sentences to defuse Proktor's anger. He may not be an easy man to like, but he was valuable and energetic, and there was no benefit to be gained from needlessly antagonizing him. In the same spirit he made a slight movement with his left hand to silence the murmurs of approval for this reprimand, and then called up a file to indicate the meeting should return to its original purpose.

The image of the target planet returned to hover briefly over the centre of the table and was replaced almost immediately by a series of moving, though disjointed, images.

"There you have it, my friends," said Taithur, leaning back in his chair. "Odd scraps of landscapes and pictures of the natives going about their daily lives. Or at least their chiefs… leaders… what you will. I'm afraid the projection quality is, as usual, not too good as we're intercepting their surface broadcasts, but I think it's important we keep them in front of us. It's too easy to forget what, or who, we're dealing with. Now, let's try and formulate some kind of policy about how we deal with these people."

The images at the centre of the table flickered and changed as Taithur looked round from face to face expectantly, but no-one spoke. The fact was, that although they had now each mastered the dominant language of the planet and had learned a great deal about the natives from the intercepted broadcasts, there was still a great deal they did not understand. Such as they did understand, and such information as they could reasonably deduce, did not fill them with any confidence.

The first surprise the planet had for them was that its dominant inhabitants were human. That had caused quite a stir when the picture signals had eventually been decoded, though familiarity gradually lessened the impact of the discovery.

That they must be the descendants of some ancient expedition became the accepted view after a while. Both history and legend were full of tales of heroes—and villains—who had flown off into the void never to return. And humanity was very old and had spread through many systems, even within known history.

"They must have been a sorry remnant when they reached here, whoever they were," was the next observation. "There's precious little sign of any real civilization down there."

It was a sombre remark, but it accurately summarized the growing feelings of the travellers as months of observations pointed inexorably towards the dangerous and unstable nature of the occupants of their intended home.

Matten spoke. "I think the feeling most of us have, Taithur, is that we should avoid these people. At least, until we're fully established and self-sufficient. All we know about them is from a few months observation of their surface communication networks. Human they seem to be by their appearance, dangerous they must surely be by such of their conduct as we've been able to see, but simple and straightforward they are not. I get the impression that their primitive little society is as complex and subtle as any in the civilized systems. We just don't know enough. We must keep away from them for as long as possible."

Several heads nodded.

"You worry too much, Matten."

Proktor's voice cut across the acquiescence. Taithur sighed inwardly. When is he going to get the sneer out of his voice, he thought. "They're savages. They can't do anything to hurt us. Not with their technology. Let's get down there and get started. Get some proper gravity under our feet. Deal with these locals as and when we meet them. If any of them cut up rough, then…"

He made a dismissive gesture.

"Then, what?" Taithur prompted.

Proktor repeated the gesture. "Then put them in their place," he shrugged.

"How?" pressed Taithur slowly and wilfully.

Proktor looked a little surprised. "Why else did we bring weapons?"

"We brought weapons for many contingencies. But slaughtering aborigines rather than learn about them and give them their rights was not one of them," replied Taithur, barely controlling his anger.

"And you're forgetting a weapon they have which we can't resist, Proktor." The voice was Hester's, Matten's wife, and its soft gentleness eased away some of the tensions building up around the table. Proktor looked at her uncertainly. Hester had been a grade 1801 operative in the Adjustment Division's Education Department and her knowledge of weapons and battle tactics was considerable.

"Numbers," she said very softly. "There are hundreds of millions of them down there, Proktor, and we are how many…?"

Proktor looked down awkwardly. "Twenty-six hundred," he mumbled.

"Or thereabouts," confirmed Hester.

Taithur looked on placidly, sending up a small prayer for forgiveness at his appreciation of Proktor's discomfiture. Hester's training made her a formidable asset in Council.

"And we're fairly certain they can co-operate and mobilize when they have to," she continued. "At least on a tribal level. If we antagonize them, they could wipe us out, there's no doubt about that. And wipe us out easily, even with their primitive technology. We don't know enough to determine accurately how well they'll organize, but my opinion, for what it's worth, is that it'll be good enough. And that's going to be the position for many years."

Taithur's slight elation faded as he accepted the implications of Hester's comments. Typical Hester, he thought. Always economical. Deflate Proktor, and tell me the only answer we can come to, both at the same time.

Hester leaned back in her chair and rested her chin on her thumb and forefinger.

Proktor scowled. "I can't accept that Hester. They're savages. We're not Adjustment Troops but we can handle anything they can do to us. Good grief, if the worst comes to the worst we can stand off in the Rithid and…" He stopped. Hester raised an eyebrow. The only heavy armament that the Rithid had were ship to ship disruptors. Used on a planet, the effects would be devastating, but uncontrollable, and the consequent resonance could quite possibly make the planet uninhabitable.

A slow, ironic, handclap came from Taithur's left. It was Alachev, a man slightly older than Proktor, and from his home planet. "Brilliant, Proktor. Halfway across the galaxy to shoot up the only place we've managed to find. I bet you were a wow on the farm. Always sawing off the branch you were sitting on."

The archaic comment made Taithur smile in spite of himself, and several others laughed outright as Proktor turned red with embarrassment.

But Taithur's amusement was soon replaced by darker thoughts. Proktor was an able and headstrong man with a growing following among the travellers. If his impatience wasn't curbed, he could lead others into rash action when they landed and, as Hester had outlined, the consequences could be dire.

# Chapter 4

For years Taithur had been an angry unhappy man, sorely burdened by the meaningless things he was asked to do and, even worse, by his almost total inability to influence any of the decisions he was being asked to implement.

"It's the way things are, Taith," his unctuous superior used to say. "It's the way things have to be. The Service knows best. Don't make waves."

Therein was the threat. Don't make waves. You make waves, you find yourself towed out to a backwater and abandoned, or worse.

"But I do know best," he said angrily to Malva. "I know my job. There's so much more we can do here to improve food production, to enrich the cycle. Why the hell won't they listen to me?"

But his wife, strong though she was, could offer him little solace as his powerful personality turned in on itself and gnawed its own wounds. And the pain he could see he was causing her doubled his burden.

Sometimes he would wake up in the night gasping for breath, his body rigid, pulling at his face as if to remove some suffocating hand.

Then one day, he had found himself alone in the far fields, not really knowing how he came to be there. The sky was lowering purple with an impending summer storm and his mind was awash with a purposeless, unfocussed rage. He was shaking his head from side to side and muttering snatches of some inner conversation with uncaring, uncomprehending superiors. His whole body resonated with the tension in the air, as if it were no longer his own and suddenly, with a terrible shudder, he felt all control slip away. Throwing back his head he released a great cry into the crushing sky. The sound seemed to come from every cell in his body, filling all the fields and echoing off the arching clouds above, to encase him in a cocoon of despair.

When the sound had faded he was on his knees and driving his hands into the soil.

"God help me," he heard himself saying. "God help me."

He looked down at his hands in the soil, wondering to whom they belonged, then his eyes lit on a small flower. He dropped down on his elbows and stared at it intently. A common weed planted elsewhere on the farm to protect a cereal crop from fungal attack. Its slender white petals radiated out from a knurled yellow centre, and both colours shone in the strange darkening stormlight.

Taithur found himself mesmerized by the tiny bright flower.

"You shouldn't be here, should you?" he whispered. "You're in the wrong place." He realized that while he knew almost everything there was to know about this simple weed, he had never seen it with such intensity. Never seen how beautiful it was. "What chance brought you here, so far away from your fellows?" But he was not aware of what he was saying. His entire being was absorbed in the beauty of the flower, a beauty that made a new whole of his knowledge of the plant. And transcended it.

A drop of water fell on his hand and absently he identified it as a tear. Others followed. Then larger, colder drops joined them as the storm in turn released its own burden.

When he returned home some time later, he was soaking wet and radiant.

"Malva forgive me," he said, embracing his wife. "Forgive me. I have to start again."

In the tiny white flower he had seen a vision that took his torments and forged them into purposefulness. For the first time in many years, Taithur turned outwards, knowing now he must set his hand to plough the furrow that had been marked out for him.

He lay awake on the stand-by bunk. For once, he was glad to be away from his wife, glad to be away from the comfort of his own quarters. Soon, the Rithid would swing into orbit around the planet and the final preparations would begin for the move to the surface. Hester's assessment of their weakness had carried great weight in the Council's many deliberations, and they decided eventually to adopt the policy of avoiding the local inhabitants for as long as possible, Proktor not dissenting. The Rithid had enormous autonomous resources: "But it has a limited capacity. We can't use it to feed our expansion down there, the cycle might tip into decay and we're too far from help to risk that." No-one could dissent from that.

They had brought sufficient to seed their scheme, knowing that growth would have to be bootstrapped, but the seeding seemed to be chillingly small now that the time was near.

"We need our unity more than ever before," said Taithur to the full company. "There's no denying that what seemed quite plausible, even exciting, when we met and planned in secret in our prayer-meets, has a different complexion in the light of this new sun, and these difficult creatures below. But we've been thorough. We've planned well, and sadly, the deaths we've had have increased our available resources. So with courage and faith we'll build our new settlements down below, and bring to life our vision of what a free society should be."

Everyone knew that a great deal of jury-rigging would be needed and they would indeed be very vulnerable for a long time. Peaceful co-existence with the natives would be essential, and from their growing knowledge of the behaviour patterns of these people, the opinion that this could best be achieved by avoiding contact with them, gradually became unanimous

There was a critical point in Hester's calculations, which she had shown to Taithur, but which by mutual agreement they kept from even the Council. As the surface community expanded it would effectively reduce the capacity of the Rithid to sustain them in an emergency.

"The bigger we become, the more planet-bound we will be. Eventually the Rithid will be incapable of taking the full community even beyond this system. According to my assessment—which may change with time of course—when this happens, we'll be large enough to be conspicuous, but still small enough, and undeveloped enough, to be vulnerable to destruction by the locals."

"We can't put more resources into defence?" Taithur asked.

Hester shook her head. "No. We're too finely balanced. That could jeopardize everything."

Taithur put his head in his hands. "In other words, if we're discovered and can't make peace with the natives, we might have to cut and run. Leave part of the community behind for the survival of the rest?"

Hester nodded. "I'm sorry Taith, but I had to tell you. I'll keep the situation under constant review. It may alter. It's quite a sensitive set of equations."

And there they had had to leave it. Nothing else could be said, or Hester would have said it.

Taithur turned in the narrow bunk. Lord give me the courage, he thought. And the wisdom to do what's right if that should happen.

However, it was not in Taithur's nature to fret excessively about matters over which he had little or no control, and with his brief prayer he consigned the problem to the future where it belonged. All he could do was improve Hester's calculations by building up the community as quickly as possible. Right now, a more urgent problem taxed him.

Following his revelation, Taithur transmitted his own new-found excitement and his sense of freedom and spiritual awakening, to anyone who cared to listen. And such was his conviction and eloquence that many did indeed care to listen. Unexpectedly, he found himself leading a religious revival that started spreading through both the central and the border systems apparently spontaneously.

The commonly held view was that while there was no great harm in his preaching, the very size of the organization that was developing would provoke the Service into doing something about it sooner or later. Religions had to be watched. They were never popular with the Service and were usually quickly institutionalized prior to fading quietly away.

However, years of blistering resentment had armed Taithur with a creative paranoia, and instinctively he ensured that the heart of his organization was both protected by the Law, and substantially funded, before it became too conspicuous.

"This bloom is not of my creating, all I can do is make sure its roots are strong and deep before it reaches out to the light."

The Service, however, was also like a living body, and sensing a threat, its many and varied protection systems came into operation automatically. Taithur and his people found themselves under a variety of attacks throughout all the systems they had reached.

Where they were weak, local planetary bye-laws were passed which effectively outlawed them, "pending appeal to the Service's religious tribunal". Groups had to meet and worship in secret and thus laid themselves open to a variety of persecutions.

Where they were strong, subtler methods were used: spot audits into the financial affairs of their protecting companies, and of key individuals; endless administrative delays and confusion over the purchases of land and buildings; difficulties with approval of their religious status; a myriad regulatory tentacles reached out to choke them. Taithur learnt that his paranoia was well founded. He was in the middle of a war.

But what he had found in that far field was not to be lightly lost, and his resolve grew stronger with each setback. Furthermore, the time was right for him. His had been a lonely torment, but he had not been alone, and people flocked to him despite the growing opposition of the Service.

For all its success, though, Taithur scarcely imagined that his crusade was in reality anything more than a minor irritation to the Service. Eventually, he believed, some form of equilibrium would be established and his followers would be allowed to practice their religion relatively unhindered. He was not an evangelist, and his vision was a gentle one, of light slowly permeating into the darker recesses of the Service to the good of all.

It came as something of a surprise therefore when he went to deal with a problem on a nearby system to find himself confronted by a Grade Six official from the Education Department. It was an experience as terrifying as it was flattering—the Service's grading levels went well into four figures, and insofar as he had any knowledge of the giddier heights, Taithur knew that even an official responsible for several systems would probably be no higher than Grade Twenty.

At their meeting, which was held in strict privacy, Taithur was almost disappointed by the peculiarly unimpressive presence of the man. Despite this, however, he remained intimidated by the Grade Six status, and although the man's manner was friendly and pleasant, there was a dead neutrality in his gaze that slowly chilled Taithur. Although he could sense no danger, or animosity even, he knew that behind those eyes must inevitably lie a cruel and ruthless assessor who was in some way testing him, and who could even now be deciding the fate of his people.

The man explained carefully and thoroughly. "I'm relying on your confidence, Taithur. I'm compromising my position just by meeting you, and I certainly shouldn't be telling you about these matters. They're highly confidential. However, we've the greatest admiration for your work and feel you should be advised of certain… difficulties that lie ahead of you." He used the words "we" and "they" frequently, in a tone that implied Taithur should understand about whom he was talking but Taithur was too daunted to ask for clarification.

"The problem in this system is not what it seems, Taithur. Necessarily I can only give you a crude simplification of the situation, but as far as you're concerned, it boils down to the fact that there's been some serious economic mismanagement here by Officials who should have known better, and to protect themselves they're intending to pass the blame onto your followers."

He raised a hand to stop Taithur's response.

"I understand, Taithur. Your movement is in no way political. You're simply legitimately exercising your right to freedom of worship. Your affairs are all in order. I've no doubt that you feel your innocence will carry you through any such calumnies. But…" He gave a slow regretful shrug. "I'm afraid you'll be ranged against powers far beyond your resources. Your organization will simply be a pawn in an inter-departmental power struggle, and as a pawn you'll be completely expendable."

Taithur unexpectedly found his throat was painfully dry. The very quietness of the man's speech, coupled with his enigmatic gaze, combined into a more terrifying whole than any amount of ranting and raging could have done. Could the official not help? Taithur ventured. Again the shrug. Very little, was the gist of the answer.

"The matter's essentially local. It would be both impossible and improper for us to interfere directly. I've only a watching brief. It's simply unfortunate that you've attracted the attention of these people."

Taithur grimaced angrily, in spite of himself, and the official looked almost sympathetic. "You're not a child Taithur," he said. "You're a man of the worlds. You're simply in the wrong place at the wrong time. To curse and fume will merely be to send your energies out of cycle."

Then, with a brief boldness, Taithur asked why the man had come here if he could not help. The official showed no sign of offence, but the conversation slowly seemed to lose direction and purpose, and the idea of the voyage gradually appeared, vague and insubstantial, like a shadow in the mist. Taithur could never fully recall how the subject arose, but soon they were discussing details.

Telling sentences ushered him along the way to a golden prospect.

"Out there, you'd be in our remit, and we could protect you."

"You'd be working for the greater good of the Service, so you'd be of no value to these people, and those you left behind would be able to follow their religion in peace."

"But…" The man had paused and looked regretful. "While the idea is sound, inspired even, you'll have to fight for it yourself. As I've said, we can't help openly, if for no other reason than that to do so would be to provoke your enemies and increase the persecution you've already been experiencing. Where we can help, we will. But you'll see none of it, and I can guarantee you nothing. Just set your heart on this goal Taithur, because only you can achieve it."

Thus, for reasons that he never paused to analyse fully, Taithur found himself dominated by a desire to lead his people to a new place. One where they could be free to practise their religion in peace, and live lives unhindered by the eternal cloying presence of the Service. His whole following began lobbying the Service passionately for an Exploration Charter.

Now, restless on the stand-by bunk, Taithur cursed this hard-fought-for Charter. From being the key to their future hopes, it seemed now it must become the instrument of their future despair, for its essence bound them still to the Law and to the Service, and following their latest discoveries, the Law must surely require their turning from this precious planet.

# Chapter 5

Taithur levered his mind away from the problem and activated the sensor display. There was no real need to do this as the sensors were routinely programmed to wake him in the event of an emergency, but he felt the need to fill his thoughts with something else if only for a few moments.

The sensor readings and recommendations floated into his field of view, apparently suspended in mid-air. In reality the images were fed directly into his visual cortex through his personal link to the stand-by bunk. He closed his eyes to eliminate the slightly disorientating effect of the subdued lighting in the cubicle, and then glanced quickly across the display. Nothing amiss, of course, all readings normal, all recommendations—"maintain". The display was more active than it had been during their long sojourn in deep space, but that was only to be expected. There was a lot to look out for once you started approaching a star system—all manner of ancient debris from the original formation, gravity distortions, peculiar emissions from the star. Taithur smiled to himself as the thought recalled Ersand's brusque dismissal of one of his junior officers.

"I don't give a damn what it says in the Manual. My manual says 'Watch your butt if you don't want it cooked', so scan the full spectrum like I told you."

That also had been unnecessary. The star was quite a commonplace one and almost Service Standard in its behaviour. Hester was all smiles. "Lot of juice in this one, boys," she said, almost gleefully. "A lot of juice. It'll see humanity out, without a doubt. Excellent."

The "Excellent" was brought about by the star's energy output. It was better than she had estimated in her earlier projections, and improved her calculations materially. Bootstrapping tended to be exponential and a good start-up period could knock years off the full programme.

Still, thought Taithur, bootstrapping was also sensitive to small negative influences, so maximum caution would have to be the order of the day for the foreseeable future.

"Maximum caution," he whispered softly. The problems they had faced in deep space and through the Darvod-hunt hops were no more than they had braced themselves for, horrific though some of them were. But since locating this star, everything had been comparatively uneventful and now everything about the planet seemed to be perfect, or at least, as perfect as they had any right to expect.

"It's odd, Malva," he had told his wife. "I keep waiting for something bad to happen. It's been so smooth lately."

Malva had laughed. "Tut tut, Taith. What's this? Your old-fashioned Hewers' work ethic, Nowt good'll come o' this idleness." Then, in a whisper, with a mocking finger discreetly pointing to the corner of the ceiling. "Or is it fear of the household gods?" He had affected an indignation, but she had cracked his sternness into a smile with more laughter. "Ord Taithur, you're just an old pagan, flying under false colours. Wait until I tell your flock."

You're probably right Malva, he thought, deactivating the sensor displays, and opening his eyes. But too many pieces of good luck still make me feel nervous. The Way isn't that straightforward. If there's a new home for us out here, then in some way we're going to have to earn it. Getting a Charter and getting away from the Service was a beginning, not an end. He swung his legs off the bunk and stretched. But we're not away from the Service are we? And this business could well be the end. Damned natives.

There had been mounting uneasiness ever since the analysers had identified the dominant language and Ersand had cobbled together an anthropological team to study the natives in detail, with a view to assessing the risks involved in direct contact.

They were reticent in their preliminary comments.

"We're still a long way away. There's a great deal of distortion and straightforward loss. A lot of the stuff we're getting just doesn't make sense. Leave it a while. It'll improve as we get closer."

28

And improve it had. At least, the reception had, and with it the consequent accuracy of their data. The conclusions, however, had not, and the reticence of the team had become conspicuous. Eventually, Taithur called on the team leader in his private quarters.

"Jion, what are you doing? What's happening? Your silence is spreading round the ship like a poisonous cloud. Whatever you've found out about these people can't be as bad as what everyone will be imagining. And you'll have to tell us sooner or later."

He regretted his hectoring tone almost immediately. Jion was a conscientious and sincere young man, very capable, but a little lost as a team leader. The look on his face wrung Taithur's heart.

"I'm sorry, Taithur. I didn't know what to do…" he began. "I…"

He stood up abruptly and went over to his computer desk. Picking up a single sheet of paper he handed it to Taithur.

"Here," he said, almost with the air of a child just admitting to some misdeed. He looked as if he were going to say something more, and Taithur waited, watching him carefully.

"Here," repeated Jion, thrusting the paper forward again. This will tell you what you want to know, said his posture. Sooner it than me.

Taithur took the paper and looked at it as if uncertain whether or not a joke was being played on him.

"A written summary, Jion? And handwritten? I didn't know you were a calligrapher."

But the man's manner told him it was no joke. Just read it, was the instruction in the nervous eyes looking down at him.

Taithur read it, and then laid it gently on his knees. He felt physically sick as a turmoil of emotions swept through him. Faith that had sustained him through all manner of dangers wavered under this unexpected assault.

It couldn't be. Not after everything that we've gone through.

He dropped his head forward onto his hands, and stared down at Jion's neat handwriting. He was a calligrapher, the thought came to him, incongruously. A young student of an old art. It was oddly reassuring. And disturbing. The writing was meticulous. And so was everything else. It was as brief a summary as it needed to be. Nothing relevant was omitted, nothing superfluous included.

"You're sure about this," he said faintly, knowing the answer.

"We've known for some time," came the reply. "We've been checking and rechecking… just vain hope… but…" He shrugged despairingly. Then an unexpected burst of emotion. "Dammit, Taithur, it's not fair. Not after everything we've been through."

The force of the young man's anger helped Taithur stifle his own.

"Faith and courage got us here Jion." he said firmly, hoping his inner sense of the lie did not show through. "It'll get us through this, have no fear." Then, more quietly, "But you did right to keep this to yourselves. It's not going to be easy, and we'll all need to think long and hard about it."

A look of exasperation came into Jion's face as weeks of fear and resentment found words. "There's nothing to be thought about Taithur, you know that. The whole venture's finished." He gesticulated angrily. "Those people. If you can call them people. Those creatures down there—they're completely out of cycle. If it wasn't happening right in front of us I'd have said that degree of decay was impossible—but it's there—like nothing any of us have ever known. They're diseased, Taithur. They're a potential menace to the entire galaxy."

Taithur sat motionless on the stand-by bunk for the short time of his duty period remaining, and then walked slowly towards the Council Room. Very quietly he had called a closed meeting of the Council after leaving Jion, and he had been in an intellectual limbo ever since. Ideas churned to and fro, but there was a conflict between his heart and his head that he could neither resolve, nor still long enough for a little peace. Sadly, he found prayer to be of little help.

This is our problem, he thought. This is a real test.

Reaching the Council Room he found he was the last to arrive. A quick glance showed him that everyone was there, and the tension in the air was almost palpable. Closed meetings were not popular. Too many reminders of Service days.

Straight to it, he thought. Defuse it before it explodes.

He closed and sealed the door. Then, setting his face, he walked briskly to his seat and began without any preliminaries.

"I have a summary of Jion's findings here." Hands reached out to activate the table's main display. "I'll read it," he continued, without pausing. The hands faltered, uncertain. Read? But before any questions could be asked he produced Jion's paper and began reading. Brows furrowed in concentration, unused to this archaic mode of presentation, until, as abruptly as he had started, Taithur finished.

There was a brief silence, though to Taithur it seemed to last interminably. Then the storm broke.

"This can't be true."

"It's not possible."

"Young Jion's made a mistake."

Taithur sat impassively. These were cries in the dark. Jion wasn't brilliant, but he was capable, conscientious and thorough, and they all knew it. And anyway, no-one could make a mistake like that. Slowly the hubbub faded and Taithur found himself at the focal point of every eye in the room. Uncharacteristically he flinched away from their expectation.

"Well. What do we do now?" he said. "The Charter binds us to the Law, and the Law is quite clear. The Service must be notified. A system with only a fraction of the divergence that this one is showing would be classed as an emergency. There's no telling what harm these creatures will do when they develop their space flight technology far enough to move into the inhabited regions of the galaxy."

There was an uncertain silence, then Hester spoke. "If the Law is clear. And I agree with you, it probably is." She glanced across at Liefer, an old Lawyer who had played a major part in the negotiations for the Charter, but he returned her gaze impassively. She continued. "If that's the case. Why do you ask us what we should do? Tell us your thoughts."

"No," Taithur said, in a tone that brooked no further discussion. "I must know your minds."

Hester looked from Taithur back to Liefer again, but neither offered her any help, and she noted that it was she who was now the centre of attention. She puckered her mouth as if she had tasted something bitter. Imitating Taithur's directness she said, "Very well. Do we obey the Law and lose everything, or do we break it and lose everything?"

God bless you Hester, thought Taithur. He looked round at the watching faces and felt the uncertainty in the room grow. Here's a test of faith indeed. What will be forged in this heat?

"There's no debate. Break it. We can't go back now. Not back to the Service. Not after everything we've been through." It was Proktor.

A fairly predictable reaction there. Taithur maintained his review of the faces around the table.

Protest came from a few people immediately.

"The Law's the Law, Proktor, we're bound by it no matter where we are."

"We're only here because the Law granted our Charter."

"If we break the Law, we'll be rooting our new lives in anarchy."

The meeting degenerated into a noisy babble as several people began to speak at once, and discussions began between neighbours.

Taithur made no effort to intervene. It was important that the Council got rid of its immediate reactions as quickly as possible.

He closed his eyes, and in the darkness it was as if the noises around him were simply his own tangled thoughts departing. Whatever happened now, he knew he was surrounded by tried and true people. He felt their support more than ever before. Even in their opposition, they supported him.

He brought the vision of his white flower to his mind, seeing again its bright colours, and smelling the dampening soil as the rain first speckled it and then turned it dark brown. Abruptly, his confusion vanished like a morning mist suddenly dispelled by the sun, and a memory of Konrad spitting on his fist rose up fleetingly to harden his new resolve.

A voice came through the darkness.

"Taithur. May I speak?"

It was Liefer.

# Chapter 6

Liefer was one of the oldest of the travellers. Small and frail, with an absent-minded manner, he gave the impression of being dried up and inconsequential, like an autumn leaf waiting to be blown away by the first breeze to come along.

But his appearance was deceptive, as a glance into his grey eyes would show. He had been a brilliant Service prosecutor in his younger days, but for reasons he never chose to divulge, he abandoned his assured career at its height and became an equally capable Human Rights lawyer, an action which brought double odium down on him.

Taithur liked and respected Liefer and his experience and knowledge had been enormously valuable to the travellers, both before and during the voyage. Occasionally he wondered why Liefer had joined the expedition. Certainly he had not intended to in the early days. He was not a young man and, follower of their religion though he was, he had frequently stated that he had no desire whatsoever to go "flitting about the galaxy"—he had plenty to do where he was, protecting individuals from the excesses of the Service.

In his darker moments it occurred to Taithur that while they had the benefit of Liefer, those left behind did not, just as they did not have the benefit of the other leading figures in the religious revival. Would they be persecuted? Would the religion wither and die? They were restless, irritating thoughts, an amalgam of feelings of guilt and betrayal mixed with reason and logic, which told him he had had no alternative. But the whole was laced together with a deep suspicion that he and everyone else had been manipulated in some way.

He mentioned it once to Liefer. The old man inclined his head to one side with a slight shrug. "It makes no difference Taith—your reason, your logic, is correct. You had no alternative. To ignore the "advice" of a grade six official would have spelt disaster for all of us. Whether it was some machination by the Service that brought us here, or we did it all for ourselves, is an… interesting problem." He smiled and raised a finger, as to a pupil. "But nothing more, nothing more." Then he chuckled at Taithur's patent dissatisfaction. "Taithur," he said, taking his arm. "Concern yourself with matters of the moment. Allow yourself only a little time now and then to ponder problems which are, by definition, almost insoluble."

Taithur nodded reluctantly, and an impish smile lit up Liefer's face. "And don't forget," he said. "While we're talking about insoluble problems, who can say who is manipulating the very Service itself?"

Now, in the noisy Council Room, Liefer's quiet, penetrating voice silenced the mounting chatter.

"Taithur. May I speak?"

Taithur opened his eyes and nodded.

"This is a great shock to us all," Liefer began. "We knew these… creatures were dangerous, but I don't think any of us imagined they would be quite this dangerous—so wildly out of cycle. It's almost as if they're not even aware of the concept." He shook his head at this bewildering notion. "It seems our fretting about whether to contact them was needless. Time alone would have provided the answer for us beyond all dispute. I suspect there's a lesson for us there somewhere… but I digress. Obviously we must study them, very carefully, and very urgently, because facts will be essential if we're to make the correct decision." It was in the nature of Liefer's delivery that people craned forward to listen. Some might argue subsequently, but none would interrupt.

"As always," he continued. "Each of us will bring his own expertise to bear on the problem. Mine, of course, will be a consideration of the legal ramifications of what has been found."

Taithur saw Hester smile slightly and lean back in her chair. Liefer's quiet statement had scythed through the turmoil that had been caused by the sudden announcement and had taken the legs from under all the amateur lawyers there.

"I suspect it may take me some time," he went on. "Certainly the matter is not simple. We are subject to the Law, of course, but our position is unique in legal history. And…" he leaned forward and tapped a finger thoughtfully on the table. "Because of this, we may have to consider the whole basis of the Law." His face became thoughtful. "For one thing, we'll have to separate, very clearly, those constraints upon us which are sound in Law… in natural justice even, and those which are merely rules, procedures etc, established for administrative convenience. The difference between the two normally tends not to matter in practice, but is quite profound. However, it's very relevant now and we'll need to do that simply to be able to see where we're going. We Lawyers tend to carry a lot of excess baggage around with us just out of habit." He smiled. "Then there'll be the question of the sovereignty of an autonomous unit such as ourselves. Then, I suspect there could be severe problems with jurisdiction over… those below. They're not, after all, citizens under our Government. Hm… interesting."

Then he looked straight at Taithur and turned his hands palms upwards in a gesture of completion.

"Thank you Taithur," he said. "I'm sorry if I've rambled on a little, but it's a long time since I've had a problem as… meaty as this. It should be quite enjoyable. I'll put my mind to it straight away."

Taithur thanked him and turned to the rest of the group. "Has anyone else got anything to add?" There was a universal shaking of heads.

"I think we've all got plenty to say," said Matten. "But nothing to add."

The observation eased away the remainder of the tension that still persisted. Taithur smiled. "Good," he said. "I propose we follow Liefer's advice. We can slow down the disembarkation preparations so that key people can work on a detailed study of these…" He shrugged. Like most of the others, Taithur found it difficult to think of the natives as humans. How could anyone, having seen the way they behaved?

"We'll keep everything informal," he continued. "I think young Jion should remain in charge of his team, and overall co-ordination. He's coming on nicely. I doubt he'll let us down. It was a nice touch, handwriting his conclusion. Keeping it out of the computers where one of the kids might ferret it out." He paused, as a thought occurred to him. Then, slowly, and almost savagely. "Talking about co-ordination… I'm sure this is superfluous, but just to ease my mind, let me remind you that I don't want any of you jumping into your little cubby holes, preparing files and sniping off memos at one another like so many

Service Scribes. If you catch yourself at it out of habit, then it will be in your best interests to deal with it before I find you."

There was a little uneasy clearing of throats around the table. Taithur might be a devout man, and a champion of freedom, but his attitude towards what he regarded as old Service habits was singularly intolerant.

As if to emphasize Taithur's comment, the room lurched slightly, and Taithur felt a wave of unease pass through him.

With an effort, he refrained from swearing. Ersand, sitting next to him, tilted his head on one side, listening to a message on his IFT.

"Sorry," he said, after a moment. "I'm afraid the gravity silo's getting a bit temperamental so near to this star." He paused, listening again. "Risk factor?" he asked his unseen informant, then he nodded. "Nothing serious," he said to Taithur. "But we'll have to step up our supervision to keep the thing in balance."

Taithur nodded acknowledgement. The gravity silo was a permanent problem they had learned to live with. Sooner or later it would have to be solved properly, but that couldn't be done until they were well established down below. The thought brought Taithur back to the present problem.

"Is the delay in disembarkation going to give you any problems, Captain?"

"No. It'll be a relief actually," Ersand replied. "We can take a wider orbit and step down from battle alert. The duty schedules will have to be re-jigged to release the key people you'll need, and I'll arrange to throw a lattice of probes round the planet to speed up the information intake. I'll also increase our veiling."

"Yes. That's vital now," said Taithur anxiously. "The effects of premature discovery don't bear thinking about."

"I realize that," Ersand said, frowning slightly. "But we needn't worry too much. For one thing they're not looking for us, they're too busy watching each other, and for another their detection beams are incredibly primitive. The D-h surface alone slides most of them round us without our doing anything."

Taithur raised a hand in apology. Ersand, he knew, needed no coaching about how to handle his ship. He turned to the rest of the group and said again. "Anything else?"

There was a short silence, then Hester spoke. "Just one thing Taith," she said. He looked at her uncertainly, then nodded. "Whatever we decide to do," she said. "This is a dreadful thing we've found. So dreadful that my heart tells me there must be a purpose in our finding it after such a journey and so far from our homes. I think we should all add some humility to our best endeavours, and some prayers for guidance."

As the group broke up and left, Liefer picked up Jion's summary and affected to look at it closely, until everyone except Taithur had gone. Taithur walked over to him and stood looking over his shoulder.

"What do you want, Liefer?" he asked.

Liefer turned and handed him the paper with a knowing smile.

"Ah, you're learning, Taith," he said. "Nicely observed. We have to talk quite urgently. Come and see me when your duty spell is finished."

# Chapter 7

Liefer eased off a display visor and laid it gently on the table as Taithur entered.

"I'm sorry," said Taithur. "I didn't mean to disturb you."

Liefer looked up at the younger man and reflected that while Taithur's courage and sincerity drew people to him, it was by such small courtesies that they were bound to him. A man of words, Liefer never quite found the one he wanted to describe this quality. Taithur was humble without being obsequious, bold and authoritative without being aggressive. Harsh in judgement of his own mistakes but compassionate and patient with those of others. He was a difficult man to encompass briefly. Not like that firebrand Konrad—explosive, was the word for him.

Then, as if triggered by the word, a surge of memories burst into his mind and in that brief instant of waiting, Liefer renewed again his inner vow. To Taithur, the man who had united them and led them though this wilderness in search of freedom and tolerance. To Konrad, who had died so impulsively, and to all the others who had worked and fought and died for what had now come to pass. He renewed his own resolve that everything he could give to these people, he must.

He smiled. "You're not disturbing me, Taith. I was just browsing, and I did ask you to call. Sit down." He indicated a seat opposite his own. Taithur sat down rather wearily.

"Are you tired?" Liefer asked.

Taithur shrugged. "No, not really," he said. Then he scowled, and shook his head. "Yes damn it, I am." Liefer chuckled. "It's my own stupid fault." Taithur continued. "I get so impatient." He threw up his hands in exasperation and slapped them noisily on his knees. "Whatever happens we've got a lifetime here. We've no emergency on our hands. An hour or two here or there isn't going to make any difference to anything, yet I fuss around like a ten thou grade clerk."

Liefer chuckled again and nodded approvingly. "Very good," he said. "I was going to give you a fatherly lecture. Suggest that you relax, spend some time with your lovely Malva, and so on, but I gather I've just been listening to her."

Taithur laughed outright. "Lawyer Liefer, you're too shrewd by half. Am I to be given no credit for self-analysis?"

"None at all," said Liefer briskly. "Just give yourself credit for having had the wit to pick the right woman."

Taithur lifted his hands slightly in an attitude of both acceptance and a desire to proceed to business. As Liefer had grown to expect, the transition was swift.

"Our real problem, Liefer," he said. "Our real legal position. What is it?"

Liefer raised his own hands in a resigned echo of Taithur's gesture. "The legal position is quite genuinely as I stated it in Council. It's complicated and interesting, and a great deal of time would be required to form even a preliminary opinion on it…"

"But?" Taithur anticipated.

"But, young man," continued Liefer with a touch of testiness at the interruption. "Our real position is a different matter from our legal one, and much more relevant." Taithur made to speak, but Liefer froze the words with a look. "Let me tell you what I think, then we'll go from there."

He raised his eyebrows as though awaiting a signal of approval. Taithur leaned back in his chair and nodded. Far too impatient, Taith, he rebuked himself, far too impatient. Liefer would not have asked me here if it were not important. And he can be a bit crusty. Just sit still and listen.

Taithur found Liefer's room very relaxing. It was almost wilfully old-fashioned, but without any sense of spurious nostalgia or desperate looking back. The lighting was subdued without being either oppressive or soporific, and even though the chair had no automatic stress relievers, Taithur found the tensions of the last few hours fading away. An image of the planet hovered in the display frame. For a brief moment he saw himself as if from a great distance, a tiny motionless speck of animate matter hovering between these thinly spread stars. It occurred to him that he should be afraid, but amidst such immensity, fear had no meaning.

Liefer's voice brought him back to the room.

"Our real position, Taith, is that our legal position is irrelevant. Our real position is one of monumental weakness, and if we look to our Charter for protection, we shall find out that it's exactly what it appears to be—a scrap of paper."

Taithur's eyes widened. Liefer continued. "We've discussed this before. The generally accepted view is that we were allowed to leave the inner systems just to get us out of the way. We'd become a nuisance, and the best way to deal with us would be to painlessly decapitate the movement. That done, the body would probably wither and die."

Taithur grimaced at the reminder, but nodded in agreement.

"But think, Taith. We weren't big really. We felt big because we did a lot and there were only a few of us. But we were nothing. The Service could have rolled over us like that." He snapped his fingers. "They wouldn't even have had to use the Education Department."

Taithur felt compelled to speak. "Some of us were very badly harassed Liefer. Don't forget that. A lot died in some systems."

Liefer linked his fingers together and tapped them thoughtfully on his mouth. "Yes," he said slowly. "That was always a puzzle. It could have been genuine local hostility of course. It could have been over-enthusiasm by some system leaders, but…" He paused, and for a moment Taithur thought he could feel the ship moving, so still did the room become.

"No evidence for this, Taith," Liefer said suddenly, speaking more quickly than usual, as if the thoughts were just occurring to him. "Let alone proof. But I know the Service. I know the things they can do better than anyone on this ship. There's an odd pattern to events looking back on them, particularly the violence." He looked slightly embarrassed. "It's almost as if we were being experimented with. Set various tests to see what we'd do—to see what others would do."

"Liefer," Taithur protested. "That's a little… far-fetched, isn't it?"

Unexpectedly, Liefer looked angry. "No, it's not," he snapped. "It makes a certain sense out of a lot of the things that happened to our people—your people—ever since you came out of that field and started preaching." He sat back and looked hard at Taithur. "Think," he said sharply. "Think. Think of the size we were. We were nothing really. Noisy, yes. Enthusiastic, yes. Many things we were. But still nothing compared with even quite a small Service Department. And you end up talking to a Grade six official. Grade six, Taith, Grade six. In all the years I worked for the Service I dealt only with high Graded officials, but the highest Grade I ever met was sixteen, and that was only the once. And he was formidable, Taithur. Formidable. An intellectual and psychological grasp that sent me out with my knees shaking and I was on his side then." His tone was rueful. "But you met a Grade six. And you come away full of this idea to take the leading lights of your flock off into the unknown reaches of the galaxy." He paused thoughtfully. "Why, Taith? Why?"

Taithur stared at him, at a loss. "We went through all this right at the beginning, Liefer," he said eventually. "Why drag it all out again? We'd no alternative if we were to avoid being destroyed. I've always presumed I was manipulated by that Grade Six official—the memories of our talk have always been oddly vague—but whether I was or not is irrelevant. The very fact that someone so high ranking came to see me shows the danger we were in. Obviously he fed me that idea for some game of his own, but what could we have done about it?"

Liefer pursed his lips. "Nothing Taith, that's quite true. But it brings us no nearer to the answer. Why send us out into the depths of space? Why all the rigmarole of an Exploration Charter—a document never issued before?" Taithur did not reply. Liefer continued. "The Service has an infinite number of ways of protecting itself against upstart organizations. I should know, I implemented more than a few in my time. If you cut away local vagaries such as incompetence or spite by local officials, petty politics, bigotries, etcetera, you'll find the essence of the Service is simply maintaining the status quo. Anything new, original—disturbing—is quietly choked out of existence or slowly worn down. And if they're too obdurate, then the Education Department will squeeze them into conformity. It's no problem. It's what the Service is for. It's soaked up and effaced countless religions over the years. One or two even in my time. So why go to all this trouble with us?"

Again Taithur sat silent. He felt nervous. These were questions he had always imagined he had answered, but Liefer's comments were unsettling. Leaning back in his chair Liefer fixed Taithur with an enigmatic stare

"What I saw in your revelation was a door through into the quiet places of my own soul. Probably what most people saw in you was something similar. Some awareness of themselves. A quality that made them sit easier in their own lives."

Taithur began to look distinctly uncomfortable.

"But the Service saw something else. Something that sent a shock wave right through, into the very highest echelons. You frightened them Taithur. You frightened them. You... found something... represented something... they couldn't cope with. I've no idea what it is, but there's no other explanation. Fear is the reason we're here. Not our fear of them, but their fear of us."

Taithur shook his head, partly in disbelief and partly to assure himself that he had heard correctly. Had anyone else cited such a possibility, he would have laughed outright, or sent them to Medical.

Liefer anticipated Taithur's reaction. "I know what you're thinking, Taith. The old man's finally cracked. To be honest, I'd never have mentioned it if it hadn't been for this business with the locals. It's taken me long enough to formulate my ideas even this badly. But I'll tell you this, I doubt you'll fault them. Just give it time."

Taithur bowed his head and rubbed his fingers across his forehead. "I'll have to take that advice Liefer, because I really don't know what to say. I can't conceive of anything intimidating the Service, least of all me. But even if you're right, what's it got to do with our present predicament?"

Liefer became lawyerlike. "Accept my premise, for the time being Taith. The Service was too frightened to assail us directly. They preferred that we wander off into space, in a leaky old tub, where the balance of probabilities was that we'd disappear without trace. That would leave the Service free of blame." He raised a finger. "Especially as it was we who pestered for the Charter against their apparent opposition."

Taithur nodded grimly.

Liefer continued. "I'd submit, however, that the decision to leave us alone was not unanimous. I've no reason to suppose that there's any less political shuffling at grade one than there is in every other grade.

So we can assume that while everyone wanted to be rid of us, there would be a lobby for our actual elimination."

Taithur nodded again.

"What then do you think the reaction will be if an emergency probe from us comes crashing out of D-h space, blaring out what we've found and that we want to be brought back?"

Taithur stared at Liefer as the old man's reasoning began to filter through to him. Liefer answered his own question. "They'll have to send the Fleet. This place is a major health hazard."

He leaned forward and emphasized his words by tapping his forefinger on his knee. "Routine procedure for dealing with large scale cycle distortion is Quarantine & Sterilisation, in other words, a complete news blackout while the Education Department's Adjustment Squads move in and 'stabilize' the situation." He flicked a thumb towards the hovering disc of the planet. "And this is more than just large. It's almost unbelievable." His voice fell almost to a whisper. "That lobby for our elimination is going to say, 'We told you so—they should have been dealt with properly—they'll all be back as heroes now—completely uncontrollable.' And the others will have little alternative but to agree. All that'll return of us will be a report that our ship was accidentally destroyed during the difficult process of adjusting the occupants of this sink-hole of a planet."

Liefer might have declared "no evidence" for his comments, but they had an icy ring of truth to them, and Taithur folded his arms tightly across his chest as if for protection. His face was white.

"Have I led us all to destruction, Liefer?" he said softly.

Liefer fidgeted idly with the display visor on the table. "Nothing I can say will stop you reproaching yourself," he said. "That's part of being a leader. I reproach myself bitterly for not having thought of all this before. Even though I know there was no conceivable reason why I should put my mind to such a hypothetical problem as..." He waved his hand towards the display frame. "As a place like that. And even though I know that my having done so couldn't have altered our present position one jot."

He stood up, nodding to himself and pursing his lips. "I suppose our distress is like grief, Taith. Grief at the death of a long-cherished love. It's an unpleasant emotion, but it's also necessary. It churns us up, makes

44

us view every thought from a new perspective. Changes and strengthens us, Taith, if we can but see it. Prepares us to face the new reality."

He looked thoughtfully at the display frame again, and a long silence fell between the two men.

Eventually Taithur spoke, softly and with a purposeful slowness.

"We're here by dint of our Charter. It binds us to the Law. It makes us an arm of the Service. We must therefore report what we've found. But if we do so, then, as you surmise, it could be the end of us. If we don't, what then?"

Liefer remained looking at the screen. "Then we have to calculate the probability of our being able to adjust these people ourselves, before it's too late."

Taithur's eyes narrowed. "Don't evade me, lawyer. You understand my meaning. What is the offence we'll be committing?"

Liefer turned slightly. The light from the image of the beautiful planet hovering motionless in the display frame made his face look pale, but he answered without hesitation.

"Failure to notify a planet so appallingly out of cycle? If we survived the Fleet's arrival, which I doubt, at the best we'd be sent to an adjustment planet for the rest of our lives."

"And if we attempt to colonize?"

The sound of children playing in the corridor outside, percolated into the room to form an arabesque around Liefer's flat and business-like reply.

"That would be rebellion, Taithur. Our destruction would be inevitable."

# Chapter 8

Proktor swore as the warning light came on. He overrode it and the console whispered gently to him.

"No, Proktor, you're too tired. I can't accept your override now. The probability of your making material errors is too high." Proktor's jaw set and he activated the override again, keying in a 'most urgent' code.

"No, Proktor," said the console, a little more firmly. "It's not 'most urgent' and you know it. Now, stop working and go to bed. You're too tired."

The fingerboard went dead under Proktor's hand and in exasperation he kicked the console viciously.

"Ooo," said the machine plaintively. Proktor swore again, very loudly, and angrily disconnected the link from the back of his hand. Damned machine, he thought. Designed to produce voice inflections that would take the user away from whatever emotional extreme they had drifted to and return them to a more efficient state. In this instance it had defused his growing tension and then uttered the little cry to remind him that what he had done was unacceptable, and to calm him with a little guilt.

That kind of manipulation was typical of the Education Department, and Hester had spent a great deal of time in the early parts of the voyage explaining how and why it was done.

"Historically, I think these techniques were quite genuinely developed to improve efficiency and safety. But now, while that remains their ostensible purpose, in reality they're purely to achieve control. Subliminal control has always been preferred by the Education Department. It's not easy, but it's less messy and more effective than direct intervention."

That remark had caused some cynical amusement in view of the

Education Department's reputation for every conceivable form of ruthless intervention, and its particular vendetta against the new religion.

"It's true, nonetheless." Hester had continued. "The only reason the techniques are not more widely used is that for complete effectiveness the body/machine link is essential. That's why they're built into every machine."

"Can't they be disconnected?" was the obvious question.

Hester shook her head. "No. They're far too elaborate, and they mesh right down into the core of the programming."

Perhaps, one day they could develop their own machines, free from such devices. One day—when they arrived at their new home. Like a great many others, this particular intention drifted into that hazy and unclear sunrise they were all heading towards—a small dream amongst many.

Proktor was at best antipathetic towards authority, and he resented the 'meddling' machines with a special bitterness. They were always right, and they always won, like some invincible, omniscient parent. Even when they calmed him down in spite of himself, and a small part of his mind managed to assert itself and disconnect the link, he could never be sure that that was not what they had in mind from the beginning.

He went through a phase at one stage when his reaction to the machines was so strong that the resultant feedback almost rendered him comatose and he became unable to do even his routine duties without some trauma occurring. Taithur had briefly considered the efficacy of prayer in such a case, but had abandoned it in favour of an old-fashioned dressing down and a short spell of punishment fatigues. Proktor's attitude towards the machines was now akin to an armed truce—still resentful, but more subdued, and rarely troublesome.

With an inner snarl, he accepted the machine's advice and went straight to his quarters. Once there, he waved the light down into rest mode and crashed down onto his bunk, his mind whirling. Like most of the group working on the study of the planet, he could scarcely believe what he was recording.

Taithur had been silent since the closed Council meeting and had vigorously discouraged debate. "The facts first," became his watchword. "All of them."

Asked what should be done about the rumours spinning ever more wildly about the ship, he quietly reduced them from hysteria to a tolerable level of apprehension by the simple expedient of honesty.

"I apologize for the closed Council Meeting, but there are serious problems with this planet that we couldn't have anticipated. The meeting decided merely to gather all the facts, and that's being done now. When these are available we'll all decide together what we must do."

But there's only one decision to be made, Proktor thought repeatedly. Independent of the facts, independent of the Law, we stay. If they send the Fleet for us, then we fight.

It was a young man's fantasy of standing alone against overwhelming odds, of dying a glorious hero's death for Right and Freedom. But even in his most impassioned moments, he realized this deep inside, and while he was not alone in his grim determination to sever forever any links with the Service, it was this nucleus of detachment which made him, like Taithur, a focal point for those of like mind.

His encounter with the machine revived all his hostilities towards the Service. Such encounters usually did, and for a while he luxuriated in a well-worn saga involving himself, now leader of the group through the unexpected death of Taithur, sweeping back across space to deal retribution to the Service until even the Grade One officials cringed at his feet and promised to mend their ways. In his darker moments, it was apt to be a bloody affair.

When the tale had run its predestined course, Proktor sat up on his bunk feeling both satisfied and foolish. He looked round at the close confines of his room. The Rithid was a spartan ship, and his room, along with everyone else's, fell far short of the comforts he was once used to, but he felt grateful for its familiar shelter. In the quietness it gave him he noted, not for the first time, a real and growing resolve, quite separate from his fantasizing and his temporary petulance. He would indeed never return to the home systems and the claustrophobic embrace of the Service. Never.

Growing in its shade were other, grimmer thoughts that surely he could never resolve, and which tormented him increasingly.

Taithur was his friend and mentor. The man who had opened so many doors for him and eased so much of his torment. He loved and respected him, probably much more than many. But... but, he was human, he was not above error. And if he made the wrong decision about this planet…?

Proktor drove his knuckles into his temple to drive the question mark from his mind.

# Chapter 9

Taithur wiped his hand across his forehead and glanced ruefully upwards. It was amazing, he thought, after all this time in the ship, how one still looked skyward when the weather conditions were troublesome.

As a token act of freedom when they were clear of the major systems, they had adjusted the ship's automatic environment control so that in the main circulation areas it now offered a wide range of average planetary weather conditions. Although there was an overall, broadly seasonal progression, daily variations were quite random, and today the computer had opted for a close, brooding stillness. Like Taithur, everyone else was wearing light clothing and wandering about a little more slowly than usual.

Inappropriate, he thought. Most inappropriate on today of all days. There was enough tension on the ship without the weather adding to it.

"Don't ask," Matthew had said with exaggerated grimness, when Taithur had entered his control area. Matthew might be an excellent engineer, with a kindly and helpful disposition, but he kept the latter well hidden under a dour, even surly, exterior, and the sight of his beetling ginger eyebrows underscoring his furrowed brow induced an acute attack of moral cowardice in Taithur, who fled, his request for an adjustment to the weather unasked.

It did not help, of course, that Matthew had advised against the adjustment of the environment control.

"It can't be clicked on and off like a light you know. It's a twenty-five-day base cycle, with all manner of sub-cycles keyed into it. You won't get balmy spring breezes all the time by any means, and if I go fiddling with it just because it's 'A little too cold' or 'A little too hot' for some bright spark, I wouldn't like to hazard a guess at what might happen." Change it and you're stuck with it, was the general tenor of his comment, although Taithur suspected his opposition was carefully balanced to ensure it would not win the day, but would leave him in a position to say "I told you so" whenever anyone complained—Matthew also had a slightly malevolent sense of humour.

Turning a corner, Taithur came suddenly into the Plaza which lay in front of the Main Hall. It was crowded, as people were arriving from several directions at once and only one door to the hall had been opened. The sight of so many people made Taithur start. It was a long time since they had held a public meeting, and a very long time since they had held one of sufficient importance to bring together everyone on the ship apart from a skeleton crew.

As an instinctive protection against the claustrophobia of prolonged space travel, people tended to avoid crowding together, and for a moment Taithur felt disorientated.

He was not alone in that feeling, and the crowd was peculiarly subdued. For weeks, groups had been arguing and debating around the ship, and even now, echoes of debate could be heard entering the Plaza from some of its tributary corridors. But each in turn faded as the protagonists encountered the crowd.

The strange unease of the crowd mingled with the humid atmosphere, and Taithur felt a sense of foreboding as he stepped forward and merged with the slow-moving crowd.

Inside the Hall, however, the atmosphere was cooler and sweeter, and as the constricted stream of people passing through the door fanned out among the circular tiered rows of seats, the emotional atmosphere also seemed to cool and the sullen silence gradually gave way to a busy hubbub.

Taithur wended his way to the central control area and with a brief greeting sat down between Ersand and Hester. He liked the Main Hall. It was the largest and highest room on the ship and its vaulted ceiling gave the feeling of drawing the spirit upwards. A good place for many things, Taithur had often thought: prayer, music, drama. Now perhaps it would lighten souls enough for the coming debate to be positive and purposeful.

Perhaps also the humid weather will serve a purpose after all, he thought. People would enter and have burdens lifted. Had it been cool and pleasant, they would have found the Hall relatively oppressive and who could say what effect that might have had? Our destinies are sometimes held by the strangest, slenderest threads.

He was about to speak to Hester when a small jolt from the damaged gravity silo passed through the ship. It was an irritating, slightly alarming experience, but they were familiar enough occurrences of late, as Matthew's engineers had been working on the main silo to improve its stability in the presence of the nearby sun. Hester, however, swore profanely, and Taithur turned to look at her, eyes wide with surprise. He became aware of Ersand chuckling as he too leaned forward to peer at Hester.

Suddenly aware of their scrutiny, Hester blushed. "Tension," she said apologetically, with an awkward cough.

Both Taithur and Ersand burst out laughing at the doleful look on her face, and their laughter seemed to infect the whole crowd as echoes of it sprang up from different groups about the Hall.

Taithur leaned back, resting an affectionate hand on Hester's arm, and looked round at the growing crowd. He was pleased to note that the tendency to sit in groups representative of their home systems which had been so apparent in their earlier meetings, seemed to have disappeared almost totally. It was a good sign. The more old habits that were abandoned, the better.

Gradually the tide of people entering the Hall dwindled into a few hurrying figures signalling various degrees of apology or irritation to waiting friends. Glancing at the monitor in front of him Taithur noted that, save for the skeleton crew and a few in Medical, virtually the whole complement of the ship was there. He knew, however, that the others would be listening on the open IFT channel.

He reached forward to open the sound system and then hesitated. On an impulse, he withdrew his hand and stood up. The Hall became suddenly quiet.

"My friends," he began. "We've a difficult decision to make today. I felt it should be discussed here, with all of us together in this splendid Hall, rather than over open IFT, because there are subtleties, nuances, in this form of debate which can't be transmitted over IFT. We can't go down to this planet—or back into space—with any equanimity, unless all of us make all our feelings known."

Several heads nodded.

"Before we start, let us pray silently for a moment. Let our minds be free from the clatter which we've all brought with us, so that we can see the Way and perhaps have the wisdom to follow it."

The silence in the Hall deepened perceptibly as everyone closed their eyes and drifted into quiet meditation, allowing no one thought or train of thoughts to linger in the mind, beckoning for pursuit.

Unbidden, Taithur's white flower drifted into his mind, the beauty of its tiny perfection sweeping away all doubts and uncertainties. In the stillness, Taithur became aware of the common hope of all the people around him, and for a timeless moment it seemed that the whole universe stood motionless, poised like a majestic pendulum at the height of its swing, waiting for that inevitable, but infinitely tiny change of balance that would send it sweeping back along its singing arc.

Is that where we are now? he thought, easing out of his meditation. Has all human history conspired to drive us here, and will our decision today determine our destiny for generations?

Part of his mind dismissed the idea as fanciful nonsense, but another, deeper part told him to remember it.

He opened his eyes and looked at the still audience.

"Who'll speak first?" he said softly.

"You must speak first, Taithur," said a voice to his right.

"Yes," agreed one from the left. "You're our Guide."

Taithur looked from one to the other. Like him, the two speakers had declined to use the Hall's sound system and were speaking directly. He realized abruptly that he had never spoken to so many people without the aid of some form of IFT. It gave him a strange, primitive feeling and he felt the hairs on his arms rise and tingle.

"My friends," he said, clearing his throat. "Insofar as I'm anything, I'm your guide, your adviser, in matters spiritual. In matters such as we have before us now I've no special competence. We must guide one another."

He glanced around, but no-one seemed inclined to interrupt. The trust of these people was the one aspect of his position that he felt most keenly. It would be so easy, at times, to deceive them and use his authority to fulfil his own whims.

I must not dominate, he recited to himself. It was an old cautionary litany.

"Very well," he said. "I'll speak first, as you ask." But I'll say nothing, he added to himself. "You now have all the facts that the Council has compiled about this benighted planet. The dominant species is human, without a doubt, although their origin here is a mystery. If they're the descendants of some ancient expedition then it must have been a sorry remnant that reached here, and a very long time ago, because they're unbelievably savage and unstable, and have either never known, or have long forgotten, any of the tenets of civilized living. As you know, the more advanced of their tribes possess a rudimentary technology—very rudimentary—but they use it in a way that betrays a lack of awareness that's staggered us all. In short, they're out of cycle. In fact, the very word cycle is inappropriate for such a linearly divergent society."

A murmur of agreement rose from various parts of the Hall. The strange, blind behaviour of the planet's inhabitants disturbed everyone at a level far beyond that of the intellect. It had a dark nightmarish quality that many of them still needed to exorcise. Taithur let the noise fade away before continuing.

"Fortunately it would appear that the damage they've done, while serious, is not irreparable and shouldn't become so for quite a few years, although…" He raised a cautionary hand. "There's a slightly exponential trend developing that will need to be watched carefully, so I don't think we should be too complacent about the time we have available. That said, I think we're left with three options. First, we leave. Start our search again and leave this planet and its people to their fate. Second, we send an emergency probe back to our home systems, wait for the Fleet, and forget the idea of a place of our own. Third, we land and start our colony as intended. Build it up until it is sufficiently strong for us to begin the re-education of the aborigines. All three of these have profound implications, and of course over everything hangs the shadow of the Law, or more correctly, the Education department. I want us to talk here today until everyone is satisfied that everything has been considered, then somehow we'll reach a decision."

He sat down suddenly and with a gesture threw the debate open.

That evening, in his own quarters, Taithur sat with his eyes closed in his favourite chair and relaxed more than he had for many weeks. He felt at once drained and excited. The meeting had been a remarkable affair, heightened considerably by the consistent use of direct speech instead of IFT. The atmosphere had been electric at times as passions rose and tempers flared. Old rivalries and bitterness surfaced to be angrily denounced or laughed to scorn. Old loyalties were lost and renewed, and new ones were forged.

Several times, Taithur had to use his authority to restore some semblance of order. At one stage he pointed to the image of the planet hovering behind the control area.

"You're as bad as them," he roared, and jabbing angrily at the panel in front of him he replaced the huge image with one taken from the planet's communication network. An incomprehensible braying filled the hall, as the picture formed to reveal a crowd of the natives bellowing and gesticulating at one another.

"This is one of their tribal assemblies," Taithur shouted through the din. "This is how they conduct their . . . government."

Taithur's rebuke, coupled with the incongruous scene before them, momentarily shocked the assembly into silence, but almost immediately, laughter and mock cheering spread through the Hall.

As the humour defused the anger that had been developing, Taithur turned down the sound but left the wild images dancing there as a constant reminder. Then a thought occurred to him.

"I didn't realize this when I turned that on…" He flicked his thumb over his shoulder towards the screen. "But we should remember that out of cycle places are classed as health hazards for good reasons. We'll have to guard against infection from these natives." The remark had sobered the gathering considerably. It had become the practice to intercept transmissions from the planet for occasional amusement, but it was indeed in questionable taste. These were, after all, a sick and potentially dangerous people.

The debate had disposed of Taithur's first alternative very quickly. Ersand did not totally share Matthew's pessimism about the Rithid's ability to undertake large scale D-h hops, but he was far from sanguine about it, and the memory of long long months following the faint signs discovered by the long-range scanners was still too fresh for the prospect to be easily faced again. And these had been the only signs that they had found. There was certainly no guarantee that they would find anywhere else in this wilderness. In addition, the place was, indisputably, a major health hazard. They could not just walk away from it.

The second and third alternatives were discussed extensively, and while he tried to maintain some impartiality, Taithur found himself swept along by the overwhelming desire of virtually everyone to land on the planet and begin its colonization. If any reservations were expressed, they were token only, and easily dismissed.

"You're sure the planet is redeemable?"

Yes, without question, but delay would not improve matters.

"Can we reach sufficient strength to protect ourselves by the time education becomes a necessity?"

In theory, yes, but the native's response to contact was a large and uncertain variable.

"It's a dreadfully dangerous place Taithur." A woman holding her child's hand.

Taithur nodded sadly. "Nowhere's really safe for us, but we have each other, and our faith, and we've survived so far…"

Gradually, the arguments became circular, and Taithur sensed the mood of the meeting moving inexorably towards formally agreeing to stay and colonize the planet. But a spectre hovered over the meeting. Everyone knew it was there, but everyone shied away from looking at it.

Then, chillingly, striking to the heart of the problem, a young man spoke. "What do we do when the Service finds out?"

Not even if they find out, thought Taithur. There was a long silence.

"That's what we must decide now," he replied reluctantly, feeling suddenly burdened. "Liefer's assessment is that the Law is vague, mainly because of the matter of jurisdiction. These natives did not subscribe to the Government. They're therefore no part of our system, but…"

This place is a major health hazard, there's no disputing that. The Adjustment Squads will be sent regardless of the Law and any fine print. And they may well wipe us out as a matter of course.

Taithur knew that Liefer had kept his opinions very strictly to himself, and was ironically heartened when he heard the same views coming independently from so many of the others.

"But what do we do?" The original questioner persisted.

Taithur opened his eyes and turned to look across at Malva and his son playing some ancient board game. Not infrequently, his son's simplicity defeated his wife's cunning and experience, a fact that caused him considerable amusement.

Taithur had looked hard at the young questioner who had pointed to the shade haunting them.

We'll plead our case, he was about to say, but that had been discussed at length, and there was precious little case to plead for failing to notify the Service about such a plague spot.

He looked at Ersand and then at Hester, but he knew he could not ask for help with the burden that was finally being placed on him.

Slowly, he stood up. "We've wandered interminably through the starways in search of a home away from the repression of the Service. We've wandered and searched and found nothing, until here, out in the wilderness we find this beautiful place, with its strange and tainted people. We find ourselves with our resources, our arguments, everything, so finely balanced that reason alone can help us only to a certain point. I cannot believe that this is the work of random chance. We have all been changed by the many things that have happened to us, as if in preparation. My heart tells me we've been brought here for some purpose, and I believe that only our faith can guide us now."

His voice was quiet and steady, and the acoustics of the Hall carried it to every listener with an intimacy far beyond that of the privacy of the IFT system.

"We're a long way from the domain of the Service. Even a Fleet Ship would find the journey difficult." He paused to let that sink in and looked again at Hester and Ersand. Both nodded slightly in acknowledgement.

"If we settle on this planet, then even though we intend no harm we may have to defend ourselves against the natives." He paused again. "If the Service finds out about us..." He emphasized the "if". "And if the Adjustment Squads are sent, then we'll defend ourselves against them also."

Taithur felt again the almost audible relief that had passed through the Hall. It mingled in his sleepy awareness with a ringing laugh from his wife and a remonstrance from his son as their game came to its conclusion.

Doubts lingered in his mind. Had he in fact used his authority to sway the people to his wish? Quite probably, he thought, with some honesty. He wouldn't be a leader if he didn't do that.

Was his wish in the best interests of them all?

Here, he fell back on the truth of his own statement. Too many things too finely balanced. Probably any decision was as good as another. They would all depend on what the people made of such opportunities as arose. But to invite in the Service was unthinkable, a negation of everything they had prayed and worked for, and to fly off into this wilderness in search of another habitable planet, even discounting the practical problems, had the feeling of blasphemy about it.

He dismissed the doubts ruthlessly. From here, there was only forward. This will be our home. It is the Way. A gift and a trial. We'll build a new, free, civilization here. We'll treat peacefully and honestly with anyone we encounter, but if need arises we'll fight to the very last.

# Chapter 10

Striking a balance between the increased risk of discovery and the improved chances of survival for at least part of the expedition, it was decided to establish four base camps on the planet. The areas chosen were those least frequented by the natives and were of necessity regions of extreme climate: two were near the equator, an arid desert, and a dense, damp jungle, the third was on the icebound southern polar continent and the fourth was to be a floating base in the vast southern ocean.

"Not ideal, by any means," Taithur sighed when they had examined and accepted the computer's choices. "But keeping out of sight is the important thing at the moment, so we'll have to make do." He grimaced at the complications that these savages necessitated at every turn.

Ersand was more sanguine. "Don't sound so down, Taith. It'll be nice to get real gravity under our feet again, and a real sky over our heads."

"Through an EC screen," Taithur reminded him glumly.

Ersand laughed and slapped him on the shoulder. "You've been long enough in space, my friend," he offered. "You should be used to environmental control by now."

"More likely too long in space," Taithur replied. "And certainly too long at the monitors, listening to their incessant, barbarous chatter." He rested a dejected head on his hand. "I think they're probably at least as depressing as they're frightening. There's a headlong lunacy about them which is almost unbelievable, even though you can actually see it happening. I wouldn't have thought such folly possible, even amongst the most primitive of people."

Ersand nodded. "Well, I can't fault that comment, Taith. You said it yourself, a place like this would be classed as a health hazard for damn good reasons. We're doing the only thing we can do—keeping away from them for as long as possible, learning about them, and building up our own reserves against the day when we have to meet them."

"I'm sorry, Ers," Taithur said, slapping his knees and standing up. "Just a passing cloud. Nothing serious." Then, pensively. "Even so, I think we'll have to be careful with our monitoring. We can play God with these creatures. We can intercept every transmission they send. We can record, analyse, project, and to some extent manipulate, but we mustn't forget we're moving into the heart of the infection. We'll be sitting right in the thick of it all, and there are some hard times ahead for us all. We mustn't wake up one day to find that we've become the same as them."

Taithur brooded enough on the thought to mention it at the next Council Meeting. Proktor and the other younger members thought his concern unnecessary, but most of the older members admitted, albeit awkwardly, to an indefinable unease about the horrors being perpetrated on the planet beneath them. Hester in particular was disturbed.

"Let's be honest," she said. "Being in cycle is more than a Service injunction. Not even the most anti-Service person amongst us would disagree about the rightness of that. It's something deeply rooted in us. The Service only codifies what most of us know instinctively is correct. It never occurs to us to think why. We're a certain type of animal, we need such and such chemicals to survive, we need to be in cycle—it's obvious. A basic fact of existence. But why?"

"Doubtless you've got a theory, Hester," said Proktor, conspicuously stifling a yawn. Taithur glowered at him, but it was unnecessary. Hester was Education Department trained and at 1801 was the highest graded person on board the Rithid. She exuded a considerable presence when she chose, and Proktor now felt the full force of it. She turned to him slowly and held his gaze with her own. In spite of himself, Taithur's mouth went dry in sympathy. Her voice was soft and patient but held overtones that made everyone sit very still lest they attract her attention. Proktor went first red, then white.

"No, Proktor," she said. "I've no theory. Just a little conjecture for us to think about. As a group we're way beyond the pale now. A vast physical distance from our old homes, a vast emotional distance from our old selves, and who can say what distance we're outside the Law and what trouble we're brewing for ourselves in the future. We're totally isolated in every sense of the word, and thrown amongst wild and dangerous savages whose conduct is the very antithesis of everything we consider to be fundamental." She leaned forward slightly and Proktor's hands tightened perceptibly on the arms of his chair. "We're going to need our every technological resource to survive—and more besides. And the only other resources we have are our intellects and our instincts. We must therefore familiarize ourselves with the noble and ancient art of thinking, and learn to practise again the even older art of listening to our inner thoughts. My inner voice says 'tell them this now.' So I offer it to you, no matter how tedious or embarrassing you find it."

She paused, and then somehow broke the tension that had held not only Proktor, but virtually everyone, motionless.

With commendable speed, Proktor struggled to win back at least a little of the ground he had just lost.

"I apologize, Hester," he said hoarsely. "I was rude."

Taithur raised an eyebrow in mild surprise while Hester inclined her head a little in acceptance.

"My conjecture," she continued, emphasizing the word, "is that our natural tendency to be in cycle is like most of our so-called natural urges. It's a trait developed by the need to survive. Presumably, once upon a time, we, humans, occupied only one planet." She raised her hands to silence the protests that were about to fly. "All right, I know, highly improbable, etcetera, but even if we started spontaneously on several planets, it doesn't affect my argument. Like all other creatures we must have evolved from some more basic disorganized state." More protest seemed imminent, but she beat it down before it started. "Just because there's no record of our being anything other than what we are today doesn't preclude our having evolved. It's merely a measure of our ability to keep records. We know we've evolved socially. I believe we've probably evolved physically as well. We can't always have been like this, can we?"

She did not wait for an answer, but hurried on. "My opinion is that our ancestors developed in many ways, and those that didn't learn to live in cycle, ultimately perished."

"That certainly is a conjecture," said Alachev pleasantly. Taithur smiled to himself. Social evolution at work, he thought. Alachev learning from Proktor's discomfiture. "But what does this mean for us here, amongst these savages."

Hester looked thoughtful. "I don't know, Alachev. You can pooh-pooh the idea of our originating on one or even a few planets. You can pooh-pooh the idea of physical evolution. But there's no denying we're a prodigiously old race, and that our real origins go back well beyond all known documentation. I think it would be unwise to assume that we weren't once like these savages here."

This did produce an uproar, as a mixture of indignation, anger and amused tolerance rose spontaneously from around the table amid much head shaking and hand waving. The consensus on the ship was that the natives were the descendants of some ill-fated exploratory venture made in the dim and distant past.

"If they're anything, they're degenerated stock, not original," someone said, summarizing the response.

"Precisely," said Hester quietly, waiting for the noise to subside. "But degenerated from what?"

She opened her arms and looked around the table, as if inviting answers. None, however, were forthcoming.

"Three things I see. One. If they've degenerated from the survivors of some ancient expedition, then it can at least be argued that the urge… drive… what you will, to live in cycle is a losable attribute. One learned late in our development. Two. If they're not degenerated stock, then the implication is that their forefathers, who must of course have been our forefathers as well, didn't have this attribute."

There was silence in the room, as many of the looks of amusement and indignation changed into uncomfortable frowns.

"And if they've developed here spontaneously," Taithur ventured. "Then, remembering they're human, it shows that living in cycle is an attribute that has to be acquired."

Hester nodded.

"Uncomfortable thoughts," Taithur continued. "But, as Alachev asked, what does it mean for us here here?"

Liefer caught Taithur's eye. Taithur nodded.

As usual, Liefer's slow voice seemed to redirect the momentum of the debate.

"I think what Hester is telling us is that if living in cycle is a trait that can be lost, then in mixing with creatures like these, so far from our home cultures, we too might lose it in time. Perhaps not us, but possibly our children."

Hester nodded. "Exactly," she said.

Several people tried to speak, but Taithur cut them short. "We haven't time for a debate on Hester's views on evolution and the origin of humanity, so let's leave that for leisure time. Even given that Hester's idea is conjecture, it has an ominous ring of plausibility about it. Obviously we haven't the facts to decide the matter once and for all, but there's no harm in considering it as a contingency. Assuming what you say is correct Hester, what can we do?"

Hester shrugged and looked almost shamefaced. "I don't know," she said. "I just spoke because I felt it was the right thing to do. My thoughts are far from clear, but the basic idea has been wandering in and out of my mind for a long time now. You know well enough that I prefer hard analysis to this kind of mushy thinking, but…"

"It's not necessary to apologize," Taithur interrupted. "We all know there are matters that don't lend themselves readily to logical analysis in the first instance. Your thinking has focused my own a little more clearly, and I think some of the others." He laid his hands flat on the table. "So, we see a potential danger of some form of contamination either from these natives, or through isolation from our own kind. Something that might cause us to slip out of cycle and set off on a path of divergent consumption." The idea provoked an emotional response in him, and he felt suddenly cold. "Apart from keeping away from these creatures I don't know what else we can do. Perhaps just knowing about it will be sufficient. At least we can be on the lookout for any untoward symptoms. Has anyone any suggestions to offer?"

There was a brief and desultory debate yielding little more than a vague declaration that a problem might well exist and that the matter should be watched carefully.

"No real facts, so no real solution," said Liefer reluctantly, as an awkward silence fell. "A vague awareness of the problem is all we have and all we can offer to deal with it."

A throat was cleared nervously. Taithur recognized the sound and turned.

"Jion," he said encouragingly. "You've something to add?"

65

Jion cleared his throat again and Proktor muttered something under his breath. "Yes Taithur," said the nervous anthropologist. "And I think it might have a bearing on this matter." Taithur nodded and gestured to him to continue.

Jion cast a nervous glance around the table and rubbed his hands together uncertainly.

"These people." Taithur noted the use of the word people, with its implication of humanity. He found it significant that Jion was using it again. "These people are indisputably human, and their various tribes show many traits which have parallels in some of our own societies. They're really quite fascinating…"

There was a satisfied introspection in his manner and, for a moment, Taithur thought the young man was going to wander off into a technical eulogy. He began searching around for a way to forestall this which would not humiliate this shy newcomer to the Council. However, it proved unnecessary.

"But," continued Jion. "This inability or unwillingness to live in cycle is a most profound difference between our two cultures." His forehead puckered as he searched for the right words. "We're going to have the greatest difficulty communicating with them. I know that our translators have most of the languages sorted out now, and that we've all learnt the dominant one, but it would be a mistake to imagine that therefore we'll understand them, and probably an even bigger mistake to imagine that they'll understand us."

"So?" said Proktor, dismissively. "Who cares? They're savages. We'll knock it into them somehow. In any case, we've spent a lot of time deciding that we'll be keeping away from them, so what's your problem, Jion?"

Surprisingly, Jion turned on him, his voice singularly free of its normal hesitancy. "One of the traits these people exhibit, Proktor, is curiosity. They wander all over their planet…"

"Poisoning as they go," interjected Proktor with a slightly nervous grin.

Jion gestured the comment aside. "Curious, Proktor. Very curious. Quite soon, for all we're hiding in the most unpleasant locations, a group of them will come wandering by and they'll find us. And what they see will most surely tell them we're not from anywhere on their planet."

Proktor affected a look of patience. "We'll have our EC screen linked to the veiling units, Jion…"

Jion's eyes narrowed. Then, sarcastically. "Yes Proktor, I'm aware of that, but, if you recall, the EC screen is less than perfect at ground level. We'll be relying on buffer zones—far from perfect—and these people have a habit of walking round on their legs, you know." He ran his first two fingers along the table in a walking action towards Proktor.

Taithur casually looked down to hide a smile at this uncharacteristic response. "Come back to your point, Jion," he said.

Jion turned away from the glowering Proktor. "My point, Taithur, is that we'll encounter these people sooner rather than later, and when we do, this gap in our respective perceptions of living in cycle will make it almost impossible for us to really understand one another. This lack of understanding will breed fear on their part, and like humans throughout the galaxy, these people will attack when they're frightened."

"It's a fair point, Jion," said Taithur. "But it really does no more than bolster our intention of keeping away from them, and learning as much as we can." He was loathe to discourage Jion in his contributions to the Council, but there was no point in endlessly justifying what was now established policy.

"I appreciate that, Taithur," replied Jion. "I mention it only because I have more accurate probability figures available now. That's why I said sooner rather than later."

The figures appeared in the central display and Hester leaned forward to examine them. After a moment she sat back, her face enigmatic. Taithur looked at her quizzically.

"Well?" he asked

"I can't tell immediately," Hester replied. "But it doesn't look good. Development before contact has always been finely balanced, and projections after contact have always been beyond reasonable analysis due to the uncertain temper of these creatures—people." She stared in concentration at the hovering figures. "This work is much more detailed than any we've had before. I'll have to study it carefully—it shouldn't take too long," she added, to forestall Taithur's impatience. "There may be mitigating elements, but it looks as if that fine balance may be even finer."

Taithur was about to speak when Jion interrupted. "There's worse," he said. Then he hesitated as all eyes in the room turned towards him. He cleared his throat. "Just as a matter of routine, we did a standard Service projection check based on the present divergence of these people."

Hester raised her eyebrows. "I'd have thought they were far beyond the limits of that," she said.

"Yes, they were, of course," Jion continued. "But it gave us a good first order approximation for a more accurate step-by-step analysis. You see Hester, if..."

"No technicalities, Jion," said Taithur firmly. "Come to the point."

Jion paused, then cleared his throat again. "Well. These people are at a strange stage. Left to their own devices they'll probably destroy themselves eventually—any one of a number of avenues lead to that conclusion. And they'll probably destroy themselves before they come anywhere near leaving this star system. But..." He raised a finger in emphasis. "While they're still very primitive, they're nonetheless at the foot of an exponential technological development. Our calculations show that if they gain access to our modern technology, they'll accelerate along that development at an appalling rate. If they get Darvod-hunt drive and even a hint of our weaponry, they'll be out into the galaxy like a plague, and with their viciousness and destructiveness and almost total lack of environmental awareness, they'll wreak untold harm."

"We won't give it to them, Jion," said Taithur. "I'm surprised you should think we would."

"You won't need to," said Hester quietly. "If Jion's projections of early contact are accurate, and I'm sure they will be, and if his observations about mutual misunderstanding are accurate, then there's every chance of violence. And as we've already discussed, they have the capacity, if only through sheer numbers, to overwhelm us. They'll take our technology, Taithur. Take it."

Taithur bent his head forward and put his hand to his forehead. Doubts threatened to crash in on him. What was he doing here, leading these people into who knew what horror? And now perhaps threatening countless systems with these savages.

Was it stubborn pride... childish ego... arrogance? Like a braying, jeering army they paraded triumphantly in front of him, and he, like a puppet general, took their salute.

Face them.

His father's admonition rang in his mind. Just another test. A twinge of self-pity emerged, but he crushed it unaided, reprimanding himself.

Who said your doubts would weaken? Who said your strength would grow? You've done what's right, and you must continue to do so. You know that you and your people must strive to achieve, the Way is never easy.

The silence in the room became oppressive. He wanted to look around at the waiting faces and ask, "What shall we do? What shall we do?" but he knew no answer lay there. He sensed the tensions all around him pulling him in every direction, pulling him apart, but not moving him. He felt as though he were an insect undergoing metamorphosis—a sudden, abrupt change of state. Somewhere nearby was the step he must take to release these tensions and move the whole venture into its next phase.

He stepped forward into a black void.

"We cannot risk that," he said. He looked at Hester. There was a glimmer of pity in her eyes which she was trying to hide for fear of offending him. She had defined the dilemma for herself.

"We'll devote more of our resources to defence," he said, simply. "If necessary, we'll go out of cycle ourselves."

# Chapter 11

Ersand adjusted the transparency of the great cowled viewport over the leisure area. The huge disc of the planet dominated the scene, and the sunlight reflecting from its surface was almost unbearable.

Looking first to the left and then to the right he could see the sleek black flanks of the Rithid.

She might be an old tub, he thought, but she's a stylish one.

Ersand was a Captain to the core, possessed of that strange deep affection for his vessel that only a Captain can know. Especially one who has nursed it against the odds through the vast, improbable distance that they had covered.

Although, like everyone else, he was excited at the coming settlement, and looking forward eagerly to his first drop down to the surface, he was oddly relieved that his special position would enable him to spend the bulk of his time aboard the ship.

Somewhere deep inside him, a small note sounded, announcing the approach of the end of his career as a starflight Captain and he found its harmony not to his liking. Whenever he heard it he pushed it rapidly to one side, and his mind rushed for solace to the splendid technicalities of his ship. The complex organization of the crew, from its engineers to its kitchen hands, from its Doctors to its entertainers, all to be fed and housed and sustained so that they meshed together into a machine every bit as efficient as the ship itself, and, he would muse, in many ways more mysterious in its workings. It was akin to playing a musical instrument.

Then there was the palm tingling eeriness of Darvod-hunt space, that no-space within space, with its haunting, indescribable vistas that flooded into all the senses, and gave Captains that slight but character-istic distance from ordinary mortals who had to be held in automatic hypnotic suspension until the ship returned to ordinary space.

Gossip in the Clubs was that D-h space was addictive, and ghostly tales abounded of Captains who had disappeared during D-h hops. "They said he was a bit subdued, preoccupied like, when they went into sus. Then when they came round—nothing—gone. Empty chair, no sign anywhere on board. And there they were. Stuck until Education could come out and rescue them. Oh it's creepy all right."

Ersand smiled to himself.

"I suppose you're pleased to see everything under way," came a voice from behind him. He turned and met Malva's laughing brown eyes. He smiled broadly. It was difficult not to be extremely fond of Malva. He knew more than many that it was her quiet, practical personality that provided an anchor for Taithur, and kept his feet firmly on the ground whenever his religious vision looked like sending his ideas whirling off into the cosmos.

"Yes and no," he replied. "I'm used to making difficult decisions. It's a normal part of my job, but there've been times recently when I felt like a recruit on his first operational tour. Relieved and burdened, excited and worried, certain and uncertain all at the same time."

Malva laughed and moved to stand beside him. She leaned on the viewport sill and looked out at the bright planet.

"Yes," she said. "I can understand that. While we were travelling we were in a sense still at home—life wasn't hedged in by the Service but it was still ordered, disciplined. It couldn't be anything else. We were held together physically and emotionally by danger and faith. Now the ties are being slackened and we're splitting up, spreading out across this strange world."

She hugged herself and smiled. "It's human nature, Ers. We want security so we build up a bureaucracy to ensure that, and then we say, 'That's too oppressive—we should be free' and we kick and scream until we are. We want life to be steady and reliable, yet we eternally change things. Just plain folks Ers, just plain folks."

A cheer from a nearby group interrupted them as a shuttle appeared above the dome and then floated vertically downwards until it was level with the leisure area. Waving figures could be seen at its sideports and the cheering and applause increased as members of the group identified friends and relatives. Then an involuntary "Ooo" rose up as the shuttle majestically rolled onto its side and silently arced down into the dazzling brightness of the planet.

Despite having seen similar sights many times before, Ersand still felt a thrill, and he noted that the exclamation came from more than just the watching children. Without a doubt, these ships were exciting to watch.

As the cheering faded and the children started to split away from the group and run about the area, mimicking the flawless flight of the shuttle, one of the men put his arm around the shoulders of the woman by his side. Her face was radiant and happy but she was crying a little and there was a slight hint of tightness about the man's mouth for all it was smiling. Ersand felt a wave of sadness pass over him, and he released the breath he had been unconsciously holding.

Malva looked at him for a moment, and laid her hand on his arm.

"The Rithid's a long way from its Return," she said. "She mightn't be doing much D-h hopping from now on, but she's still got a lot to do and so have you. She'll be floating here for generations yet."

Ersand's forehead wrinkled. He was about to profess ignorance of what she meant, but her touch and her eyes evaporated the lie before it formed.

"You're too perceptive by half, Malva," he said ruefully. She passed her arm through his and turned to walk him round the edge of the leisure area.

"I don't have to be perceptive to know how you feel about your ship. Are all Captain's the same?" she said.

"More or less," Ersand replied. "Running a ship's not something you can do half-heartedly."

She nodded, then, "Will it bother you? No more D-h hops?"

Ersand chuckled. "Do you mean 'Is D-h space addictive?'"

"Now who's being perceptive?"

Ersand laughed outright. "I don't need to be perceptive to know what people say about D-h space," he said.

Malva squeezed his arm affectionately. "Seriously, Ers. Will it bother you—cause you problems?"

Ersand looked thoughtful. "I don't know Malva," he said, eventually.

"It's an experience beyond description, that's why no-one ever talks about it at length. Once you've been through it, there's no denying that you'll want to do it again. But I don't think the desire is so strong you'd call it an addiction." He paused, searching for words. "You see," he said self-consciously. "You tongue-tie me, making me try to explain it to you."

They walked in silence for a time, eventually rising up onto one of the high walkways that overlooked the leisure area. Leaning on the guardrail Ersand spoke again.

"I'll miss it without a doubt," he said at last. "How serious that will be for me? If I'm honest, I don't know. Only time will tell."

He fell silent again and stared down at the people below.

"My only consolation will be that I've been in D-h space. Something that only a tiny few can ever hope to do. I've made contact with—I've been—an entirely different reality."

"But?" Malva offered. There was another silence.

"But there's no denying, there's a strange tiny piece of me, deep inside—inside all of us—Captains, that is—that just wants to disappear into D-h space for ever."

Malva opened her mouth to speak, but catching the strange distant look on Ersand's face, changed her mind.

"I'm sorry, Ers," she said. "I didn't mean to pry. I was just concerned. I didn't want you to think that no-one cared about the Rithid, or your… peculiar loss, in our haste to make a new beginning."

Ersand's enigmatic expression faded and he smiled. "I understand, Malva. And I appreciate your concern. But I'm afraid there's nothing anyone can do about the problem except me, and I'm sure I'll be able to cope—I'll certainly have plenty to do."

The noise from the hall rose up and, surrounding them, carried away their introspection. Below them a few people were playing games but most were gathered around the edge looking out at the planet or at the maintenance crews crawling over the Rithid's glistening surface.

"The ship's going to feel empty with so many gone," said Malva, glad of the opportunity to return to normal. Ersand grunted slightly and stood up, straightening his tunic that had creased up against the guardrail.

"It might feel empty," he said. "But it's going to be busy. Busier than we've been since we set out. Especially during initial establishment—the data from ground probes will be enormous—and the quarantine problems…" He shook his head. Quarantine procedures worried Ersand. Years of sometimes hard experience had taught him that the consequences of neglecting them could be profoundly serious. But equally, that same experience had taught him that they were all too easily neglected. Again, Malva seemed to intercept his thoughts.

"I wouldn't worry too much about quarantine, Ers," she said. "Not after that red-handed briefing you gave us all. I think you've made your point more than vividly. By the way, where in the world did you get those old projections?"

Ersand could not help smiling.

"I've had those for years," he said, turning to move along the walkway. "Our instructor at College didn't think astro-health was a topic to be learnt calmly in a 'Psychologically Optimal Environment.' He beat it into us. 'You can learn your procedures from your Manuals,' he'd say, 'but you've got to learn the need here.'" Ersand smacked his stomach in imitation of his old tutor. "'A wrong piece of DNA in the wrong place and phut, you're gone—and like as not, your crew. Sometimes whole communities. And gone none too nicely I might add.' Then he'd launch into a catalogue of horrors that was guaranteed to make a lifetime's impression." Ersand paused and shook his head with an amused grimace. "On a strong day he'd have a third of his class either passing out or fleeing the room. He was a tartar, but he knew his job without a doubt, although I only appreciated that when I actually saw the effects of an infestation." Ersand's face darkened briefly, but the mood passed almost immediately. "Anyway, I just gave you the edited version of one of his lectures. I thought it was enough for a civilian audience."

Malva puffed out her cheeks. "It certainly was," she said. "Neither Taith nor I slept at all well that night."

Ersand chuckled. "Good," he said, unsympathetically. "Let's hope it had the same effect on everyone else, then maybe they'll remember when it really counts."

Malva looked half inclined to argue the point, but a shadow fell on them as they walked down the final ramp to the floor of the leisure area. Looking up, they saw two shuttles hanging silently between them and the planet.

"I thought it was a cloud," said Malva, with a self-conscious smile.

"So did I," admitted Ersand.

Like all the others before them, the two shuttles were moving slowly downwards to come level with the leisure area before starting their drop onto the planet's surface. The pilot of the first shuttle had done it on a whim and the others had followed suit by popular demand. It added a carnival atmosphere to the departures.

"Those were the last," said Ersand when the shuttles had disappeared into the glare of the planet and the cheering had died down. He moved to the edge of the area and rested his forehead on the viewport, his lined face gaunt in the harsh planetlight.

Malva watched him, her face concerned. Not for the first time she seemed to sense an appalling loneliness in him, but she knew she could offer no solace. She was not even sure that it was loneliness, but she was sure that whatever it was, it was private and unassailable and a necessary part of the man. All she could do was wait.

"Incredible," he said after a long silence. Malva's expression turned to one of surprise.

"Incredible," he repeated. "All this way. All this work. All the fears and the endless meetings, and calculations and discussion. And now we're here, and we're starting. Incredible." He turned to look at her, his face alive. "Taithur's led us out of the grip of the Service, he's led us to an oasis in the wilderness. We're free, Malva. Actually free. And I can't quell this feeling inside that we're going to succeed. I feel as if I'm part of a huge unstoppable mass rolling downhill. We're going to struggle against unimaginable problems, and we're going to win. We're going to turn this planet into a paradise. I haven't been so excited since I did my first solo hop."

# Chapter 12

The establishment of the four main bases went broadly according to plan. The first few weeks were both exciting and frantic as the pioneer teams worked to establish the environmental control screens. Until these were activated, not only had the teams to work in appalling conditions, but their temporary work camps, though small, were visible from above.

On board the Rithid, monitoring of the broadcasts from the planet was increased radically. Now the travellers were listening not only for the loud indications that would surely signal the discovery of one of the base camps, but for more subtle signs that would indicate a risk of discovery in the near future.

Jion's face became strained as he began to grapple with the implications of this new work, and Hester too became reserved and offhand, almost to the point of rudeness.

"These... people are so restless and fretful," she reflected one day after sitting still and silent in her chair for an unusually long time.

Matten's sensitive ear caught the need for release in his wife's voice, and encouraged it with an attentive look and a husbandly grunt.

"It's as if they're looking for something," Hester continued, almost to herself. "As if they know something's wrong but they're trying to run away from it rather than face it."

Matten nodded. "They're human," he said. "They must realize what they're doing, surely. If they share our ancestry then there must be some residual knowledge deep inside that's trying to set them on the right path, and if they're in some way original to this planet perhaps that faculty is beginning to develop."

"Maybe," said Hester, doubtfully. "But it's all too slow. They're destroying faster than they're learning to repair." She fell silent again and Matten waited.

After a while she wriggled herself upright in her chair and furrowed her brow. "It's their unpredictability that's so difficult to deal with. That, and their incredible curiosity. They've got little groups of people wandering all over the globe for the strangest of reasons." She threw open her arms in a gesture of resigned surprise. "Do you know, Matten, they've actually got people within a few hundred miles of our base camps at the south pole and in that desert. When you look how our pioneers are suffering, with our technology, it's almost unbelievable that these primitives would even think of venturing into such places. But they do—with their pathetic equipment."

Matten did not seem too surprised. "Well, as you said, they're an inquisitive people. We all do things against our better judgement at times."

Hester waved the comment aside with a scowl that made Matten smile. I hadn't finished, it said. "The point is," she continued, leaning forward and tapping the arm of her chair in emphasis, "some of these groups are scientists after a fashion. All very crude of course, but it's a hopeful sign. The others are, guess what?" Matten shrugged. "Warriors," said Hester in a tone of bewildered resignation. "I ask you. Soldiers, learning how to fight and kill one another in places that hardly anyone on the planet would even want to visit. And they're nothing like the soldiers I've trained. Such ferocity. Such paranoia."

She flopped back in her chair. "I have this feeling that they're reaching out for something they sense they need, but at the same time, I can't avoid the feeling that when they find it, they'll smash it. One way or another, malice or clumsiness, they'll smash it."

Matten's smile broadened. "You're tired Hester," he said. "The kind of projection work you and Jion are doing would be difficult enough on a civilized planet, let alone here."

Hester's mood eased. "They're human," she mimicked. Matten acknowledged her irony with a nod.

"Yes," he said. "But they've formed a very alien culture as you've just admirably demonstrated. You and Jion are doing original, not routine work, and I don't think you've realized that yet. These people are all exceptions and no rules."

It was a phrase that passed rapidly into the language of the travellers.

While Jion and Hester and their team were occupied with the monitoring and projection analyses, Ersand was concerned with more immediate problems. The logistical problems of positioning the Rithid and moving people and materials to and from the surface proved to be more complex than he had envisaged.

The inhabitants of the planet had girdled their world with a plethora of satellites in a wide variety of orbits, and although a minimal amount of veiling shielded the Rithid from their primitive probes, she was not invisible. It was thus imperative to keep the ship from even the peripheral vision of various camera satellites and two small manned satellites. In addition, Ersand had to ensure that the Rithid did not pass in front of the planet's single large moon.

These constraints restricted movement quite severely and prevented the easy access to the base camps that Ersand would have preferred. In addition, great care had also to be exercised by the shuttles as they did not have D-h surfaces and were working on jury-rigged veiling mechanisms.

The consequent delays were not to anyone's taste, and Ersand had some problems with one or two of his younger officers who, with the typical optimism of youth, did not seem to be able to absorb the consequences of too premature a meeting with the natives.

At Ersand's request, Hester incorporated a factor to cover this problem and ran her calculations again. Her verdict was simple.

"Get them into line, Ers. Tell them why—explain it as well as you can to those who don't have the maths—but get them into line whether they understand it or not." Then a flash of her Service training with the Education Department. "Full field punishment for anyone who deviates from procedure. We're working from first principles here, not nit-picking some inappropriate Service Manual."

Ersand passed the observation to his officers. His formal manner and the shade of Hester in the background had more effect than any ranting he could have risen to, and the brighter sparks in his crew had to content themselves henceforth with shining in private.

Once the environmental screens had been installed and tested, the base camps became increasingly autonomous, and the number of essential shuttle journeys was reduced considerably. Life on the Rithid fell gradually into a routine and Ersand found himself able to instigate a much-needed programme of maintenance. It would be difficult to make the Rithid space-worthy enough for extensive hops without the full dock facilities of a major Service port but she could be rendered fit for hops to local systems, and Ersand realized that that would be more than useful if the Service ever did find out where they were and what they were doing.

A combination of experience and imagination enabled Matthew and his engineers to effect substantial repairs to the gravity silo, and this gave Ersand the chance he had been seeking to take the Rithid near to their new sun in order to revitalize the ship's semi-organic D-h surface and sere out any residual Irm spore.

Taithur and Malva joined Ersand in the leisure area as the ship eased past the battered innermost planet of the system, and began its spiralling tour of the star. As they flew on, a strange stillness began to pervade the whole ship, and Malva looked about her in wonder.

"It's the shields," Ersand said in reply to her unspoken question. "They're working on automatic feedback—increasing in strength in proportion to the intensity of the various radiations that strike them." His voice was flat and dead, totally without resonance, and Malva had to lean forward to hear him. He smiled. "Because they need to be so strong this near to a star, they're apt to develop these odd induction fields within the ship."

"It's not unpleasant," said Malva, her voice strange in her own ears. "In fact, it's very relaxing."

"This one is," said Ersand. "But they tend to be a bit of a mystery. Some of them can be quite alarming—it depends on all sorts of things—what kind of star it is, what kind of radiation has to be let through to the surface, what kind reflected, what kind stored…" He let his comments tail off as he saw Malva's attention drift to the huge horizon of the star just rising into view.

The great domed viewport immediately adjusted its transparency to reduce the brilliance that flooded around the watchers. The effect was disorientating and brought an involuntary gasp from the watchers. Malva took her husband's hand and together they stood in the deep stillness and watched as the curved edge rose slowly above them until it seemed that the whole universe was dominated by the face of their new home sun. It was a sight that few had been privileged to see: the furious swirling face of creation.

Malva turned briefly to Ersand, but her question died unasked. In the flickering strangled sunlight she saw tears gathered in the man's eyes, tears of neither sadness nor elation. And there was that look on his face which showed him to be apart from other mortals. She wondered again whether the strange knowledge that fell to starflight Captains would sustain Ersand when he had to face leaving his allotted task and adapt to being planet-bound.

Abruptly, the image before them shifted, and there were muffled cries in the stillness as several people staggered and fell.

Ersand chuckled, and uttered an insincere apology.

"Sorry," he said. "The gravity effects are always a bit odd so close. Just hold on to something, or better still, sit down. We'll be beginning our searing tour in a moment. Be careful how you watch the sun. We'll be spinning quite fast and some people find it very disconcerting."

Slowly the scene in front of them shifted and the edge of the sun came into view again. Then, without any perceptible sensation within the Rithid, they were hurtling forward. Whether it was some effect of gravity, or whether it was just a psychological effect brought on by the sight of the sun's surface rushing below them, Malva could not have said, but the sense of overwhelming speed made her grasp the arms of her chair.

She heard her husband laugh quietly in the muffled stillness and looking at him she saw he too was clutching his chair.

As the ship spun, so the image of the sun rotated in front of them, but Malva did not find this disturbing. Rather, it was hypnotic, and she felt the warm dissociating glow pervading her body that her reasoning mind identified as deep relaxation. All sense of time left her.

"Malva."

Ersand's voice was clear and distinct, quite unaffected by the muffling effects of the shield induced field, but it was faint and distant as if he were speaking from some other place. It held no urgency.

"Listen," it said, and Malva felt herself sinking deeper. It seemed that she heard a sound like a wind blowing, far away. Or was it the sound of wordless singing voices? Or fine trembling strings? But it did not matter. It was a haunting siren song from regions which the human soul cannot know save in the rarest of moments. Malva listened and knew.

The Rithid swam and twisted in the sun's thundering atmosphere like a great exulting fish battling against a raging torrent. Its route determined and controlled by harsh scientific reality, it pursued its inexorable destiny while its human cargo sat in unearthly silence and waited.

Without any conscious awareness of the fact, Malva realized suddenly that the sound had faded and was gone. The sun dropped below the viewport for the last time and the transparency of the viewport cleared to reveal the stars as the Rithid turned for home.

The sound of her own movement and the stirring of others around her seemed raucous and awkward after the infinite subtlety of what she had just heard, and she felt a profound wave of regret pass over her. She turned to look at Ersand. His gaze held hers and he nodded but did not speak.

Taithur took his wife's hand gently. "I heard it too," he said softly. "An affirmation. I heard the music of my flower in the heart of that sun." Malva raised the hand and held it against her cheek.

Her reverie was ended by a sharp intake of breath from Ersand. His face distorted as if he were in pain.

"Just a moment," he said, and leaning forward he gestured to Taithur to link in his IFT. Malva joined the two men in the link.

"Repeat," said Ersand.

A premonition filled Malva the very instant before the voice of the duty officer sounded in her head.

"Proktor's group have made contact with the natives. One of them has been killed."

# Chapter 13

Taithur had thought deeply before placing Proktor in charge of the establishment of a base camp. He was the youngest member of the Council, and though clever and capable he betrayed most of the faults of youth: impetuosity, thoughtlessness, stubbornness, and an impatience which verged at times on intolerance.

However, he had also the energy, imagination and courage of youth and was sufficiently perceptive to be aware of at least some of his own failings. This latter, coupled with a willingness to learn and an intuitive insight into needs and wishes of others, finally swayed Taithur in his recommendation to the Council.

Little came out in the Council meeting that Taithur had not already agonized over, and Proktor conducted himself well enough through the peculiar ordeal of having his character publicly discussed and analysed. At the end, when Taithur's recommendation had been accepted, Proktor's open delight broke through the reserve he had been maintaining, and seemed to illuminate the whole room.

Taithur was happy to see this effect, as he felt it vindicated his own judgement of the man, but even as he smiled he felt a twinge of regret worming inside him. It was small but it was deep, and felt like a meanness of soul. Its presence distressed him. Initially he thought it was envy, but later he decided it was fear. Proktor, for all his faults, had the potential to be a considerable leader, and it would probably be he who would replace Taithur in due course.

Meditating later that night, Taithur opened his mind to all his innermost resentments about Proktor and looked at them squarely. He looked also, as far as he was able, at his own motivation. His main purpose was still clear and undimmed. Through the miracle of a tiny flower, the Way had been made known to him, and from that time he had had no alternative but to follow it.

But fringing the edges of this purpose were many human flaws. The chief amongst them, he decided, was his enjoyment of the power he had. Proktor would take this power from him one day and it was this that he feared.

In a crucial instant he spoke out into the darkness of his private cell. "I don't want to lose this authority. I don't want to lose the respect…" He faltered. "The… awe, that others have of me because of it. I don't want Proktor—or anyone—to take it from me. I must speak this out loud like a petty child or it'll destroy me from the inside. I will—I must—relinquish my power when I have to and I must concentrate on helping Proktor to become fit to inherit it. My heart resents it, but my head knows it's right and the latter will school the former in time."

He heard his words sounding flat and foolish in the stillness. They were quite inadequate to describe the complexity of the thoughts and emotions that lay beneath them like the bulk of a huge iceberg, but he was glad he had spoken them, and his inner self soared as if relieved of a great burden.

There had been little need for debate about which base camp Proktor would command. While the travellers had to be divided into separate groups for protection in the event of discovery, the unity of the whole group was vital, for the same reason. Hester and Jion calculated that while fragmentation was not initially a high risk, it could be critical in certain circumstances, and accordingly it was decided that the development of excessive loyalty to individual camps and Council members should be discouraged. This was achieved by the comparatively simple expedient of rotating all personnel between the four surface bases and the ship. This way the intense group feeling that had developed through the long voyage would be maintained in some degree and, equally importantly, every family and every individual would be familiar with the peculiarities of each base camp.

Not that there were many differences between the camps, once established, for all their widely different locations. The control screens produced broadly the same environment in each, such differences as there were being associated with the particular resources available in each area.

It was thus a matter of pure chance that Proktor was placed in charge of the camp situated in the equatorial rain forest. The only complication that arose was Proktor's wish to be part of the pioneer team that made the initial establishment. Taithur did not need to see the horrified look on the team leader's face before replying.

"No, Proktor," he said, unequivocally. "You've been watching too many old Ent shows. Pioneer work's highly specialized and very dangerous. They need to know and trust one another completely. First-footing a new planet needs a second nature knowledge of countless procedures, that's why team members are generally related to one another. You've not even done basic training. You'll be killed sure as fate... or you'll get someone else killed and we've far too few pioneers to risk that."

Proktor protested. "Taithur. It's an almost Service Standard planet—it's not dangerous..."

Taithur stopped him with a look. "I'm not debating this, Proktor," he said decisively. "Pioneer work's always dangerous as you know full well. In any event, the decision isn't just mine, the team leader has the final say."

Taithur looked at the team leader, but before he could speak, Proktor interrupted. "We have to spread our skills," he said. It was one of Taithur's favourite expressions for dealing with the small eruptions of Service departmentalism that occurred among the travellers from time to time.

Taithur was tired, and took the point with a bad grace. "There's all the difference between learned skills and hereditary ones, Proktor, and pioneering's largely a family business," he replied, with mounting irritability.

Proktor's jaw set, and it looked for a moment as if he were considering meeting Taithur head-on, but the Pioneer team leader spared them both further aggravation. She laid a hand on Taithur's arm. "It's all right, Taithur," she said quietly. "Proktor can come as an observer. We'll put him in a remote suit with low output. That way he can stay safe in the shuttle and still get some idea of what it's all about."

Taithur felt a confiding squeeze on his arm and caught the slight wink. "Very well," he said to Proktor. "But just remember who's in charge down there. One step out of line and so help me, Council member or no, I'll put you on field punishment."

As the two left, the team leader turned and winked again at Taithur, this time broadly. Taithur flopped into his chair and spun round to stare out of the viewport at the curve of the planet's horizon. The planet's light illuminated a smile. From the more distant reaches of his mind had come the memory of his own limited experience of pioneering. Or, more correctly, the memory of the pioneering families who had instructed him. He chuckled to himself. That'll teach you not to stamp your foot and scream, Proktor, he thought.

The pioneers were so necessary and their skills were so peculiarly unteachable that they were virtually beyond the control of the Service. Taithur often wondered whether his early and brief contact with these people had not laid the seeds of his own subsequent independent turn of mind. They had the specialist's smiling disdain for outsiders, and were notorious for their extensive repertoire of practical jokes on those who ventured into their domain.

Most of their work was done inside large articulated vehicles which they referred to as 'suits' because of their approximately human shape. In fact the 'suits' were a sophisticated combination of protective clothing and remote handling technology. They cocooned the occupants from adverse conditions outside while at the same time enabling them to perform any manual task with increased dexterity and sensitivity. Long tapering fingers could pick up a butterfly with such delicacy that scarcely a single scale would fall from its wings. But, equally, those same hands could crush a granite block or tear up a tree.

The real value of the suit, however, lay in the intimate bond between the machine and its occupant. Once inside and fully connected, trained pioneers simply had to move normally and the machine would faithfully reproduce their actions. A less well trained operator was a different matter, as the correct use of the suit required that the occupant be totally aware of his or, more usually her, body.

If the task in hand was liable to be particularly dangerous, then a remote would be used, thus enabling the operator to remain in some place of safety while remaining connected to the machine. Remotes were not popular with pioneers, being intrinsically harder to use and less sensitive in operation. However, they were suitable for rough work and as they allowed dual control they were invaluable for training purposes. The trainee would sit in his own linked control module while the instructor would don the suit and demonstrate its use out on the training area.

Taithur remembered the eerie feeling of knowing that he was in reality motionless inside an isolated module while every part of him felt as if he were walking about outside. It would have been dreamlike had it not been for the constant commentary by the controller who was actually wearing the suit. At the instructor's desire, the amount of control given to the student could be varied from none to total, although it was rare that any pioneer would permit his student to have much more than half control.

It was at zero control that most of the pranks occurred. In his case he had found himself walking to the edge of a cliff, then gazing unsteadily over... then jumping.

Even now, sitting comfortably on the Rithid, he found himself gripping the arms of his chair. Bastards, he thought ruefully as he recalled his first words when he was helped from his module. His instructor was a small and jolly blond.

"Tut, tut," she said, with an infectious laugh. "That's no way to speak to your venerable instructor." Then, wrinkling her nose as she peered into the module, she clicked her tongue. "House rules, Taithur. I'm afraid you'll have to clean that up yourself."

"Penny for your thoughts."

Taithur started slightly. It was Malva, her smile barely disguising the anxiety they all felt. For a moment, Taithur's forehead frowned, then recognition dawned.

"Ah, yes," he said, standing up. "It's one of their expressions isn't it? You've quite a flair for retaining these strange idioms." He shook his head distractedly. "But you don't have to pay for my thoughts at the moment do you? Or anybody's."

The trip back from the sun had taken only minutes—"A couple of nano-hops will help run the surface in," Ersand had said—but on arrival at the planet they were obliged to remain in orbit for some hours due to an unfortunate disposition of satellites. For a similar reason they had also to maintain a communications silence.

It was not an easy time. Proktor's message hung in the air like a stale smell. "Contact made. One dead. Return." It had slipped through just before the communications silence became necessary and had been relayed by one of the shuttles which were holding station with emergency crews in the absence of the Rithid.

It was virtually impossible for Taithur and the others not to worry this brief enigmatic morsel relentlessly, even though they knew nothing could be done safely until communications were open again.

"Why's he not coming through in code. It's not like Proktor to be so careless about procedures."

"Perhaps he can't."

"Who could have died? And how? There was supposed to be no-one in the area."

"It might not be one of the natives who's been killed, it might be one of ours."

That did not go down too well, nor did most of the other imaginative flights that were made through the limbo of waiting time. Eventually Taithur took as calm and reassuring stand as he could manage.

"Look, there's nothing we can do. If Proktor's seen fit to observe the silence, then we must do the same. It's probably a good sign. If anything massive had happened we'd probably have picked it up on the general monitoring by now. We must wait as patiently as we can. Fretting and idle conjecture will gain us nothing but fatigue, and we may need all our energies shortly."

But he did not take his own advice and when Malva entered she noted the fading after-image of some of Hester's calculations hanging in the air. She put her arms around his neck and rested her forehead against his.

"Not long now," she said. Taithur let out a noisy breath. "I hope Proktor's not done anything stupid," he said, as if it were the continuation of a long conversation. For a moment Malva considered reproaching him, but she decided to let the matter lie. The consequences of what might have happened were too serious for her to expect anything other than Taithur's complete absorption in them, independent of whether he could do anything or not.

After a seemingly interminable time, an asthmatic crackle on the shipwide communicator indicated the re-opening of ship to planet transmissions.

"We're through, Proktor," came the slightly relieved voice of one of the base camp operators. It faded slightly as he apparently turned away to address Proktor, and for a moment the sound of Proktor's approaching footsteps filled the Rithid. Aware of the many listeners, Taithur forced a calm purposefulness into his voice.

"Report, Proktor," he said. "You're on shipwide link. Tell us what's happened."

Proktor's voice was controlled, but strained.

"We've killed one of the natives, Taithur. I'm sending a simultaneous report directly into the computer now for everyone to examine, but I'd like you to come down right away..." He was interrupted by someone entering the room and bringing with him the noise and clatter of the busy camp. There was some hissing for silence and a muffled apology, then Proktor spoke again. "Taithur. Bring someone down from Medical to examine the body."

# Chapter 14

"Poor devil," said Taithur, gazing down at the body in front of him. In the subdued lighting of the quarantine unit his face looked drawn and tired.

He glanced again at the preliminary medical report and then turned to Andreas, the duty Medical Officer who had come down with him from the Rithid.

"So much for quarantine," he said grimly. "It's one aspect we didn't give as much thought to as we should have done."

Andreas nodded his head slightly. "It's not usually a problem," he said. "There was no reason we should have. In any event it wouldn't have prevented this."

Taithur looked doubtful. This time Andreas shook his head. "No," he said firmly. "The camp Medical unit did everything they could. The man was simply beyond all help." He reached out to the control panel and increased the intensity of the lighting.

Taithur sighed. "Well the least we can do is give him an honourable Return," he said. "See that he is fully analysed. We must learn everything that is to be learnt from this incident. There are appalling implications here."

"Indeed," agreed Andreas, reaching up to pull his visor down over his face. Then he paused and cast an enquiring look at the report. "Is that enough for now?" he asked.

"Yes," Taithur replied. "More than enough. You carry on. Take whatever time you need, and if you need any special equipment, get it sent down—battle priority, my order."

Andreas muttered an acknowledgement, and sliding the visor down, he bent forward over the body.

As he was about to step into the sterilizing exit bay, Taithur turned and looked again at the corpse floating in now bright lighting. As Andreas moved, the light caught his visor, and briefly Taithur had the impression of a large predatory insect hovering over the body.

When he stepped out of the irritating crackle of the bay he was still scowling. Proktor misunderstood. "That's Ersand, Taith," he said. "I think he got the cook to set the bays. He's so cautious about quarantine." Taithur looked at him vacantly for a moment until the meaning of his words sank in. Proktor's well-meant humour jarred, and scattered the already confused jumble of thoughts that were vying for his attention. He shook his head and waved his arm as if to dismiss them.

"Quite right too," he said, for the sake of something to say. "Look what happens when it goes wrong."

Proktor stood silent and uncertain, unwilling to catch Taithur's eye, and anxious about what might happen next. Taithur looked at him and then, for the first time since he had landed, became aware of the sun, warm on his face, and the air carrying strange scents to him.

Real gravity under your feet, Ersand had said, and with the memory of those words Taithur felt the tension of the last few hours slip away from him.

Lifting his face skyward he closed his eyes and breathed in deeply. Something very old stirred within him, stretching as if from a long sleep.

"And the heart shall dance to the music of the morning air," he said softly.

"I'm sorry?" said Proktor, puzzled. Taithur opened his eyes and smiled.

"It's all right, Proktor," he said. "I was talking to myself. A little personal prayer."

Even though he felt the presence of the dead native, pregnant with awful possibilities, he wanted to shout a great paean of joy up into the sunny air and out into the empty starways.

"Come what may, we're here. This is our home and our future. Thank you."

The sound echoed in his mind, but he said nothing. The whole base seemed to glow with life and vigour.

"It's looking good Proktor," he said, adopting a more businesslike tone. "Take me round and tell me exactly what happened again. Only slowly this time."

Proktor raised his hand to a passing vehicle, but Taithur waved it on as it turned towards them.

"Let's walk while we talk Proktor. I want to feel what's happening as well as see it."

Proktor took a risk. "You're in a fey mood Taithur," he said.

Taithur laughed explosively. "Fey means I'm in high spirits because I'm about to die," he said. Then, seeing Proktor's discomfiture, he took him by the arm and propelled him along the dusty roadway. "That may be the case, Proktor, who can tell? But as far as I'm concerned I'm in high spirits because I'm in high spirits. I need no other reason in this sunshine and this air." And he laughed again.

Proktor smiled in spite of himself. "I don't understand," he said. "I'd have thought that you'd have been a little more concerned at our first contact with the natives, especially under these circumstances."

"I am," said Taithur, more quietly. "But that die is cast now, for better or for worse, and we can weigh the consequences at our leisure." He looked around at the bustling activity of the base: its growing buildings and roads; people walking, running; vehicles careening back and forth. And the occasional incongruously soft hiss of one of the pioneer suits passing by.

He could not find the words to explain to Proktor the sense of optimism and forward movement he could feel. He realized there was a factor at work that could not be included even in Jion and Hester's most sophisticated calculations. It was as if all the travellers had been restrained by some unseen force throughout their long journey, and were now bursting out like the waters of a breached dam. The premature and tragic contact with the natives was like a boulder in the flood. It would cause turbulence and diversions, but it would not, could not, stop the flow now gathering momentum. It would roll and roll until it found its place of equilibrium in the history of these unfolding events where it would remain as a small monument to times gone.

Slowly he felt his euphoria slipping away, just as his earlier tension had gone, and his mind returned to the problem in hand. No matter where this boulder was going to end up, it was his job here and now to make sure it did as little damage as possible.

"Down here," he said, indicating a roadway that led towards the perimeter of the base, the buffer zone. "Tell me as we walk."

Proktor told his tale quickly and simply. The dead man had been a passenger in a small aircraft that had flown into the EC screen and subsequently crashed. Why the craft was flying in that area, so far from the routes that these people normally flew, was a mystery. Its presence had been picked up routinely by the security monitors, but had only given rise to serious alarm when it suddenly changed direction and headed towards the base.

"We mapped out a contingency plan for this based on simple instrument interference, but I'm afraid it didn't work," said Proktor. "I don't know why they headed straight towards us. Their instruments must have been going wild. In fact, everything must have been going wild when they hit the screen's automatic defences, but the monitoring of their on-board talk wasn't very clear."

Taithur stopped and shot a worried glance at Proktor who shrugged apologetically. "They were all highly excited—understandably I suppose—all four of them talking—shouting, at once—and in some obscure dialect. Then there was the engine noise..." He paused. Taithur motioned him to continue and strode out again, his eyes fixed on his shadow undulating on the increasingly uneven ground. He did not want to disturb Proktor's report, but he made a note to have this aspect of language looked into further. Although one language dominated the planet, there were many others widely used, and countless local variations and dialects. It was essential that they understand all of these.

"Anyway, they just kept coming," continued Proktor. "There was nothing we could do. They only skimmed the top of the EC screen, but the eddy currents tore the aircraft almost in two." He paused, his face suddenly tense. Then, very softly: "Two of them fell straight out."

Taithur did not want to hear, but knew he had to. "Into the screen?" he said. Proktor nodded. Taithur felt his face go cold as the blood drained from it. He sat down on a nearby wall and put his head in his hands until the first horror had passed. Proktor winced at the pain on his face when he looked up.

"We must do more Proktor," he said quietly. "These people have no conception of our technology. Things whose dangers are blatantly obvious to us mean nothing to them." He looked up at the bright blue

94

sky. Up through the virtually invisible environmental control screen, that huge and terrible energy field. He shuddered.

"Carry on," he said. "Why didn't the aircraft fall in as well?"

Proktor shrugged. "I haven't had a sub-analysis taken," he said. "I didn't think there was much point." He made a tight bitter smile. "I think the two others just got lucky. The aircraft was thrown up and out, and tumbled into the jungle a couple of miles away."

The dense jungle canopy eased the fall of the shattered craft but not sufficiently to prevent one of the two survivors breaking his neck.

"To be honest," said Proktor. "I didn't think anyone could have survived that crash. We just put the monitors on it to confirm they were both dead. And there he was. Battered, and as far as we could judge, very shocked, but otherwise uninjured."

Proktor walked a few steps away from Taithur and stood looking out into the increasing tangle of growth that marked the beginnings of the buffer zone. He was uneasy about the similar tangle of motives in himself for seeking out the remaining survivor. The man had to be rescued as a matter of basic humanity. Equally, it was necessary to know what he had seen, why the aircraft had changed course, and for that matter why it was in the area at all, and of course it was essential to find out what interpretation the man had put on what had happened. Also, a great deal of valuable information could be obtained from this real specimen of the local natives. Interrogation and examination would add greatly to their knowledge of both the physiology and psychology of these people, and could prove invaluable.

It disturbed Proktor that he could not be sure that the first motive, the one he considered needed no defence, was dominant.

"Well?" said Taithur, standing up and walking over to him.

Proktor snapped out of his reverie. "We went in and collected him."

"We?" said Taithur, in mild disbelief. "Don't you mean the pioneers."

Proktor turned to him. "No," he said, in a slightly injured tone. "Me, a medical officer and two others. In a surface car."

Taithur had to admit to being pleasantly surprised. Standard quarantine suits and a surface car could be attributable to the local technology with some judicious lying, but a pioneer suit never.

The man was conscious when they arrived, and after being lifted delicately down from the canopy he assailed them with a stream of language that they deduced to be a mixture of gratitude, relief, and bewilderment, mixed possibly with alarm at their unusual appearance. The rescuers for their part muttered words of comfort in the dominant language and tapped anxiously on their translators, all of which were proving to be singularly inadequate.

Eventually the man began to speak in faltering dominant and was persuaded to lie quietly on the Emergency Treatment Litter while they returned to the base.

"He went through quarantine clean as a whistle," said Proktor.

"That's hardly surprising," said Taithur. "In view of what the bays have been set for."

Proktor shrugged regretfully. "The rest you know. We thought we'd let him have a good night's sleep before examining him. He was perfectly all right when I saw him last—euphoric in fact. I should have realized then that something was wrong. The small amount of tranquiliser he was given to quieten him down and get him through the forest shouldn't have had that much effect on him. Anyway, he developed a fever within a few hours and then simply died—poof, just like that. Left our medics in complete disarray—we weren't even monitoring his health signs. It scared me I can tell you. We sealed him up immediately and called you."

Taithur nodded. "According to Andreas' first observations, he was euphoric for another reason," he said. "But that's of no consequence at the moment. For what it's worth you can take some consolation in the fact that Andreas also thinks that no amount of monitoring would have helped him. We may as well have had one of the pioneers tread on him. It would have been just as effective and perhaps a lot kinder."

"What's it going to mean?" asked Proktor.

Taithur looked at him. "That's what we've got to work out, Proktor. In the short term we have to find out why that aircraft was here and whether it will be missed—will there be search parties out looking for it? Then we've got to work out far better and longer-range defences. Probably the remains of the aircraft will help with that. Then we've got to decide whether what happened to this man is exceptional or normal. If it's the latter, then God help us."

"We'll be safe," said Proktor reassuringly.

"Oh yes," replied Taithur, a bitter edge to his voice. "We'll be safe. But it's not what we had in mind is it? Our whole presence here is based on the premise that if we can have enough time to become established and strong, and if we can avoid slaughtering them in open warfare, we can educate and train these people to live correctly. Briefly, we can save their planet for them. Now it seems there might be a strong possibility that we'll wipe them out. Wipe them out with diseases that are so trivial we never even consider having them treated. What a grim irony. These people are potentially the biggest single health hazard in the galaxy and we, the healthy ones, come along and kill them with a plague."

Proktor did not reply. In the distance he could see a flock of birds erupting out of the Jungle canopy, disturbed by some predator. Once again he found himself prey to thoughts he would rather not have. Could this be a punishment on these people for their behaviour? Was it the justice of the Way?

# Chapter 15

Newin was excited. This was his first duty spell as a fully-fledged Apprentice Officer. Throughout the long journey, the travellers had maintained a strict training programme for all manner of disciplines. This was an obvious necessity from the point of view of survival, not only on the ship, but subsequently when they arrived at their destination. However they had added a component uniquely theirs. In addition to training for specific tasks in the time-honoured manner, they implemented a programme of inter-disciplinary training which was the very antithesis of normal Service practice.

Many interesting things had occurred as a result of this, but the broad sweep of community policy meant nothing to Newin. All he knew was that like the other travellers' children, he had taken some tests early in the journey and then found himself the centre of some unusual attention.

His father had always said he could train to be an environmental control engineer when he passed out of Preliminary, but suddenly everything changed.

He still remembered the strange thrill when Captain Ersand—the Captain—had crouched down in front of him and looked searchingly into his face.

"Newin," he had said very softly. "It seems that there is a possibility you might be suitable for training as a Captain. That's a rare thing, Newin. Very rare. Most people want to be Captains at some time or other, but only a few are actually suitable for it. Look at me carefully and tell me truly. Is that what you would want?"

Then he had found himself looking straight into Ersand's eyes.

Unbidden, his hands had reached out to touch Ersand's lined face, and from somewhere deep inside him had come a childish, "Yes please."

After that, nothing very special seemed to happen although he had had to do extra tests now and then that his contemporaries had not, and on leaving Preliminary he had gone straight to Officer Training without being asked for his opinion on the matter. Looking back now he saw the extra tests and the occasional, apparently casual, conversations with Ersand as part of some coherent scheme, the true nature of which was only slowly becoming clear to him.

The ability to handle conscious flight in D-h space was rare and was scattered through the populations of all the systems in a random manner that defied all attempts at analysis. Those with this ability were thus rarer even than pioneers, whose abilities at least tended to be hereditary. Further, out of those who could handle the peculiar ordeal of D-h flight, only about one in ten could be trained in the difficult skills required by a Captain.

Because of the importance of these people, the standard Service practice was to test all children for those slight signs which foretold the development of this ability after puberty. When the Service had arbitrarily prevented one particular family from joining the Rithid, Taithur had seen no special significance in the deed. It was only later, in less flurried times, that he realized why it had been done, piecing together evidence that emerged during casual conversation with friends of the family. He confirmed his suspicions with Ersand.

"It sounds as if the child was a potential waker," Ersand said. "It's always been a risk having only one person capable of handling the ship through hops, but it looks as if they've played a long-term contingency shot there by stacking the odds against us even further."

Taithur's face showed an almost snarling distaste as he struck through to the heart of the problem. "So even if we found somewhere to live and started building ships, the probability would be that we'd have no-one to fly them."

Ersand nodded. "Such is the subtle malice of the castrator," he said.

"A real Service trick," Hester had commented ironically.

The discovery that Newin might be a waker came to Taithur not only as a relief, but as a re-affirmation of the rightness of their venture, and he had quietly put the boy under intense supervision, to ensure he would develop the many other skills he would need to become a Captain.

Newin himself knew nothing of the scrutiny to which he was being subjected. He considered himself to be a more or less ordinary cadet, now Apprentice Officer, like the others who were training with him. The possibility that any of them might become Captains was an occasional topic for idle debate, but not one to be pursued seriously, although it carried its own special mystique. It was a well-known fact, rumour had it, that wakers were segregated and sent to 'special' places for 'special' training. Newin kept his peace about his conversation with Ersand, though scarcely a day passed when he did not remember it. Looking into Ersand's eyes he had felt a strange certainty awaken in him that he knew separated him from others and that had stayed with him ever since. Some deep inner sense told him that this was not a subject for idle boasting, or even one to which he should be clinging the way he did. Whatever his unspoken need was for, its very nature precluded its being discovered by normal intellectual endeavour, but all steps, he knew, would lead him to it.

Now, having become an Apprentice Officer, shining prospects of a more tangible character occupied him. A full watch. His first solo watch in the Rithid's long-range monitoring room. He refused to be deterred by the fact that he was to spend his time watching instruments that looked back across the last part of their long journey. Looked through a deserted and barren sector of space in which nothing was going to happen. He was on duty. He had his orders and he had the procedures to follow. He had his responsibilities. The protection of a part of this great ship and this great project fell to him.

After looking round to ensure he was alone, he scanned the control panel and, grinning broadly, rubbed his hands together in excitement as he identified each of the instruments arrayed before him. Then, in a more dignified manner, he settled himself into the comfortable, if rather large, chair and checked that the panel's main link was clipped to the back of his hand.

Activating his IFT to the main duty Officer, he cleared his throat and, frowning slightly, unearthed as deep a voice as he could manage.

"Apprentice Officer Newin reporting commencement of Back Watch, Sir."

"Acknowledged," came the businesslike reply. Then, "You all right Newin? You haven't caught a cold have you?"

Andreas' final report on the death of the native had thrown a sadness over the Council meeting.

"I suppose this could reasonably have been projected from the lack of problems we've been having with quarantine generally..." Even Ersand was beginning to acknowledge that none of the micro-organisms they were encountering presented any real threat to the community. "But that's by the by. The most important finding, as indicated in the preliminary work, is that the immune systems of these natives are simply not as well developed as ours. At least those of the two samples in the plane weren't, and there's no reason to presume that they were materially different from the rest of the population. Obviously, this has considerable advantages..."

Taithur waved him to silence. "I can see the advantages, Andreas," he said, his voice flat and his manner pained. "But the disadvantages for the natives are far more serious and we must consider them carefully."

Since his revelation in that quiet field so long ago, Taithur had grown used to being faced with threatening and apparently insurmountable obstacles. It was something he now regarded as normal and his faith was buttressed by a fatalistic optimism that refused to allow him to be overwhelmed. Now finding himself an unwitting and potentially disastrous threat to others, he felt strangely helpless.

"And guilty, Malva," he had confided to his wife. "I don't seem to be able to accept that we... we, who in time could bring civilization and hope to these savages, could also be the bringers of death and destruction. I've got such mixed feelings about it. On the one hand it removes a great burden of caution from us. It'll save time and resources that are precious to us. That's marvellous, it puts entirely new factors into the calculations for our survival here. It makes me want to shout out for joy. But at the same time I feel sick inside when I think that these demented people might die in thousands because they'll find it almost impossible to deal with infections that we shrug off almost without a thought."

He had made a conscious decision not to discuss this emotional disorientation at the Council meeting but, looking round, he could tell that many of the Council members were feeling a concern that was disproportionate to the simple facts of the case. He touched on the matter obliquely to acknowledge to the others their common bond, then veered off like a bird flitting nervously from an uncertain branch.

"Andreas tells us this might have been foreseeable. I suppose that's possible, but I don't think it would have helped us a great deal… although it might have saved that native. I think we all feel very strange about it. Alien even. Knowing oppression and threat as we all do, it's something we'd never have wanted to happen. But it has, and we have to live with it. Let's deal with the facts of the matter here, and give ourselves time to accommodate the emotional consequences."

No-one seemed inclined to disagree with Taithur's suggestion, but when Andreas finished his report the meeting lapsed into a resigned silence.

"Well, if it's any consolation, at least we've found out why they ignored the instrument distortion and most of the screen's automatic warning."

Proktor's voice was that of a man who had found something he did not expect to find, and it broke the spell that seemed to have bound them all.

"I didn't fully understand that," said Liefer. "Were they really flying that machine while they were under the influence of some kind of drug? Literally not in control of their senses?"

Andreas nodded but offered no amplification.

"I wouldn't blame them for that," came a voice. "I'd certainly need to be drugged before I'd go up in a machine like that. It's an unbelievably dangerous contraption." Matthew's dry delivery further lightened the mood in the room and Taithur took the opportunity to push the meeting forward.

"We can study the details of Andreas' report later. And Matthew's," he added. "What I'd like to do now is spend a little time discussing such immediate implications as we can see."

Liefer caught his eye.

"I'm intrigued by this drug the two natives had been using." He looked down at his monitor displaying Andreas' report. "I have difficulty imagining the way these people think. Matthew's comments aside, can anyone explain to me why they should addle their brains to such an extent that they could ignore the EC screen's automatic defences, while they were flying such a dangerous craft. Is it possible they were drugged specifically to be able to fly so close to our base?"

It was an uncomfortable thought.

Andreas frowned and twisted his lower lip between his thumb and forefinger. "I can't answer that, Liefer," he said. "That kind of military psychology is far out of my field. Perhaps Hester can. All I can say is that as far as I can tell, the drug they were using would render them euphoric and would probably be addictive—seriously addictive. That's born out to some extent by evidence that both of them had been taking the drug for a long time. I don't think anyone under its influence would be of any value as a... spy... an observer. I'd go so far as to say that had they not crashed into our screen, they'd have crashed somewhere else anyway."

Hester nodded. "These people do have a certain tradition of using drugs and sacrificial troops in war, but I don't think this was a case of either. According to Matthew's report they had no weapons and neither maps nor communication equipment worth speaking of. There were just the four of them and a large quantity of the drug. Far more than any of them needed, I'm sure."

Andreas nodded. Jion coughed nervously and Taithur motioned him to speak.

"I don't have anything very positive on this, because I've had to cut down on my general studying since we moved onto the surface, but I seem to recall that some tribes have severe problems with widespread drug addiction. Perhaps these people might have been something to do with that?"

The discussion drifted on for a little while until Taithur cut it short. "Hester. Pursue Liefer's idea a little further will you. Step up monitoring of local broadcasts. If Jion's idea is right, then we can forget about it, but if Liefer's right we may have a problem. Matthew, I appreciate that you're particularly busy now, but would you re-examine the reports we have on their technology in the light of what you've found in that aircraft. It's not much, but it's the first solid input we've had and I think that could be very useful."

Then, unexpectedly, the horror of what had happened returned to him and twisted a knot inside him. Reluctantly, he broached the topic. "Before we break up this meeting can we briefly consider the implications of what we've discovered about the physiology of these people?"

Hester gave him a cold look. "They're simple, Taithur," she said. "As Andreas was about to say when you shut him up, the weakness of these people gives us an unexpected strategic advantage." Taithur's eyes widened angrily. Hester could not meet his gaze, but she raised her voice and continued speaking. "I'm sorry, Taithur, I know you don't want to hear this, but I'm sure you've worked it out for yourself and it has to be said here, in Council."

Taithur made to speak, but this time Hester did meet his gaze. "Taithur, we've survived this journey so far because you've made us wring advantage out of even the direst extremity—even poor Konrad's death and the D-h distortion fevers. And thanks to that we're here and hanging on by the skin of our teeth. But it is only by the skin of our teeth, we still need our every resource and more, and some good luck wouldn't go amiss. I can understand your reluctance about what we've found, but we must accept it for what it is. The weakness of these people is our good fortune."

Taithur's face set, but Hester ploughed on.

"We can run down our quarantine procedures almost immediately, at a tremendous saving in time and resources, and we can develop chemical and biological means of subduing these people if we have to."

Taithur jumped to his feet sending his chair floating crazily across the room. "Hester!" his voice was filled with both anger and dismay. The action brought Hester to her feet also and for an interminable moment she held his gaze firm and unwavering. Taithur's chair stabilized itself and, floating back, gently touched the back of his legs.

It was like a signal, and abruptly he seemed to yield to something in Hester's manner. He put his hand to his face and lowered himself wearily into the chair.

"Hester," he said softly. "No."

When he looked up, his eyes were shining with tears, and when he spoke, his voice was low and strained.

"Hester... that's a terrible demon you've given freedom. Can we here contend with it?"

Hester's voice too was uneasy and the resolution of a few moments ago had faded as if it had never existed.

"It's no demon, Taithur. It's an idea. An idea based on a reality and one that would inevitably arise from what we've learnt. Nothing can cage ideas. Least of all any of us. We who've spent so much time encouraging and releasing them."

Taithur moved his head from side to side, as if looking for somewhere to escape. Hester continued.

"Time and circumstances are not on our side, Taithur. Let's have the idea out and a debate begun now rather than later." She paused and looked earnestly at Taithur. "You've said so many times yourself—these things are tests. It's the nature of the Way. We must expect nothing easy. We'll not make a future for ourselves without facing the unfaceable…"

Taithur raised his hand a little from the table. "Give me a moment, Hester. Please."

Hester sat back and closed her eyes. Silence hung in the room like the massive presence of the nearby planet. No-one moved.

Slowly Taithur leaned forward. His voice was still soft, but it carried that purposeful quality that advised all present to listen well.

"I'd be lying if I said I was content with what's just been said. I can feel nothing but terrible misgivings. Perhaps it is indeed another test. We've survived others and grown stronger for them, though none, I fancy, have been as bleak as this. However, I can't imagine being able to find solace or reassurance in prayer, so I, we, must accept the harsher solace of logic until such times as the Way grants us a deeper peace."

He looked around the table, and felt again the loneliness of his peculiar position. How could that small flower have led him to this bitter moment. But, coming unbidden into his mind, the very memory of the flower seemed to draw tension from him and ease away pain he had not realized he was feeling.

Nodding, he said, "Yes," as if to some inner conversation. "Yes. Logic will have to suffice."

The mood in the room also eased as the Council members felt their guide and leader recovering his inner stability. "You were right to thrust it in my face Hester. I'm in your debt. To ignore an obscenity is no way to deal with it. It would surely only have festered and given us more difficult problems in the future. Probably at some time when we had even less time for considered debate."

Hester bowed her head in acknowledgement.

Taithur continued. "We must obviously increase our endeavours to ensure that contact with the natives is avoided. Not only for our own sakes now, but for theirs. To wilfully assail these people in their weakness through some dire need will be evil enough, but to do it by accident..." He shook his head, leaving the sentence unfinished. "But I'm sure that needs no debate. Looking at Hester's strategic observations I suppose, if we're honest, we must admit that in the final analysis we'd be prepared to destroy these people if they threatened our actual survival. I can think of no moral justification for that, especially as we're the interlopers here, but..."

"These natives are a source of plague, Taithur," Proktor volunteered, but his voice died away as Taithur turned and glared at him.

"I didn't say I couldn't think of excuses, Proktor," he said angrily. "God knows, that's easy enough. I'm talking about morality, not expediency. It only needs two ounces of that kind of reasoning and we'll soon talk ourselves into seeding the atmosphere with some short-lived bacteria and then standing off in space for a few days until they're all dead."

Proktor winced, and Taithur relented.

"I'm sorry, Proktor," Taithur said, more quietly. "I apologize. I shouldn't inflict my anger at myself onto you. You deserve better."

Proktor cast his eyes down. For all that he was prepared to disagree and argue with Taithur, he still looked to him as his leader and he was deeply unsettled by Taithur's patent uncertainty and distress over this problem with the natives.

Taithur continued. "As I was saying. Independent of moral considerations I suppose we must accept, however repellent the idea, that should we be seriously threatened, then we'd use whatever weapons we could devise. And obviously we'd look to strike where the enemy was weakest." He paused, and again turned his head as if looking for release. "I suppose, giving justice to Proktor's comment, that we've a greater obligation to the rest of the galaxy than we have to these people. They are a source of infection and there's no doubt that given time they might break out into inter-stellar flight and then they'll either do immense damage or run headlong into the Education Department's Adjustment squads. Or more likely both." He looked at Hester who nodded. "I suppose that in turn puts an obligation on us to prevent this happening if possible. We're here. We've the ability and the will. And with luck, we may have the opportunity to do it comparatively peacefully. The fact that it's also in our own best interests doesn't necessarily mean that our motives are wholly selfish. Perhaps, indeed, we've been sent here not for the establishing of a new home for ourselves, but as the..." He gave a weak smile. "I was going to say saviours. You must forgive me. I'm having the greatest difficulty in deciding whether I'm talking morality or just hiding our self-interest under a cloak of spurious reason."

"It doesn't matter, Taithur." The voice, unexpectedly, was Jion's. Taithur turned to him in some surprise.

A slight tingling in his hand and the sound of a reproach fading away, made Newin sit upright and look around guiltily. That was the second time the chair had had to prevent him from going to sleep. But something else was catching his attention. Something was not in order. Nervously he checked the time and the log. That was all in order. Then he scanned the panel, even more certain that something was wrong. Everything seemed to be stable. There was no reason why any of it should change. After all, it had not changed since the journey had begun. Then he saw a faint warning light flickering unsteadily. His mouth went dry.

"It doesn't matter," Jion repeated. "It's too difficult for any of us. We've nothing left. We'll have to go as far as our reason will take us, and then use our hearts to make our decision."

So the pupil teaches the teacher, thought Taithur. "Thank you Jion," he said. "I suppose that puts the truth of the matter as clearly as we can hope for." Then, in an almost offhand manner: "The fact is, I suppose, that no matter how we talk, we'll not leave this planet, nor will we be driven from it. But we must fully accept the consequences of that. Andreas, look into the possibility of a chemical or biological agent that can be used against these people—something incapacitating, not fatal if possible, but . . . Hester, will you consider its deployment? Class the work as low priority. There's no urgency for this, and I want nothing to stand in the way of the continuing establishment of the bases."

He looked around the table. "Has anyone else anything to offer?"

Ersand tilted his head to one side and then sat upright.

"Switch to Council Members and repeat," he said.

Immediately a voice rang in Taithur's head. It was formal but tense.

"Duty Officer reporting. Apprentice Officer Newin has just reported a signal on the long-range scanners." There was a pause and a little muttering, then, "It's at the extremity of their range but it doesn't appear to be an instrument fault."

# Chapter 16

Newin found himself hovering on the fringes of the anxious and noisy crowd of Council Members that had squeezed into the long-range monitoring room.

Ersand and Taithur were studying the control panel, Ersand speaking quietly on IFT to the Duty Officer in the main control room. Abruptly an elaborate display appeared in the frame above the panel and all eyes turned to this from the still flickering warning light.

Ersand peered into it intently. "More magnification," he said, and the display started to expand outwards as if it were about to burst out of the limits of its frame. Dots and symbols and lines grew and vanished from the display with increasing rapidity and for a moment Newin felt as though he were falling into a great pit. He turned his face slightly, so that he could still see the movement without being disturbed by its accelerating perspective.

At Ersand's command the expansion slowed and stopped and he leaned forward to study it closely. The details on it were less well focused than before and seemed to be shifting slightly as if viewed through sun-warmed air. After a moment Ersand shook his head.

"We'll run a full check, of course, but I don't think it's an instrument fault. There definitely seems to be something there."

The alarmed clamour in the little room rose, everyone speaking at once.

"Is it the Fleet?" seemed to be the predominant query.

"More to the point, how far away is it, and is it on our route?" Taithur asked, only marginally more calmly.

Ersand scowled. "For heaven's sake look at that display," he said,

111

irritably. "This might be sophisticated equipment, but you can see it's working well beyond its design range. I can't answer questions like that right now. If this signal stays on frame and if it indicates any substantial movement, then with a lot of analysis and checking we might be able to determine where it is, and perhaps where it's going. From that, we might be able to deduce what it is."

"But you must have some idea," someone said.

Ersand did not bother to identify the speaker but turning round spoke angrily: "Why don't you listen..." he began, but the sight of the anxious faces of his friends took the anger out of him in a heavy sigh.

"No. I've no idea what it is," he said. "All we have at the moment is a signal indicating that there's a ship, or ships, somewhere on our old route and a long way out from the inner systems. It's the first time this equipment has been activated in years so we'll check further to confirm that it's not an instrument fault, then we'll just have to wait and see."

Taithur bit back the many questions demanding voice. He had sufficient knowledge of the long-range scanner to realize that if the signal was genuine, then whatever was causing it was a prodigious distance away. It was some consolation and it would have to suffice until Ersand and his crew produced a proper account of the matter. Looking round at his fellow Council Members he could see that several of them were already beginning to feel slightly embarrassed at the near panic which had sent them almost running through the long elaborate corridors of the Rithid.

He put a hand on Ersand's shoulder. "Carry on Ers," he said quietly. Then, more lightheartedly, to the rest: "Well, at least the Fleet's not come bursting out of D-h right on our tails. I think all we can do now is take Ersand's advice and leave him to it. We'll know soon enough what's happening, and fretting over it's not going to help."

There was little else he could have said to any purpose and the group broke up awkwardly. So quiet and sudden was their departure that Newin was reminded of the clouds that he had watched when he was on the surface. They drifted along silently, changing shape and even disappearing, though he never actually managed to see it happening. The room seemed suddenly much larger and, alone with the intent figure of Ersand, he felt peculiarly exposed. He coughed.

Ersand turned and looked at him. He had that strange expression in his eyes that spoke to Newin in ways he could not begin to understand.

"How are you feeling, Newin?" he said. The bland question caught Newin unawares after the tension of the last few minutes.

"Fine, Captain," he managed to stammer. "A little bit tired. A little bit... excited." He grinned in spite of himself. Ersand smiled and glanced back at the swaying, slightly fuzzy display.

"Yes," he said. "We've all had a little excitement tonight. Excitement we could all have done without. Still..." He glanced down at the control panel. "I see from the monitor that apart from the odd little slip you've maintained a high level of concentration. That's good, Newin. You've done very well." Then the strange expression returned to his eyes again, but this time more intense than Newin had ever seen before. Newin met the gaze without flinching, sensing the imminence of a momentous decision.

Ersand spoke some quiet orders on IFT to the Duty Officer, repeating one of them, and then beckoned Newin. "I need your help, Newin," he said. "I've a short flight to make. How's your navigation?"

Newin grimaced. "It's not my strongest subject, Captain. I find reconciling extended D-h meridians... difficult..."

Ersand laughed. "Don't worry," he said. "We won't be going that far. Do you think you can get us round this system safely?"

Newin looked puzzled. "Yes Captain," he said. "But all the local routes are in the computers..."

Ersand raised a finger to silence him. "That's all very well, Apprentice Officer Newin, but in addition to your formal navigation lessons, please note for your future reference that as far as I'm concerned all the local routes also have to be in the seat of your trousers. Do you understand?"

"Yes Captain," Newin lied. "But what about my watch?"

"Come on," said Ersand, heading for the door. "Don't worry about your watch. The navigators and analysts will have to take over now anyway. That..." he reproached, "is standard procedure, is it not? Besides, there'll be nothing more spectacular than you've already seen."

Newin heard the last remarks as the Captain disappeared into the corridor. Hastily, he snatched up his tunic and ran after him.

Taithur had not realized how small in his mind had become the Service, the inner systems, and all the events of his earlier life, until that faint signal had illuminated the tenuous path leading back to it all. Although he had given little or no outward sign, the shock had been appalling, and after leaving the long-range monitoring room he had returned to his quarters in a torment of self-doubt, guilt and fear.

Slowly, and with much faltering, his stronger nature had reasserted itself and he had fallen to prayer and meditation. As usual in times of trial, he found the memory of Konrad returning. Konrad, slamming and bolting a door and driving his fist into his hand preparatory to "discussing theology" with some gang of thugs who were trying to break up the meeting. Konrad, who had looked to him for so many things and who by his honesty and passion had given so much in return that his influence persisted still.

Sitting now in the main control room, Taithur said silent thanks to the courage he had learned from his dead friend as he pondered the latest analysis of the signal. He took some pride in the fact that he had successfully taken his own advice and avoided fretting over these analyses. Their conclusions were still frightening, but time and personal resolution had put the fear into a different perspective.

Later, Ersand's initial opinion was confirmed. The signal was not due to an instrument malfunction. Almost certainly it was a ship—or ships—but he was cautious.

"It's all fairly vague," he said. "We're working on one or two ideas to improve clarity, but it's not easy. Really we're only talking about probabilities until whatever it is comes nearer to the design range of the equipment."

However, vague though the information might have been, it gradually accumulated to indicate that the ship was largely following the same route that the travellers had followed. Ersand's opinion was that it seemed to be nosing a cautious way through D-h space, seeking out the tiny lingering traces left by the Rithid's passage.

"That means very sophisticated equipment, doesn't it?" said Taithur.

"Not necessarily," Ersand replied. "Not in that region. Don't forget it's well out from the inner systems and all the normal traffic that usually muddies the water, as it were. I'd think our wake should be quite easy to detect for a long time yet."

Taithur did not find the prospect comforting. Ersand saw the questions in his face and knowing his strictures about idle speculation, spared him the embarrassment of asking them.

"It seems to be moving no faster than we did," he said, speaking softly and sitting down by Taithur's side. "Perhaps even slower. That means we have time—a few years probably—before it gets here, even allowing for them speeding up if they develop their tracking techniques."

Taithur almost whispered. "What if it's the Fleet?" he said.

Ersand made a small gesture of resignation. "It won't make a great deal of difference. They risk losing our trail entirely if they try to short circuit any of our hops. The only chance they have of speeding up is if they target our destination star, and they won't be able to do that with certainty for a long time yet."

Taithur was surprised at Ersand's apparently easy acceptance of the situation.

"You seem unperturbed about it," he said, almost sulkily.

Ersand smiled. "I'm only taking your advice, Taith," he said.

Taithur narrowed his eyes distrustfully. "Ers," he said warningly.

Ersand slapped him on the arm. "Come on," he said. "Let's walk a little. It's been a bit rough for you lately, you need to relax."

"Ers," repeated Taithur. "I know you too well. You've got something up your sleeve."

Ersand raised his hands in mock surrender. "Yes," he said. "You've caught me out, but come along anyway, there's a couple of things I want to tell you and I don't like sitting whispering when I'm surrounded by my crew."

Taithur flicked off the latest analysis and watched the hovering figures fade into nothingness. Then he turned to follow his friend.

Walking down one of the main longitudinal corridors of the ship, Taithur was pleased that Ersand had suggested the walk. Thinking back, it was a long time since he had deliberately set out to walk simply for walking's sake. He made a note to do more in future.

It was made even more pleasant by Environmental Control having selected a mild summer's day, and a pleasant breeze greeted the two men as they joined the spacious corridor.

For a moment, Taithur stood and looked up and down the corridor, breathing deeply.

There were a few children playing and one or two adults either strolling or sitting about talking. The reduction in the number of people on the ship was very apparent in this normally busy thoroughfare.

Scattered already, thought Taithur. Making new streets in new cities on our new home planet. He smiled involuntarily.

"Told you it would do you good," said Ersand. "A little bit of fresh air and exercise."

"Never mind that," replied Taithur, striding out. "Tell me what you're up to."

"It's nothing spectacular," said Ersand. "In spite of your instructions not to waste time in idle conjecture, I've been thinking about what all this means—this ship following us."

"And?" said Taithur.

"Well, we have to assume it means trouble, haven't we?" replied Ersand. "So let's assume it's the Fleet. We needn't consider why they might be coming, that's irrelevant. Let's just assume they are."

Taithur nodded and Ersand continued.

"It's not as bleak as you might think. I know the reputation of the Education Department, but we've got to remember they're only human. That's a long journey they're making. Far longer than any other ship has ever made, as far as we know. I can't imagine any commander undertaking such a journey without establishing a supply chain right back into the inner systems. He'll need it to serve his battle front and to relieve crews on the journey. Think of the expense of that, and the complexity, Taith. All those desert outposts to be manned and serviced."

Abruptly his tone became more serious. "Think about this too. When they arrive, they'll be a group of men years away from home, fighting in the middle of a wilderness against people who know the area and have nothing to lose."

Taithur looked a little disappointed. "It's something we've considered before Ers."

"No, Taith, we haven't," Ersand replied. "Not even Hester. Not properly. We made a collective decision to colonize this planet in spite of our Charter and in spite of the Service's health regulations, as an act of despair as much as of faith."

Taithur started slightly, but Ersand ploughed on.

"Insofar as we thought about the Fleet, it was only in terms of some glorious last stand." He waved aside Taithur's impending objection. "It's true and you know it. Just think back and remember the state we were in all those months ago. Desperately tired, keeping going by hope and faith alone. We didn't realize we were like that, but compare us then with the way we are now."

Taithur felt a surge of anger at this unexpected outburst, with its implicit criticism of him as leader. However, there was a blunt honesty in Ersand's remarks and a strange feeling of confidence about him that made him pause.

"What are you trying to say, Ers,?" he managed eventually.

"I think we're on the verge of making a serious mistake," said Ersand, after a deep breath. "It only really dawned on me as we pieced together the progress of that ship. Out of all our figures, all that hard mathematics, came a peculiarly human feeling. The feeling of people, fumbling their way towards us in the dark."

Taithur gently disentangled himself from a small child that had careened into him. It uttered a hasty and insincere apology and ran off.

"Go on…" he said.

Ersand became unusually intense. "We've this image of the Fleet as some invincible corrective force which implements the Service's will when all else fails. We looked at this image, waved a tired fist at it." He mimicked the action. "And started colonizing this planet in the almost childlike belief that nothing would ever really happen."

Taithur did not reply.

"We're avoiding the truth, Taith. We've allowed ourselves to become totally preoccupied with the development of the bases. No-one even considers external defence, and such efforts as we make to defend ourselves against the natives are made grudgingly."

Taithur felt himself being cut adrift by his friend. He had been uncomfortable for some time about resources allocated for defence being too easily sacrificed to the increasing clamour from the bases. But he had been too busy himself to take any action, and such reallocations were invariably accompanied by very plausible reasoning. Again he felt a surge of anger. He had better things to do with his time than listen to Ersand theorizing. Besides, how could they stand against the Fl…

He stopped walking. The thought had burst into his head like a child's mocking Jack-in-a-box. And he'd expressly ordered everyone not to speculate on the nature of this approaching ship. A ship that could only belong to the Fleet. He was hiding from the truth, while pretending not to. The rhetoric and posturing that had been made against the

117

Service were empty gestures. He'd not led his exhausted people into a brave new future, he'd told them what they wanted to hear and given no regard to the true consequences.

"Oh God," he said softly.

Ersand looked concerned. "What's the matter Taith?" he said, taking his arm.

Taithur shook his head and moved over to a seat by a viewport. Sitting down, he turned the seat away from the bright summery corridor so that he was looking out through the port at the stars and the skein of light which marked the heart of the galaxy.

"Are you ill?" asked Ersand anxiously, adjusting his IFT. Taithur stopped him with a gesture.

"No," he said. "I'm fine." Then, wearily. "I was just about to lose my temper with you when I thought, 'Who can stand against the Fleet?' It's a good question isn't it, Ers? And you're right, I have avoided it. We've all avoided it."

He leaned forward, resting his chin in his hands.

"Granted, we were tired and weary, but that's no real excuse is it? Certainly it shouldn't have been for me. And we're not tired and weary any more, are we? Not in the same way. We might be fatigued with work, but emotionally, spiritually we're as strong as we've ever been. But we've ignored defence, probably to the point of folly."

He closed his eyes and became very still. Ersand waited, uncertain now where the end of the path he had started Taithur along would be.

"These endless connections, Ers," Taithur said eventually, still with his eyes closed. "An adjustment here is a distortion there. Every least movement swings the whole Universe. Who can say what will be the consequences of any act. I think the best that any human hand can achieve carries almost as much harm in its wake as good."

He opened his eyes and gave a grim smile. "What is it these people say?" He flicked a thumb over his shoulder in the direction of the unseen planet. "'Three steps forward, two steps back,' isn't it? Very apt. I think for all their savagery they have a shrewder grasp of cosmic affairs than we care to believe."

Ersand's eyes wrinkled in distress at his friend's pain. He wanted to help him but knew he could not. Only Taithur could do that.

"I suppose it's a reaction, Ers," Taithur continued. "Years of constraint by the Service, then desperate years under ship discipline, then suddenly we're here. Free to pursue our own destinies on this rich, if maggoty, apple. We've blundered in like children, and within months are becoming as foolish as the natives. I remember saying that, if needs be, we'd go out of cycle to defend ourselves against these natives, because they were so dangerous."

He shook his head. "First signs of an infection, Ers. First signs." Then he turned to face his friend. "Now we've postponed our first resources audit. Do you realize what that means?"

"It's Establishment time Taith," said Ersand. "There's so much..."

"No." Taithur interrupted vehemently. "No more excuses. You started this, let's take it to the end. No more excuses. I don't need Jion to tell me where we'll finish if we start off like this. We say 'There's only a few of us, it'll be all right'. But it won't. We'll be at least as bad as these people, only cleverer and even more destructive."

He stood up suddenly and started off back along the corridor at a brisk pace. Ersand had to run a little to catch up with him.

"Get everyone back," said Taithur. "Immediately. I want a full Council meeting, plus observers, and no excuses from anyone. We'll cut this serpent's head off before it winds even one more coil around us. I can use the threat of the Fleet to re-establish our old discipline. We need to learn from this." Then he stopped and snapped his fingers. "What was it you wanted to tell me?"

Ersand felt the renewed strength of his friend. "Oh, nothing special," he said with wilful casualness. "Just that I took Newin out on a trial run the other day. He had no problems in D-h space. If we look after him, we've got our second Captain there."

# Chapter 17

The meeting was more like one of Taithur's old Prayer Meetings than a Council Meeting, its central feature being a prolonged and unanswerable sermon focusing around the ease with which the travellers were "falling from grace".

"The Way couldn't be made more clear than it is on this strange oasis that we've found. Now we're here, we see vividly the results of the continuing corruption these people seem to revel in. We see them poison their atmosphere, poison their seas, their lands, sometimes so effectively that even we would have difficulty bringing back balance. They obliterate whole species with a disregard that beggars description, and fight amongst themselves for the right to do more harm. They even take pains to choose leaders who will ensure this folly can continue. And we realize now that they know what they're doing—they know what they are doing." Taithur repeated the phrase slowly and paused to let his audience consider its implications. "They console themselves by looking outwards—outwards to their sister planets. There lies a source of sustenance for them when they've reduced this world to a barren shell."

He gazed sternly at his listeners. "And what do we do? We, with our superior technology and our superior moral sense. We with our civilization and our inner knowledge of the True Way. We look down on them. Call them natives—savages. Look to the day when we needn't fear their numbers and their ferocity and can take them in hand like erring children. Bring them into the Way. Show them how to live in cycle, how to live so that this tiny speck of cosmic dust will house and feed them lavishly for countless generations. This is what we do, isn't it?"

Taithur's delivery was heavy with irony and a considerable tension had built up in the room. There was some awkward shuffling as his listeners waited for the thunderclap.

"And how do we do it, my friends? How do we do it? How do we prepare for this great day?"

The shuffling stopped and all eyes were locked onto him apprehensively. He pointed to the central display. Slowly, writing began to appear, followed by the familiar symbols and calculations of a Resource Audit. Each of the four bases was represented by a sub-audit and then the sum total was presented. It was obviously an approximate, hastily prepared audit, containing many estimates and uncertain projections, but its final conclusion could not refuted. They were living out of cycle. They were consuming more resources from their environment than they were returning. Not as the result of a temporary defence emergency or through adopting an ordered loan and repayment scheme, but through incautiousness and neglect.

Taithur's voice was quiet and sad, and its effect was more disturbing than any thunderous declamation could have been.

"I must bear the greater part of the reproach myself. How can we have so soon lost our way as to commit this kind of folly?"

There were arguments that could have been raised to justify what had happened, but for shame's sake, no-one could speak them.

"The Way is never easy, but surely it teaches us to see things as they are, not as we think they are, or as we'd like them to be. We must learn a great lesson from this or I fear we'll be doomed. Let's look at these people the way they are. Let's look at ourselves the way we are. They're not erring bewildered children, and we're not flawless paragons come for their effortless correction. They're wild, unrestrained, appallingly dangerous humans, and we're a small band of frightened pilgrims following a hope through the wastes of the galaxy and stretched to our very limits just to survive. Who can say how far back in our own past these people belong? What chords they strike in us? We fondly believe that living in cycle is written into our very genes, but after just watching these people for the briefest of times we find we follow where they lead."

His voice rose. "We follow them."

There was a long silence.

"They must stir some aspect of our nature so ancient that we can't begin to understand it. But it's there and we must accept it whether we understand it or not. And we must realize the dangers we face." He raised his extended right hand. "Out there, some years away yet, as far as we can tell, is a ship that can only belong to the Fleet. Sooner or later we must face it: with sound arguments, or force if needs be." He raised his left hand. "Out there lie these demented and dangerous people. Our ancient cousins perhaps. Sooner or later we must face them: with sound arguments, or force if needs be." Then bringing his hands together on his chest. "And here, we have ourselves. A handspan away from our dreams, and beset with more dangers than we've known since we began this journey. If we're to survive the dangers and seize the dream, then we must face ourselves now."

No-one could argue with Taithur's analysis of the situation, and no-one tried, although by the time he had finished, everyone had received some blow to his or her pride. Taithur, for his part, came away satisfied that he had destroyed most of the rot simply by exposing it, but, not for the first time, he was humbled by the honesty and trust of his friends and pained by the knowledge that he too had been seduced into neglecting his responsibilities. In addition he had to accept that the avoidance of similar problems in the future would require continuous vigilance, and in thinking of how their society might develop he realized for the first time how a bureaucracy like the Service could begin to develop.

He had intended the meeting to be no more than a morale booster and "head-clouting" session, but in the event it marked a watershed in the affairs of the travellers. They had recovered from their great odyssey and in turn recovered from the euphoria of finding a home and successfully establishing the four bases. Now, with clearer, wiser eyes they began to look at the realities of their position.

Within hours, an accurate Resource Audit was prepared and steps taken to ensure that the errors it exposed would be quickly corrected and that the risk of similar errors occurring in the future would be minimized.

Subsequently the travellers reaffirmed and strengthened the policy they had decided upon before commencing colonization—all contact with the natives was to be avoided. The two peoples were a menace to one another in ways that were both known and unknown. In the light of what had happened to them, the travellers decided even to reduce their monitoring of the natives to the minimum necessary for security.

Taithur regretted that, but had to acknowledge its correctness.

"There's such a lot we need to know for the future," he said. "So many things we can learn just by watching them."

"A great many dangerous things," retorted Hester. "We can't risk the kind of subtle infection we've just experienced, particularly as we'll be growing rapidly from now on. In fact I've increased the accuracy of the Resource Audit to Service Standard One and doubled the frequency."

Taithur nodded resignedly. "It'll slow things down a little, but I suppose we should've done that from the start; we're small enough. And it'll keep everyone on their toes."

Uncharacteristically, Hester shuffled awkwardly, then, "I want to set up a programme to monitor our monitors."

Taithur pulled a sour face. Hester laid a hand on his arm. "Not like the Service, Taith." she said. "Nothing underhand. We'll let everyone know what's happening, for all our sakes."

Taithur looked into her earnest face. "This slip has really frightened you, hasn't it?" he said.

Hester nodded. "Yes," she said, with an unexpected passion. "Not what everyone else did, I'm used to accommodating other people's mistakes. It's part of my training." She hammered her fingers into her chest. "But I was part of it and didn't realize. That's what's frightened me."

Taithur took her hand. "Do what you have to do, Hester. I think all this has chastened everyone. It'll do us no harm in the long run. I'm sure it will make us all stronger." Then he turned away from her and looked out through the viewport. The planet's battered moon hung there pale and sterile, a sight he always found eerily beautiful, symbolic in some way of their own spartan isolation.

"Besides," he said. "One way or another we'll have to treat with the Fleet when it arrives. There'll be no chance of negotiating if we're showing any signs of infection, and our already poor chances in a fight will be reduced to zero if we're having to fight the natives at the same time; especially with the numbers they can muster."

He remained silent for a while, tapping his fingers on the arm of his chair. Then he nodded to himself and, standing up, began to pace up and down the room. Briefly Hester felt the surge of the personality that had smashed into her closed life and shown her the truth so many years ago. Time and proximity had mellowed her earlier awe into respect and affection, but she felt strangely relieved at this sudden reminder of the power that had led her out across the galaxy. Taithur was half addressing her and half thinking out loud.

"Yes," he said. "Do what you have to do. We must watch these natives and we must watch one another. We've finished our journeying, but we've a long way to travel yet. We mustn't allow ourselves to be drawn away from shipboard discipline by the comforts we're building in our bases. Nor must we allow ourselves the luxury of thinking we've plenty of time just because the Fleet is so far away."

Abruptly, he stopped pacing and turned to face her, his face enigmatic. "Where does the next step lead, Hester?" he said.

She made a vague gesture. "What do you mean?" she asked.

Taithur offered no explanation, but answered his own question. "It leads into darkness, Hester," he said. "Every step leads into darkness. Logic and probability are modest guides, but only our faith, our intuition, cuts through and shows the Way."

Hester waited.

"My heart tells me there's something strange in this approaching Fleet. We can prevail, I'm sure, but we must use every second and every intellectual, emotional and spiritual resource to its full. Our entire community must go to Battle Alert."

## Chapter 18

Following his call to Battle Alert, Taithur outlined the way forward that he felt should be followed. He had not reached his insight through strict logical analysis so he offered no close reasoning in justification, leaving it to those who wished to sketch in such structure as they felt might be there.

He simply asked his followers to listen to him and then, if their hearts so led them, to accept his guidance. He was completely unaware of the fact that when he spoke in this way he carried far more authority than that which the travellers had formally vested in him. Such opposition as might have occurred, due to the natural fragmentation of the group now they were away from the ship, simply melted away.

Thus the travellers imposed a discipline on themselves far more severe than any they had known on their home planets and, in many ways, more severe than they had known while aboard the Rithid.

They were helped in their acceptance of Taithur's advice by the fact that while it was derived without formal analysis, it was nonetheless very difficult to reject logically.

When he said, "We need children now. We must return to normal family life. We must expand the base camps and establish new ones. We must pray for peace but prepare for war," Hester and Jion observed that he was increasing the traveller's involvement with the planet; their sense of ownership. He was channelling their fear into creative work, and at the same time turning the planet from an oasis into a well-stocked fortress, with its hidden bases and determined occupants.

"There's a dubious morality in using new-born children as hostages to fortune," Matten remarked to his wife one night as they lay in the balmy air looking up at the flickering ionization bursting high above the southern polar icecap base.

Hester did not answer immediately and Matten thought she had fallen asleep. Then he felt her move by his side.

"It's not a soluble problem," she said drowsily. "We can't solve it, and neither can the Service. The children complicate the legalities enormously. They'll bind us together and bind us here. We'll protect them with our worldliness, and they'll protect us with their innocence..." Her voice faded away as her mind chased the problem her husband had released into the shifting leafy groves of her dreams. "...born into infection... but in sterile... trust Taith... residential qualify..." Then abruptly she sat bolt upright. "If they're not born now, then they'll be slaughtered for sure." Her voice was clear and strong, but after a perfunctory nod of agreement with herself she thudded back down onto her pillow and was immediately sound asleep.

Matten covered her gently and chuckled to himself as he lay back to watch the dancing, coloured sky above.

As part of the preparation for the arrival of the Fleet, Taithur set Ersand and Hester to considering its probable condition when it finally arrived. Ersand expounded his view that the Fleet would be stretched to previously unheard-of limits and unable to mount an extensive Adjustment campaign and, too, that the morale of its crew would be suspect.

Hester agreed about the logistical complexity of such a long-range operation and that there would probably be difficulties with morale.

"In fact," she said, "it's really a considerable puzzle to me why they should be pursuing us after such a delay. I don't know whether it bodes well or ill. There's no possible way they could have found out about these people and their threat, and that's the most likely reason I can think of for their coming. The only other reason is some major political change since we left, but there's no point in even conjecturing about that."

Ersand smiled. "Perhaps they're coming to welcome us back to the fold," he said.

Hester too smiled at the thought. "That'd be just our luck," she said. "They come with a promise of peace and freedom on some paradise planet somewhere in the inner systems, and then they have to Adjust us because we're sitting in this place." The thought seemed to grow on her and she burst out laughing infectiously.

Such light moments, however, were rare. The ever-present signal on the long-range monitors nagged like a decaying tooth, and Taithur maintained a ruthless pressure on everyone, himself included, to consolidate their position on the planet.

"We can't afford even the suggestion that we've plenty of time, or that we've done enough."

Doubters forcing themselves into his presence to complain on behalf of exhausted work crews came away reproaching themselves for their selfishness, and more determined than ever to improve their progress.

Ersand's and Hester's considerations about the Fleet, however, steered through waters so perilously rocky that fatal collision was virtually inevitable. They were not helped by the fact that the Fleet was too far away for even the crudest estimate of the extent of its force. Also, while Hester's knowledge of weapons and tactics was considerable, she had little or no experience as a field commander, and Ersand had no illusions about either his ability to fly the Rithid as a battleship or the Rithid's capacity to take the physical strain.

"She's stylish, but she's old and battered, with a jury-rigged gravity silo. Since we've been in orbit we've upgraded her a lot, but gentle hopping to the local systems is all we can really expect. Combat flying, crash hops…" He shook his head.

And their weapons. Konrad's surreptitious dealings in the darker reaches of the Service's Arms Supply Division had served them well, and Hester was pleasantly surprised when she prepared a full inventory. It was far larger than the token entitlement allowed under the Charter, but, "It's mainly anti-personnel stuff. Some of it's quite heavy—useful against drones and probes, small machines generally—very necessary for the conditions we might reasonably have been expected to encounter, but almost all of it is really for surface use. It'll be difficult to adapt them for use in space."

Fortunately they did have ship-to-ship disruptors. Old and rather crude, they were nonetheless extremely formidable weapons, and unequivocally well outside the terms of the Charter. They represented the culmination of Konrad's obsessive distrust for the Service, and his grim determination not to be cast out into space defenceless.

Taithur's first reaction when he found they had been installed was an angry one, and he turned on both Konrad and Ersand, accusing them of jeopardizing the mission.

"You and your schoolboy fantasies. If the Service catches even a sniff of this we'll be vaporized without so much as a warning shot. And you, Ers, what were you thinking of to let this overgrown adolescent persuade you into this?"

However, when he eventually exploded in frustration, banging both his fists on the table and shouting, "Ye gods, Konrad, this is supposed to be a mission in search of peace and freedom and... and tranquillity..." Konrad wrapped his massive arms around him in a crushing embrace, and laughed.

"You're splendid when you get going, Taith," he said. "But we're too far out now. You can't go trailing back saying 'Please sirs we're sorry, Konrad's been scrumping disruptors' can you? And no-one here's going to send any worried messages back if for no other reason than the one you've just stated." Then, more seriously. "Besides, you're wrong. I might well be an adolescent, but I'm not naive, and at times you are. That's why I didn't tell you, and why I persuaded Ers to keep quiet. Those bastards will give us trouble sooner or later. Trust me like I trust you. You'll not regret having disruptors aboard. I guarantee you."

It was the combination of Konrad's boisterous conviction, Ersand's quieter though similarly reasoned position, and the irreversibility of the deed that gradually quietened Taithur.

Now, he freely admitted he had been wrong, and wondered more than once what mistakes he might be making now, without the noisy guidance of his friend.

But even the disruptors offered only a slight respite from Ersand's and Hester gloomy projections.

"They'll not expect us to have them," said Ersand. "So we'll have a considerable advantage in surprise. If we hit and hop we could probably do some damage, perhaps even a lot, but it would only be a holding action. They're sure to have more than one ship and they'd swat us like flies sooner or later."

"And even if we destroyed them," said Hester, "they'd get messages back and the next contingent would be both bigger and able to travel more directly." The intractability of her own reasoning angered her.

"Besides, if we use the surprise, then there'll be no question of negotiating," she added bitterly.

Both of them were depressed and weary when they presented their report to Taithur. He, however, did not seem to be in the least perturbed by their conclusions.

"Very good," he said, extending an appreciative arm to the display figures floating above the table. "Very thorough, very carefully thought out."

Misconstruing Taithur's ease of manner, Hester leaned forward, her face distressed. "Taith," she said. "You don't have to put on a bold front for us. We know this is bad news. Ers and I have searched all around the facts, but looking at it from different angles doesn't change the reality of the situation."

Taithur smiled. "I wouldn't dream of putting on a bold front, Hester," he said. "Your report is more or less what I'd have expected. I'm sure your reasoning is as near flawless as can be managed given the vagueness of the information we have about the forces heading our way."

He switched off the display and turned to Hester. "It's not all that long ago since you said something like 'We're going to need our every technological resource to survive here, and more besides, and that means developing the ancient and noble art of thinking and the even older art of listening to our inner thoughts.' Granted, I think it was in connection with dealing with the natives rather than the Service, but it made quite an impression on me. I think you were a little cross at Proktor for some reason."

"That could put it anywhere in the last several years," Hester replied with ironic resignation. "But I recall the remark. What about it?"

"Well, I think you're going to have to take your own advice. Set aside what you've been doing for a while—forget about it—perhaps take on a new base assignment for a week or so. The urgent part of the work is done. Now it needs time to mature."

Hester was wilfully patient. "Taith, the facts are the facts. Every line of analysis leads to the same conclusion—our eventual defeat in any confrontation with the Fleet. Nothing can alter that, whatever means we use to compute it."

Taithur in turn did not argue. "I agree with you, Hester." Then, leaning forward. "In fact, I'll make things easier for you. You can forget about the analyses which involve any form of surprise attack. Apart from being as futile as all the others, they'd be morally indefensible."

Hester scowled and waved a dismissive hand. "Easier?" she snorted. "I suppose if we're playing word games, then reducing the number of negative options can be called a positive move, but what are you talking about? We need to retain and consider every option we have."

Taithur ignored Hester's irritation and turned to Ersand. "You're not saying anything, Ers," he said pleasantly.

"I'm listening," Ersand replied. "Hester can handle an argument better than I can. But I must admit I don't know what you're after. You seem to be taking our report remarkably calmly. I just feel trapped."

"Calmness is our only hope," Taithur said softly, looking down at his hands resting on the table for a moment. Then, briskly, "But you're misunderstanding me. Or rather, I'm teasing you." He looked at them both intently. "Violence is a strange thing. Its causes may or may not be reasonable, but violence itself is intrinsically unreasonable—it's actually outside reason. Presumably it must have existed before our capacity to reason developed." He raised his eyebrows as if expecting some comment, but none came. Hester's scowl darkened. Taithur continued. "Thus, it's an ancient trait, and our attitudes towards it have roots that go very deep. They draw up sustenance from dark strata, strata well below the ordered topsoil of reasoning, thinking minds."

Hester seemed moved to speak, but Taithur's voice and manner stopped her. His intensity seemed to fill the entire room.

"You'll not die," he said. "Neither of you. Not willingly. You're human. You'll cling to life with unbelievable tenacity. Your own personal will to survive will ensure that, independent of any responsibilities you feel for others. And that will goes even deeper than the roots of violence. I'm not playing word games, Hester, or rejecting the rightness of your various analyses. How could I? But I do reject your contention that you have looked at every aspect of our position. You need a new insight, and I'm making it easier for you to find it by eliminating the available logical options. You feel trapped now, Ers, but you two are the best people we've got to deal with this, and you know it. That knowledge will push you further and further into that trap—as it'll push me too—until you break through into some other truth."

Ersand nodded slowly. His experience as a Captain gave him a view of other realities unattainable by others and beyond description. He could wait and trust. But Hester looked troubled. Her scowl had changed from one of irritation to one of self doubt. She shook her head. "I don't understand, Taith. I have such difficulty understanding the Way. Something seems to elude me always. Once or twice I've seen a flash of something when my mind's been quiet in meditation, but when I reach for it, it's gone. I really don't understand." She stood up, suddenly distressed. Taithur walked around the table and taking hold of her hands lowered her back into her chair. The strange intensity that had emanated from him had faded as quickly as it had appeared, and in its place was a simple gentle caring.

"You understand far more than you know," he said, kneeling beside her. "Far more. It's just that you're unaware of it. You needn't fear your own ability. It will manifest itself in spite of anything you can do. If you can't trust yourself, then do as you've always done: trust me. You have to search and think but what you seek will come unbidden when you least expect it. Now, both of you, leave this subject. Let go. Get some rest. Re-assign yourselves for a week or so if you think it'll help. Don't pursue anything that clatters into your mind, understood? We'll talk again in a few weeks."

When they had left, Taithur placed his fingers to his temples and breathed out heavily. He had largely anticipated the contents of the report; nothing else could reasonably have been expected. But to see the logic of it laid out so vividly was almost nightmarish. Beyond all reasoned doubt there would be no hope for them when the Fleet arrived.

# Chapter 19

The community grew and prospered. The world they had landed on was, despite its aboriginal inhabitants, rich in many resources and, in places, very beautiful. The four main bases were expanded and several others of various sizes established as the population increased.

Taithur's exhortation to the travellers that they should end their years of self-imposed restraint and begin having children again may have been open to debate on moral grounds, but it chimed with the mood of the people and they set to with a will.

Jion was fascinated by the behaviour of his own tribe. "It gives one a great deal to ponder," he said, studying a batch of population statistics. "These figures are remarkable. What a pity we can't set up a properly controlled experiment." He rubbed his chin thoughtfully. "We must have suffered some peculiar collective frustration being cooped up all those years in the ship. It's as if the gap that developed in the very young age groups acted like a genetic vacuum."

Ersand's eyes lit up mischievously. He wrinkled his forehead and looked at Jion paternally. "It's nothing peculiar, Jion," he said solemnly. "Just real gravity under their feet, that's all. And a real sun and real air. Nothing profound. What happens is…"

But Jion refused to be drawn out as a target for Ersand's dry humour, and contenting himself with a non-committal grunt by way of reply, bent earnestly to his figures. Given time, he was sure he could glean some very revealing data from this development, for all the lack of a control. It would make a most interesting paper.

Taithur for his part was also indifferent to the anthropological implications of the population growth. The new arrivals might have wreaked havoc with the average age of the community, but they had almost doubled its size and he could feel the travellers pushing down a tangle of tiny roots, each one anchoring them to this new home. He saw it as a confirmation of the rightness of their being there, and a promise of great hope for the future.

He was not, however, without doubts about this expansion that he had sanctioned. The reaction of the Fleet when it arrived was something about which he could not conjecture, but he was certain that at worst the children would not be physically harmed. Not that he had any great faith in the protection of the Law so far from the inner systems, but he was quite sure that even Education Department security could not keep secret any armed assault on a community containing so many young children. That, he reasoned, would be a considerable protection.

However, to still the conflict between his head and his heart, he took the precaution of preparing unmanned emergency probes which could reach the inner systems in one hop and blast the news onto all the main communication networks before anyone could stop them, should anything untoward be threatened.

The intense activity involved in expanding the main bases and in developing new ones, together with the ordinary problems of administering such lively growing communities, had another beneficial effect that Taithur had hoped for. It preserved much of the unity that had existed on board the Rithid. The rotation of personnel between bases necessarily declined as families grew and individual communities became more complex, but very little rivalry arose between bases and such as did was, in the main, friendly.

But the unity was not total, and as time passed, Taithur and the Council found it increasingly difficult to maintain what they considered to be an appropriate sense of urgency about the approach of the Fleet. A small but vocal minority began to take the view that the resources being allocated to defence could be better used elsewhere.

At the heart of this minority lay a group of strident malcontents, people who looked ever outwards for someone or something to bring them peace, and who could never accept that the cause of their pain lay in themselves. Taithur had encountered many such in his travels through the inner systems and they had often caused him great distress, it being their nature to turn on their chosen healer when their pain returned.

Despite a wary eye being kept open for such unhappy souls, a few had found their way onto the Rithid. They had been well content there, in spite of the physical and emotional discomfort, but once released from the constraining discipline of the ship and faced with the responsibility of comparative freedom, inner stresses had cracked outer shells and the world had become again a malevolent agency intent on depriving them of a happiness which should have been theirs.

Authorship of this persecution, once vested in the Service, was freely transferred to Taithur, and the allocation of resources for defence became the focus of their pain.

"We can't possibly fight the Fleet. These natives won't be any trouble, so why should we waste these resources? If they weren't being spent thus, then we could have this... or that..." and so on. And for a while they assailed Taithur relentlessly, using a mixture of half truths and misunderstandings baked solid in a heat of passion.

Patiently he took them through the various Resource Audits and Projections. He explained the real and terrible threat the natives posed in the event of premature contact, and how the precautions to be taken against them could with comparatively little adaptation be used to provide at least some resistance to the Fleet if need arose.

"Defence against the natives is essential. Defence against the Fleet will be useful. The two systems are interlinked, they benefit one another."

Though he considered it obvious, he even explained how important it was to be able to offer resistance to the Fleet if they were going to be able to negotiate. However, it soon became apparent that he was talking to closed minds.

"I wish we could hand them to the Fleet," he said irritably, after one particularly protracted session. "They'd destroy morale in a week." Then he relented. "But they're unhappy creatures. I should be more patient. There's a germ of validity in their argument."

Other Council members were less charitable. Alachev and Proktor seemed particularly incensed and formed an unusual alliance. Proktor, as usual, was blunt. "No-one denies there's an argument to be made, Taith, but it's up to us to make it, not them, and certainly not the way they do. You'll have to take drastic action sooner or later. People like that are corrosive. They're not content unless they're making more of their own kind." He warmed to his topic. "The very existence of a few extremists tends to move the whole community their way, even if only slightly. We can't afford that. We're too vulnerable. You've been more than fair with them and you can't be wasting your time dealing with such nonsense. Give them a warning and if they don't step into line, put them on field punishment."

Taithur hesitated. Proktor's manner when dealing with people still left a great deal to be desired; he could spoil a good case effortlessly simply by abrasive presentation. But Taithur had considerable regard for his intuitive insight into what motivated people, and he was anxious to encourage the young man's growing maturity. It was indeed some measure of this maturity that Proktor had gained his old rival Alachev as an ally.

Taithur could not decide which of the two was using the other. Whether Proktor was sending Alachev in to absorb the opposition's first fire, or whether Alachev was using Proktor's brash forthrightness to carry his own views forward under the guise of protected messenger. But either way, it added a little lightness to an increasingly gloomy topic and he was grateful for their advice even though he did not like it.

It was Alachev who summarized the position. "So many things are going so well for us, Taithur, but we're still bootstrapping, still walking a tightrope. We need our unity. We can't afford the risk of the kind of social disruption these people can cause. We've a great deal of freedom here in our new communities, but we've no pretensions about being a truly free people yet. It's too early. There mightn't be orbiting battleships blocking out the sunlight, but we're still at status four Battle Alert, and you're still Leader in Council. Leader by virtue of the Charter and as confirmed by the people. You must do something before they get out of hand."

Taithur accepted Alachev's reasoning, albeit unhappily. It was true that their freedom was in many ways illusory. They were not hemmed in by the countless arbitrary Service regulations that typified life in the inner systems, but the figures of the Resource Audits remorselessly emphasized the need for everyone to contribute to the full.

He looked up and caught Proktor's eye. Proktor gave a slight shrug of regretful resignation.

Taithur's reluctance fought a slight rearguard action. "I might be Leader in Council, but I can't use my authority on an arbitrary whim.

I respect your judgement, both of you, but these people are still only expressing an opinion."

"Show Taithur their individual work audits, please Alachev," Proktor said. In spite of his immediate concerns, the word "please" coming from Proktor brought an involuntary smile to Taithur's mouth which he had to cover with a casual hand movement.

A small bright light appeared in mid-air and the audit figures expanded from it to hover in front of him, clear and unequivocal.

"It's started already," Proktor said, leaning forward and pointing out the summary. "And I'll wager if we run the audits for their immediate family and friends we'll find the same. These people aren't pulling their weight, they're beginning to be a drain." He peered at the figures. "It's not large yet by any means, but it's there without a doubt. I wonder what we'll get if we do a sector analysis?"

As he reached for the console, Taithur stopped him with a gesture.

"Don't bother, Proktor," he said with a grimace. "That's quite clear, and it's probably all I'll need. No, wait. Run me a back analysis… baseline say, twelve months ago." Proktor raised an eyebrow in appreciation and adjusting the console settings, he spoke into the display unit. The figures changed instantly.

Taithur studied them thoughtfully and then sat back. The deterioration was accelerating. For a moment it occurred to him to ask why this had not been picked up routinely, then he remembered and reproached himself. That's a real old Service reflex showing, he thought—automatic individual monitoring.

"That clinches it," he said. He was saddened by the results of this search, but also a little relieved. Now at least he had grounds for action. He was also beginning to be angry. Angry at himself for allowing this situation to develop and, in spite of himself, angry at the individuals responsible. For these people to turn their faces from the truth about themselves so resolutely was one thing, but to act in such a way as to jeopardize others was a different matter altogether.

He flicked the figures off. "Get them up here," he said brusquely. "I'll have to read them the Riot Act for this." Proktor stood up to leave but paused as Taithur raised his hand. His look was distant but bleak, and Proktor felt a twinge of fear. Although he was actually looking down on Taithur, he had the feeling that he was in the presence of someone much taller. Not for the first time he reminded himself that he must not allow his constant proximity to Taithur the man to blur his vision of the powerful and driving personality of Taithur the Leader and Guide.

"Check the individual audits of their friends, families and work colleagues, and bring them to me as a matter of urgency. Then put them all on daily check and let them know why you're doing it. If we've got the rot setting in then, as you've said, we'll have to deal with it quickly." Taithur's tone brooked no dispute, nor did his final words.

"Proktor. Alachev. Thank you for what you've done. You were right to press your point. But Proktor, you in particular, mind your manners with these people. I know they're a pain, but this is an unhappy business, and needs careful handling. Whether these people improve or deteriorate will depend to a large extent on how you put the matter to them; whether you invoke their resentment or their consciences. If any of them crash out because of your impatience, I'll transfer the loss to your own audits, is that clear?"

Taithur's firm treatment of this problem was debated and discussed hotly throughout the community, but caused little real divisiveness. Such resentment as there was, was over the use made of the individual work audits, but this was offset by Taithur's openness and by the implications of the particular audits examined. Freedom of expression was one thing, but not pulling your weight was another when everyone was in the same boat. On balance, his action improved the unity of the community because it served to remind everyone of the reality of their position.

Capitalizing on this, Taithur and the Council judged that more was now to be gained than lost by emphasizing the proximity of the approaching Fleet. Initially they had encouraged progress by utilizing the sense of release felt by the community at being able to leave the Rithid. Then had come progress through population growth and the natural drive to improve living conditions for the new generation.

Now, however, it was decided that these very improvements would serve as an effective incentive to build up a spirit of resistance to the Fleet. Physically, emotionally and spiritually, the travellers now had far more to lose than ever before, and would need little, if any, encouragement to defend it. Where once the threat of the Fleet might have crushed them, now it would rouse them. The watchword of the community became mobilization, and Taithur missed no opportunity to reiterate the arguments showing the rightness of their cause.

"It's true, we made a serious mistake when we first arrived here; when we were vulnerable after our great journey. However, we diagnosed ourselves, we cured ourselves, and since then we've monitored ourselves. We've had no further direct contact with the natives, and only such exposure to their 'culture' as has been necessary for our security so we've contracted no infection. Our bases are well founded, well hidden, and thriving. Each week that passes sees us moving nearer to the time when we can contact these people with impunity and begin their Adjustment."

He expounded his intention of treating with the Fleet. "But we can't negotiate from weakness. True, it would be foolish to consider facing the Fleet in direct combat, but we can ensure that a price will have to be paid for our destruction, and the higher we make that price, the more we're likely to be listened to."

Then he gave the travellers a wider vision. "We mustn't forget that we've left friends as well as enemies back in the inner systems. Our action here will determine their fate as well as our own. We must send a message across the starways that says to our enemies, 'We offer you no harm. Leave us alone, or there will be consequences–we will hurt you.' And to our friends, 'There is hope.'"

The Fleet itself was at the middle of its journey, just easing into the normal design limit of the long-range scanners, and its every move was being scrutinized obsessively. It became clear that, as expected, there was more than one ship, though it was still not possible to determine how many. Ersand was still puzzled at what he considered their slow progress.

"It seems to take them a long time to pick up our trail," he would say periodically. But he did not vest any great hope in this. "Maybe the Rithid was smoother than I thought. Maybe there's some turbulence in the D-h. Maybe they're having to wait for crew changes. It could be any of a dozen things. Still, the longer they take, the better."

Ersand and Hester conferred frequently over tactics, but still seemed as far as ever from Taithur's promise of a revelation. They boxed themselves into a corner and stayed there, shuffling awkwardly for position, although after Taithur's pronouncement they never again fell into despair.

Hester busied herself with the Rithid's computers, extending her already considerable knowledge of weapons and tactics, and at Taithur's insistence she instructed the Council in the same. There were one or two protests but Taithur was unequivocal.

"I know we came here for peace and freedom and that none of us want to do this, but we've no alternative. I know, you're a farmer, you're a lawyer, you're an environmental mechanic. Good grief, I know we're none of us generals, but we've all done basic Adjustment training at some time in our youth, and, more importantly, we're all we've got. We're too few to risk putting all our faith in one trained person, so listen and learn. Hester's no field commander but we're lucky to have someone as capable as her to instruct us."

Slowly a nucleus formed consisting of Council members and others who showed some aptitude for military thinking, and from this spread out a training regime that involved every member of the community. Such protests as arose were dealt with as Taithur had dealt with them in Council—there was no alternative.

Compulsion generally was avoided, due to Taithur's skilful use of social pressures, but Hester insisted on one thing. "Everyone must know how to use, maintain and field repair all of our weapons." She had made a cautious study of the fighting tactics of some of the natives and assuming that the Fleet would choose to send in troops rather than destroy the planet wholesale, or destroy their bases by bombardment, then they would be best opposed by a large number of small, organized and armed opponents with considerable knowledge of the terrain. Arguably such a force would be indestructible, and while outright victory might not be possible, so would outright defeat.

Ersand for his part concentrated on training Newin. "He's not exceptional," he told the Council. "But he's not stupid, and he's enthusiastic. And I can give him almost my entire attention. We've been very lucky. He'll make a Captain."

Lucky or no, Ersand insisted to Taithur that a constant and thorough search be maintained for potential wakers

"We're going to need them if we manage to survive. We mustn't forget we're living in a desert here. We can't risk losing our capacity for D-h

142

flight. There's more years left in the Rithid than there is in me. She can't take us far, but she'll do the local systems comfortably enough and we have to have people coming along who can handle her."

Taithur found it increasingly difficult to think beyond the arrival of the Fleet, but agreed with Ersand. Besides, he thought. If the worst comes to the worst, wakers will serve as more bargaining counters with the Fleet. He watched the thought in horror as it passed through his mind, but let it go unhindered. Like his thoughts about the children, it left a trail of regret and shame like some crawling swamp dweller.

However, with the prospect of a second Captain came an unexpected hope. The technology of shipbuilding was too commonplace for the Service to be able to prevent its being taken on board the Rithid, but just as they tried to prevent the travellers taking any potential wakers, so they forbade their taking any scientific data on the manufacture of the special surfaces which permitted D-h flight.

At one time it seemed as though they might even forbid the taking of the repair kits that were carried as standard on all ships. Ersand, however, sent a blast of cold fury towards the source of that idea, threatening a Captain's moot at the very thought of such a breach of the most basic safety procedures. The idea faded into the nothingness from which it had appeared, but not before Konrad had acquired some extra kits, and some most eccentric cargo in the farm of old written manuals.

The manufacture of the D-h surfaces was more of an art than a science and a substantial part of that art resided in the wakers. Some demonstrated those traits which would lead them to become Captains, guiding ships in and through the eerie no-distance between the stars. Others, of quieter disposition generally, touched nearer that part of the life force which dwelt there, and cultivated the strange lichen-like spores that bridged the two spaces. From these came the sleek semi-organic surfaces that characterized all interstellar ships and the maintenance of which was the pride and joy of each Captain's heart.

Ersand experimented cautiously before he approached Taithur, using everything he could remember of the limited instruction and practice he had had while a cadet. One thing he knew—he was too old and too clouded in his mind to effect the metamorphosis that was necessary, but Newin was a different matter. He could not instruct him, but with care he might be able to lead him to find it for himself.

One day, following an exhausting piece of instruction, he said, "Take my shuttle. Go for a sun hop. It'll relax you after all that."

Then, casually, like an afterthought, he rooted in his locker and unearthed a small white bowl containing a small quantity of a fine grey powder.

"Ah," he said with some satisfaction. "I thought so." He handed the bowl to Newin. "Haven't seen this for years," he lied. "Just came across it the other day."

Newin stared into the bowl blankly. "What is it?" he asked. Ersand gave him a conspiratorial wink. "This is an old Captain's game," he said.

"Game?" queried Newin, both puzzled and pleased by the camaraderie of Ersand's manner. Ersand looked round as if to make sure no-one was listening, then he bent forward and spoke softly.

"It's more of a trick than a game," he said. "Give it a try. You'll find it interesting. When you're near the fold of the sun and the song's steady, hold the bowl in one hand and place the fingers of the other hand in the powder, thus…" He demonstrated. "Close your eyes, listen to the song and then sing it yourself."

Newin's eyes narrowed sceptically. "You're having me on," he said. "This is some old Captain's practical joke if it's anything."

Ersand laughed. "No," he said. "Truly. Try it. I've never managed to do it very well myself, but I've seen it done, and I think you'll be able to do it."

Still suspicious, Newin took the bowl. He'd take his chance on this nonsense. Whatever it was, it would be little enough to pay for a solo sun hop in the Captain's shuttle. Besides, if he ended up looking ridiculous, no-one would see him.

When he returned, his face was flushed with excitement. Ersand was affecting an air of forgetful indifference, working over a maintenance report.

"It's incredible." Newin was almost spluttering.

"What's that?" said Ersand, maintaining his forgetfulness. "Feel better for your hop? No problems?"

Newin waved the questions aside. "No. No problems," he said. "Look. Look at this." He pushed the bowl into Ersand's face. Its smooth white surface was now an iridescent black with a strange appearance of great depth, and it shimmered as if it were alive.

144

Ersand concealed his excitement with a broad smile. "There you are," he said. "I told you it was a good trick. You lucky young devil, I never managed to do it properly."

Later, in the quiet of his own spartan cabin, Ersand found himself almost crying, so moved was he by what had happened. It seemed to him almost as if his entire life had been a preparation for the way in which he had drawn out Newin's natural talent. Looking back, he saw it had been a small act of perfection and he felt at once elated and humbled.

Following this first success, Ersand took a friendly but apparently casual interest in Newin's hobby, giving him various articles to coat and studying each with obvious pleasure. Eventually, at Ersand's request, he sang layer upon layer around a small sphere, and when he reported that it was apparently growing on its own, without the grey powder, Ersand went to look at it. Nodding, he said, "That's interesting, Newin." Then he almost ran to Taithur.

"Newin has revivified sterile spore from one of the repair kits," he burst out.

Taithur gazed at him uncomprehendingly. Ersand looked skyward in a gesture of impatience. Taithur scowled. "I'm busy Ers, what are you talking about?"

Ersand raised his hands in a placatory gesture, and spoke very slowly and quietly. "I'm sorry Taith," he said. "I've been so absorbed in this. I forget it's beyond most people."

He explained what Newin had been achieving, putting the first bowl into Taithur's hands.

"It's beautiful," said Taithur, turning it round gingerly. "And it looks familiar. What's so special about it?"

Ersand tapped his knuckle on the bowl. "This is the organic base for a D-h surface, Taith, and reasonable quality too considering where it came from. Newin's cultivated to a self-sustaining level."

Taithur's expression changed.

Ersand continued. "With what I can remember, and what's in those peculiar manuals that Konrad acquired, we can make our own D-h surfaces. Not perfect by any means, they'll need a lot of careful maintenance, but good enough for local hopping. We can surface our shuttles and any new ships we make."

The soft bell-like tone of the watch signal interrupted him, and through the viewport he saw a bright line appear as the sun rose around the curve of the planet. Taithur dimmed the port. He felt a little disorientated by Ersand's news and the rush of concerns that followed it. Ersand anticipated him.

"It won't tilt the balance against the Fleet, Taith. Power is power, and we're only talking transport. But it must improve things for us." He gripped Taithur's arm. "It feels like a first thin line across a chasm. It's our first contact with the future."

# Chapter 20

"We have their probable time of arrival and point of final exit."

Taithur started nervously and touched his ear as the IFT sounded the message in his head. The uneasy stillness of the control centre became an uneasy movement, as people exchanged glances and then returned to their instruments.

"Is it within the estimated limits?" Ersand asked quietly.

"Yes."

"Have Newin hop the shuttles out to their assigned positions, then set course and move us out at cruise speed."

There was a slight vibration as the Rithid's engines cut from idling to drive and the tension in the room eased. Another stage in the commitment had been made. Click by click, like some great ratchet, Taithur thought. We move inexorably towards our confrontation.

As time had passed and the Fleet had continued its steady approach, the attitude of the travellers had hardened proportionately. The four main bases had been well established and though under-populated, could almost be regarded as cities. Twelve large sub-bases had also been established and were beginning to develop their own characters, and a large number of small, well-hidden and heavily fortified submarine and subterranean camps had been prepared for use in emergencies. The travellers had thrown their every effort into the work, and now had a great deal to defend.

Paradoxes fretted at Taithur from time to time. Had the Fleet not pursued them, would they have made this much progress so soon and so efficiently? Would they have maintained this unity? Would they have so assiduously avoided contact with the natives? Why indeed had they found new peace and harmony in preparing for war? He found no satisfactory answer to this last question in particular, and had to content himself with acceptance of the reality.

The travellers were as well trained in military skills as could be expected of a random selection of civilians whose main common feature was the following of a peaceful religion. Here, however, Taithur was much clearer in his mind. Strength had been a priority need, ever since they decided to colonize this planet with its wild inhabitants.

Admittedly, the reason for it had changed, but what they had achieved would have had to be achieved, Fleet or no. Strength, he knew, was dangerous, but it was not a commitment to violence, it simply offered more alternatives. Its use was a matter of judgement, his judgement, he thought with a twinge, as he watched the shuttles flicker hesitantly out of existence.

Before their after-images had faded, Taithur knew they would be at the estimated rendezvous point. Linked to Newin's craft and with their pilots in suspension, the shuttles would be carried through D-h space and brought out into normal space to watch and to report on any scout ships or probes that might be vanguard to the Fleet and that might warrant the Rithid retreating or taking evasive action.

"All's quiet," came Newin's voice eventually.

"Good," replied Ersand. "Are the pilots OK?" There was a short silence and the scanners in the control room indicated ship to ship communications at the rendezvous point. Ersand scowled slightly, then Newin spoke again.

"Some of them are a bit dizzy. I brought them round a little too quickly, but they'll be all right."

Ersand's scowl did not change. He was about to reply when Taithur spoke. "Switch me into your IFT, Newin, your ears only." After a moment Taithur tilted his head as he heard the click of the connection and Newin's call code.

"Newin," he said angrily. "Take more care of your men. D-h travel is dangerous and unpleasant for them. They're not like you. A few seconds extra in sus and a slower waking makes a lot of difference. If you don't think about them, they mightn't think about you when the action starts and it's their job to protect you. Don't forget that." He cut the link before Newin could reply.

Ersand nodded approvingly. "Maintain your stations and your watch, all of you. With luck you'll have quite a wait."

Taithur stood up and walked across the darkened control centre to watch the planet visibly shrinking as they cruised away from it. Would he see it again, he wondered? Or if he did, would it be as a captive? For an instant, a host of regrets and worries swirled around his mind, but he dismissed them almost effortlessly. If every step in life is a step into blackness, what is so frightening about this? This die is well and truly cast.

He turned and looked round at the people manning the centre. A few were occupied with instruments, but the majority had little or nothing to do until they arrived at the rendezvous point. The tension was beginning to seep back.

"I'm afraid there's no cure for waiting, friends," he said, walking back to his seat. "As far as we can tell, we've done everything that can be done, and if we haven't, it's too bad. We've plotted out a great many contingencies, but the only one we can be certain of is that we're going to have to think on our feet. So stay loose."

"It would help if we knew a little bit more about them," said Jion, in spite of himself. Taithur nodded, but made no reply. None was necessary. Jion's remark touched on an old sore, but now it was little more than a nervous twitch.

It had been a difficult decision, and to most of the Council members an unexpected one. All they knew was that their scanning equipment was of a high quality and should therefore be able to tell them a great deal about the nature of the Fleet as it drew nearer. Ersand had to explain otherwise.

"It's civilian equipment," he said. "As you say, probably the best available, but it's intended for planetary searches. It has no security screens." The blank looks that greeted this information turned gradually to disappointment and anger as he explained further.

As the Fleet neared, so the presence of their scanning, unprotected by security screens, would become apparent. "Screening a scanning beam is difficult even with the right equipment. Our civilian scanners will be like a direct broadcast to them. We've been reducing power and frequency ever since they came within design limits. Now we're down to very brief passes, very infrequently, in the hope they'll not be expecting scanning and will take it for background noise."

"All of which means?" asked Proktor unpleasantly, his mouth tight.

Ersand squashed a momentary surge of irritation at Proktor's manner. "It means, Proktor," he said quietly. "That all we can risk doing is keeping an eye on their general progress." Proktor swore, and Taithur reprimanded him.

"You mean that we'll not be able to get details of their strength, or monitor their communications?" he said.

Ersand shook his head. "I'm sorry Taith, but yes. If they catch one of our scanning beams they'll locate us almost immediately. That'll shorten their journey considerably, and they'll be able to scan us in turn."

Now, reflected Taithur, that old disappointment had joined many others to cower in the dustier corners of their memories, dwarfed and forgotten by the looming reality of the approaching Fleet. In any event, it had not made any serious difference to their planning. Even if the Fleet was sending only one battleship, it would be more than they could reasonably be expected to defeat. Planning had always centred around negotiations, with holding and damage limitation actions if they failed. "Hit and run," was a phrase that Hester rooted up from somewhere.

The thought of Hester heartened Taithur. She had been the most resolute amongst them. Working long, dedicated hours, studying intently and intensively, anything that might possibly add to their ability to fight and resist the Fleet. Raising morale wherever she went and drawing hidden reserves out of exhausted men and women to bring them to some new awareness of the task in hand. Taithur imagined her now, waiting patiently down in the southern polar base, probably meditating, using even this dead time to prepare herself mentally and physically for whatever was to come.

The image moved him. He always found it difficult to find the words of thanks that he felt should be made whenever he thought of people such as Hester, who had thrown their lives so totally into his vision. What was it in him that drew so much out of them? He felt no extraordinary power in himself. Often, he felt only weakness and inadequacy. And yet they looked to him. He, who all too frequently felt awed in their presence.

His reverie was broken by the soft bell-like reverberation of the watch signal.

"Old habits," said Ersand with a slightly rueful smile. He turned and signalled one of his officers to switch off the signal. There would be no changes of watch today. The Rithid was manned by only a skeleton crew of volunteers and everyone had their allotted task, which would last until the mission was completed.

The crew consisted of Taithur, Ersand and Jion from the Council and a handful of men and women drawn mainly from the older travellers. Taithur reasoned that during the tense initial contact with the Fleet, older, more mature minds would be a greater asset to him than young impetuous ones. Others had argued differently.

"You may need to take quick decisive action," was the tenor of their concern. "You'll need young people for that." But he had insisted. Half-jokingly he said. "No, no. Older people value their lives more than young ones. They'll certainly not provoke a fight, and they'll talk longer and faster to avoid one. That's the kind of attitude we're going to need." Then, more seriously: "Besides, if we have to fight, I doubt the Rithid will last too long and the real war will be here, on the surface. We… you… will need young people then. You'll be fighting battles where youthful characteristics will be important—courage, strength, stamina. Apart from a little courage, we'll need none of these in a space battle."

So the Rithid soared away from its adopted home, leaving the remaining Council members and other key personnel scattered throughout their new bases and camps.

Taithur was glad to think that Malva would be in the southern polar base with Hester, but it had been an unexpected wrench to part from her that morning. Too full of words and thoughts, his normal eloquence had deserted him, leaving him to make a fumbling and awkward farewell, and concluding with a nervous, almost brusque parting from her embrace. Periodically the scene returned to him and a little knot of grief turned in his stomach. It was no way to have parted from her at such a time. He knew that she understood but, even so…

Only with an effort could he take the distress and lay it gently to one side.

It did not help that they had no communication with the planet. Few had argued about that. Any two-way communication signal would lead to the bases being pin-pointed almost immediately. In the event of a battle developing, Newin was to fire emergency probes which would break out of D-h space near the planet and transmit a simple codeword across a wide frequency band. The bases would then assume the Rithid lost and prepare for ground resistance. Newin himself would crash hop back and take refuge on a base built under the surface of the planet's moon. He had bridled a little at this order, but Taithur had been blunt. "You'll be this colony's only Captain, Newin. You've no choice but to preserve yourself."

Taithur still had reservations about Newin being at the rendezvous point, but the tactical arguments had been overwhelming and he had conceded. However, he selected the other shuttle pilots with the greatest care, and told only Ersand of the briefing he had given them.

"Newin thinks you're just part of his patrol. What you really are is his bodyguard. He must get back to the moon base safely—at any cost. Any cost," he emphasized. "And that includes your lives. If any firing starts, it'll be your job to put yourselves between him and the Fleet. If you can't do that, then say so now and you'll be assigned other duties. It's certainly no dishonour to decline such a task."

Not one had demurred, and once again Taithur had felt smaller than the people he was leading.

"Can you remember your welcome speech?" Ersand's voice brought him back to the control room.

He shook his head as if to clear it, and smiled. "I'm sorry. What did you say? I keep drifting off. You should've given me something to do. I'm at too much of a loose end being the only passenger."

"I don't think so," said Ersand. "You were never very reliable at routine duties."

Taithur's forehead knotted. "That's a calumny," he said, with heavy indignation.

Ersand looked up at him, eyebrows raised. "Shall I flash up your duty record?" he said.

Taithur shook a finger at him hastily. "No thanks," he said. "One war at a time." Ersand gave a victorious and understanding nod and turned back to his instruments.

"How much longer?" asked Taithur.

"Before we get there or before they get there?" Ersand replied.

"Both," said Taithur. Ersand glanced at the array before him.

"We'll be about two hours," he said. "They'll probably be about an hour later."

"Probably?" queried Taithur.

Ersand shrugged slightly. "They've followed our route almost exactly, right up to the very last hop. Our latest scan was desperately brief but it indicated that they were continuing that way, in which case, as I say, they'll be at the rendezvous point about an hour after we arrive. But I'm still puzzled."

"By what?" Taithur asked.

Ersand shrugged again, and wriggled into a more comfortable position. "By their tactics," he said. "They won't have faulty gravity silos, and they must surely have deduced we were on that planet a long time ago. They could've reached us in a third of the hops that they've actually taken."

"Perhaps it's a good sign," Taithur offered.

"The Fleet's never a good sign," Ersand replied without hesitation. "It's some tactical devilment on their part for sure, but I can't think what it might be."

"Perhaps you're overestimating them," said Taithur. "We've always coded and directed our ship to surface communications to avoid the attention of the natives, and we were only one ship amongst quite a mass of general space junk. Perhaps they haven't scanned us after all. If you remember, there's a prodigious amount of artificial transmission coming out of that place—we'd be quite difficult to find."

"That's a possibility," admitted Ersand. "But even so they could've worked out we could only be here. There's just nowhere else we could have gone. Looking back, it was wild good fortune we found this place—it's so lonely and desolated."

Taithur sat down. "It's academic anyway," he said. "They're here, and we're here and that's all that matters. It's probably no more than a severe case of Service thinking. Orders probably say, 'Locate the trail and follow,' and some stiff old Fleet Captain is doing just that. It's not up to him to use his imagination or his wits."

Ersand did not reply but nodded slightly in agreement. "If that's the case," he said, "let's hope the rest of his orders read 'and negotiate' not 'and adjust'."

Their conversation had been held in undertones; not because they were discussing anything particularly profound, but because the tension in the control centre was steadily rising as they neared the rendezvous, and normal speech sounded raucous in the heightened atmosphere. Now all became silent, except for the occasional cluck of an instrument or the splutter from one of the local scanners picking out some piece of debris.

Taithur took what he imagined Hester's advice would be, and tried to meditate. But though quiet and still, the atmosphere around him was heavily laden with the subtle scents of fear, and his mind would not let go.

Fighting my animal nature, he thought. The body knows there's too much danger about to allow the mind the luxury of wandering off.

After a while, he stood up and paced over to the viewport again. There was no sign of their new home now. Just a bright point of light that was their sun, and the meagre scattering of stars he had gradually become used to. It had a certain spartan charm, he thought, but very different from the crowded glittering skies that would greet a night walker on his home world.

"Taithur."

Ersand's voice was urgent. Taithur moved across to him quickly.

"Newin's patrol have just reported fore-shadows. It looks like our estimate of their position is right."

Fore-shadows, those strange mirage-like images, at once vivid and fleeting, that preceded the exit of a ship from D-h space. Although a well-known phenomenon, they had never been caught by any recording device and always seemed to occur in the peripheral vision of the observer. Debate about their nature had been long and profound ever since they had been noted, but analysis was as elusive as the images themselves.

"Good," said Taithur. "How much longer now?"

"We'll be there in minutes," said Ersand.

He spoke to Newin. "How many fore-shadows have you had so far?"

There was a pause. "Difficult to judge. I've not seen that many, but I think they're tertiaries and there's a lot of overlap," came the reply. "And there were a few small ones, then a clutch—maybe a dozen or more—all at once, then odd ones trailing after."

Taithur looked at Ersand enquiringly. Ersand scowled. "It's difficult," he said. "It takes a lot of practice to read shadows, but they seem

154

to have sent quite a force to tackle us." He paused and rubbed his chin. "Though it's an odd pattern."

The remaining time went surprisingly quickly. The Rithid went into formation with the watching shuttles and the crew checked their battle station procedures.

Somewhat sulkily, Newin took up a position well to the rear and prepared to fire his probes and then crash hop back to the planet. With a similar reluctance, Taithur donned his battle suit.

These had been developed from ordinary maintenance suits, and were a considerable tribute to the ingenuity of Hester's motley group of designers and engineers. They allowed great freedom of movement and would also give a prolonged survival period in deep space, but Taithur did not like them and his distaste struggled bitterly with his gratitude as he went through the elaborate connection routine.

The suit joined him intimately to all parts of the battlefield through the other suit wearers and various probes, but at the same time he felt profoundly isolated, as if he were in the comfort of his quarters watching an old Ent show. He feared that in some extremity he might simply stand and watch visor and visual cortex displays with such detachment that he would forget his own involvement.

"You won't," was the brusque reply that Hester had offered when he mentioned this. "Believe me, you won't." But she had declined to elaborate.

Momentarily lost in his inner plaint about his suit, Taithur was startled by a sudden flicker of light coming through the viewport. It cast eerie shadows around the control room.

"Primaries. Ten seconds." Ersand's voice sounded in his head and brought him back to full awareness. Looking through the plethora of suit signals, as Matthew had taught him, Taithur looked out of the viewport and prepared to make the brief speech of welcome that he and Council had decided would be the best way to greet the Fleet.

His stomach turned into a cold, painful, knot of fear.

Then they were there. In the blink of an eye, the long-awaited ships appeared as if from nowhere, to face the Rithid and its tiny escort.

Ersand stepped forward and placed his hands on the viewport as if for support. His eyes were wide.

"Ye gods," he whispered.

# Chapter 21

Through the connections of his battle suit, Taithur could feel Ersand's pulse racing. He could also hear him talking to himself.

"A G class freighter, and an E... a Spiral class schooner... Two, three, barges... tugs... Good grief, an old Blackstar Liner..."

Taithur was receiving surges of information through Ersand's suit link that he could not understand and his immediate thought was that one of their suits had malfunctioned.

Before he could speak, however, Ersand was issuing orders, his voice urgent.

"All ships. Arm all weapons. Full external lights and flares. I repeat—arm all weapons. Full external lights and flares. Observation, take full scan of all ships."

Taithur noted the responses on his visor display at the same time as he felt the slight vibration of the Rithid's flares being fired. The sudden intense illumination made him blink before his visor adjusted its transparency.

He was horror-struck. "What are you doing, Ers?" he managed to gasp. "They'll vaporize us, they won't even..."

Ersand made a reassuring but slightly impatient hand signal and opened the communication circuits. To his further horror, Taithur saw he had opened the circuits not only to the shuttles and the Fleet, but also back to all the planetary bases.

A terrible thought formed suddenly. Ersand's a traitor, a Service spy. He crushed it angrily, but for all its folly it was reluctant to leave him.

"Cut your engines and identify yourselves."

Ersand's voice boomed into Taithur's head through his suit

communicator. Its tone and its volume drove out the unpleasant speculation, but his shocked surprise was being replaced by anger.

"What are you doing?" he hissed, seizing Ersand's arm with a gloved hand.

Ersand cut the link to the waiting ships but left all the others open. "It's not the Fleet," he said, and as he turned round from the viewport, Taithur could see his face. The body function signals he was receiving now made sense. Ersand's fear responses had been radically reduced and he was showing excitement almost to the point of elation. Taithur released his grip.

Not the Fleet? The words hung in his mind but refused to register. He heard himself saying "But…"

"Say again, Ers." Hester's voice interrupted him, sharp, distinct and urgent. As cold as the ice field that surrounded her polar base city.

"Give them full visual," said Ersand, signalling to the communications officer.

There was a brief silence, then, "Good Lord." Hester's voice showed an almost girlish surprise. "They're civilian craft. All sorts… That's an old Blackstar liner isn't it?"

"When you two have finished ship spotting, perhaps you'll tell me what's happening," said Taithur angrily.

"Identify yourselves, or we will fire on you." Ersand's voice rang out on a circuit to the stationary ships with an authority that Taithur had never heard before.

"They're civilian craft, Taith," Ersand said. "It's not the Fleet. I don't know who they are, but they're not the Fleet."

"Trap… possibly?" Hester's voice was tentative.

"No," said Ersand, almost disparagingly. "Your visuals probably aren't very good. They're civilian craft and they're battered. You can't fake that kind of wear; they've come a long way. And anyway, why would the Fleet disguise itself out here?"

There was a faint grunt of agreement from Hester.

"Civilians," said Taithur to himself.

"Is that the Rithid?" Instinctively, Taithur looked out of the viewport, as if to see who was speaking.

Ersand ignored the question. "You've had fair warning," he said, still stern and forceful. "Identify yourselves or we'll fire on you."

"Ers..." pleaded Taithur.

"Look at the scan data," said Ersand urgently. Taithur closed his eyes and read the information being relayed directly to him from the scanners.

"We're refugees," came the voice again. "Don't fire. We mean no harm. We've no weapons, and we've women and children aboard."

There must be ten thousand of them, thought Taithur as he tried to interpret the mass of information he was receiving. He heard a soft whistle from the base as if in confirmation. Through it he sensed the watching eyes and listening ears of every person on the planet.

"Refugees from what?" said Ersand, still unbending. "What do you want?"

"We're looking for the Rithid. Taithur's expedition. We've been travelling for years."

"Who are you and what do you want?" repeated Ersand.

"We're from all over," said the voice. "We need help. We've had a lot of D-h fever. We're short on supplies. Most of our ships need repair. We're..." The speaker hesitated.

"Out of cycle," anticipated Hester softly.

"...out of cycle," said the voice eventually.

"We see that," said Ersand, more gently. "Don't worry. You'll come to no harm if you obey my orders. Hold your stations."

He cut the circuit and, breathing out a long breath, turned to Taithur. Even in the peculiar isolation of his battle suit, Taithur could feel the conflict of emotions affecting everyone around him. There was obvious relief. Relief that they were not now either dead or struggling to make a feeble bargain with some stone-faced Adjustment Squad Commander. But there was shock and surprise at the nature and extent of the new arrivals. Taithur was also taken aback by the swiftness with which Ersand had taken control of the situation and by the severity of his manner.

Ersand anticipated his pique. "I'm sorry Taith," he said. "I had to act straight away. As soon as I saw what it was I knew we'd avoided one problem and found another."

"I don't understand," said Taithur.

"Numbers, Taith," came the reply. "Numbers. A convoy that size was bound to have a lot of people on board. And just from the state of the ships, I could have guessed they'd be in a parlous condition."

Taithur fiddled impatiently with his helmet, he couldn't think straight inside the damn thing.

"That's better," he said, as it came free and one of the crew took it from him. Running his hands through his hair, he moved towards the main console and began struggling with his suit fastenings.

"I wouldn't take that off yet," said Ersand. "You might need it before we're through here."

Taithur looked at him, puzzled. "What do you mean?" he said. "I don't know who that lot are, but I've seen enough to see they need help. They're not even armed, or barely so, if I read that scanner data correctly. What do we need battle suits for?"

Ersand shook his head irritably and opened his mouth to speak.

"Take care. You're all in shock." Hester's voice sliced authoritatively through the control room. "You were keyed up for battle and it's not happened. This development's been a jolt to us down here and we weren't under the pressure you were. Give yourselves a moment's pause to adjust. Those ships will do as they're told for a little while yet, I'd think. They're not rigged for battle, and they're making no signs that they intend to start one. But keep up your own Status One Battle Alert."

Her voice was like a splash of cold water, and for a moment there was complete stillness in the control centre. Then Taithur nodded and slowly began to re-fasten his suit, using the act as a focus for his whirling mind.

"Thank you, Hester," he said. "That was a timely observation."

He moved back to the viewport and looked out at the waiting ships seemingly pinioned by the glare of the light from the Rithid and the shuttles. He always had difficulty with his sense of scale when looking at objects in space. Even the smallest ships were so large, and the shortest distances so long by planetary standards. Could he actually see signs of movement at some of the viewports? He dismissed the idea and turned back to Ersand and the others.

Once again he felt himself the centre of their enquiries. But while this usually unnerved him somewhat, he found now that it had the benefit of being pleasantly familiar.

"It's the Way, friends," he said. "We lay plans to fight our old foe, coming, as we thought, in malice, across the years. And we find these souls, whoever they might be, apparently more lost than we ever were. My heart tells me we've a battle on our hands that may be less bloody than we envisaged, but could prove almost as painful. What shall we do with these people?"

Several voices spoke at once, some from the control centre crew, some from the planet. Taithur held up his hands until the hubbub spluttered out.

"Taithur?" Davar was acting communications officer for the Rithid. Taithur nodded to him.

"I've been monitoring their transmissions. They all seem to be very frightened and alarmed."

"Are they all ship to ship?" asked Ersand. "Have any probes gone out?"

Davar consulted his console. "No," he said. "Not unless it was immediately at the point of exit and that seems unlikely."

"Alarmed you say?" Taithur asked.

Davar nodded. "Yes, very alarmed."

Taithur frowned and looked at Ersand. "We must do something quickly," he said. "I've no taste for being the cause of other people's suffering."

"Nor I," replied Ersand. "But we must be careful. There's so many of them. We must contain them until we find out more about them. If they start drifting off towards the planet there'll be chaos and worse. We may well have to destroy them."

Taithur's frown deepened but Ersand continued. "If their ships are in such a state, and they're out of cycle, I'll lay odds they haven't remotely enough resources to establish their own bases—properly protected bases—especially for that number of people. And we haven't got enough to take more than a few into our bases. Even taking them into orbit may not be possible with all the satellites those natives have pointing in every direction. It's hard enough with just the one ship."

Taithur grimaced. He had the feeling of a trap closing about him, of going back to the middle of their own long journey when only faith had kept him moving forward through the wilderness, carrying the burden of the future of his people. He uttered a silent prayer. Give me the strength to face all that again.

"Taithur." It was Malva. "Talk to them. Talk to their leader, they must have one. You can't decide what to do until you know what they need."

Taithur nodded and signalled to Davar. "Open that circuit again, and find out if they've any immediate needs—food, medical supplies

161

or treatment, that sort of thing. Then invite their leader over for discussions. Tell him he can come in his own shuttle if he wishes…"

"But unarmed," interrupted Ersand.

"Unarmed," confirmed Taithur.

# Chapter 22

The leader of the newcomers styled himself Commander; an affectation that raised a few eyebrows. And despite his best endeavours Taithur found himself instinctively distrusting the man, with his restless watchful eyes and his hunched shoulders.

After introductions, the two men faced one another in one of the Rithid's more spartan wardrooms. The Commander, sitting stiffly opposite Taithur, was discreetly guarded by two of the Rithid's crew while Taithur was flanked by Jion and Ersand. Taithur spoke.

"Commander Vronic, I asked you aboard so that you could tell us who you are, where you're from, where you're intending to go, and to see how we can help you. I apologize for the rather fierce greeting we had to give you, but... well, no matter. It was necessary, and remains necessary. However, I can assure you that no violent action will be taken against your convoy while it remains here, providing you obey our instructions."

The Commander nodded, but whether it was an acknowledgement of his remarks or just a nervous twitch, Taithur could not tell. He continued. "We should be in a position to get some of the things you need immediately fairly soon, and they'll be sent straight across, but that done, it seems to me that maximum priority should be given to preparing a full Resource Audit as soon as possible."

Vronic bridled. "Taithur, that's so much Service claptrap. I can't be wasting time with Resource Audits. We've got urgent problems and we need to establish planetary bases as soon as possible to sort them out."

Taithur's eyes flashed for a moment. "Commander," he said slowly. "We're no great lovers of the Service ourselves. But we're here by virtue of their goodwill and a legal Charter. And for our own sakes we prepare Resource Audits to a far higher degree of accuracy than Service Standard requires. Out here that's anything but claptrap. It's essential for survival. Look around you. This place is a wilderness. No civilized life within years of us. You should know yourself after the journey you've just made that even the slightest slip out of cycle can have the direst long term consequences."

"Well," Vronic replied, almost snarling. "I suppose we'll have to do whatever you want. But I want urgent action for my people. They're space weary. Our scanners are good enough to show us there's plenty of space on that planet and we'll want to get down there as soon as possible."

Ersand's voice whispered into Taithur's head on the IFT. "I've put all this on open transmission to their ships. I think these people had better find out what kind of a 'Commander' they've got."

Taithur nodded. "I think they probably know already," he replied quietly. Then, to Vronic. "Commander. We're both a long way from our old homes and our old ways. It's a difficult and dangerous piece of space we've found to live in and we've learnt some hard lessons over the past years. I'm not going to go into details here, it's too complex, but we've a very delicate situation with the indigenous population and it'll not be possible to establish any new bases for a very long time."

Vronic's sneer broke through. "Indigenous population," he said. "If you mean those savages, they'll be no problem. We might be a little bit off track, but they're unbelievable. You should've exterminated them. You'll have to do it sooner or later."

Taithur felt the cold lump of fear return to his stomach. This man might be objectionable in his manner, and doubtless in many other respects, but Taithur felt a dreadful premonition when he heard this last remark. He set it aside, and rounded on Vronic angrily.

"There's no denying these people are savages and a major health risk," he said. "But they're also human, and while they don't know any better, they're redeemable given time and care. You're the unbelievable one. You do know better, and you've been massively negligent. You're not a little bit off track, you're way out of cycle—even our scanners picked that up—God knows what a detailed audit will find. How could you get in such a mess..." He waved his hand before Vronic could speak. "Don't bother. It's not relevant now. It's a problem for your people. The point is that we've taken a careful and calculated risk because nothing else could be done. You come flying in here, a mobile sink hole, and calmly talk about genocide…" He stopped and looked at Vronic carefully. The man was totally unmoved. Taithur found a hardness inside himself he had never suspected before. "Let's understand one another, Vronic. We'll help your people as much as we can. You've got women and children on that convoy and we could do no less. But I want a full Audit right now. I want a complete personnel list—Service Standard," he emphasized. "And I want the full documentation approving this trip of yours."

Vronic's eyes narrowed. "I thought you were a religious man, Taithur." he said. "The holy man leading his people to a beautiful new world. I've got people on those ships who've given up their entire lives just to come trailing after you. What am I supposed to tell them now we've found you? 'Yes, here's the great man, but he's keeping what he's found to himself, and he's playing Service games to keep us out.'"

Ersand leaned forward. "No-one's playing any games, Vronic. Just looking at your ships I can see more breaches of major safety regulations than I can count, and our scanners are pulling in some appalling information about your passenger conditions. We'll look after those who need looking after, but you're going nowhere until we find out who you are."

Vronic scowled, then conceded. "Very well," he said. "It's not the welcome I thought we'd get. I thought we'd got away from the Service, but I'll get back to my ship and have the information prepared for you."

Taithur put his head in his hands when Vronic had left. "What do you make of that?" he asked no-one in particular.

"He's a criminal." Liefer and Hester spoke almost simultaneously and then spent a confused moment apologizing to one another.

"He certainly is, judging from the state of his convoy," Taithur said.

"No, no," said Liefer. "Not just criminal in his behaviour. I'll lay odds he's a felon. Probably escaped from one of the penal systems."

Taithur looked up in surprise. "What makes you say that?" he said.

"Just gut reaction, Taith," came the slightly embarrassed reply. "If I'm allowed to have one at this distance."

Taithur could not help smiling. "But how could an escaped criminal mount an expedition like that?" he asked. "It might be ramshackle but it must have cost far more than ours, and that took some funding."

A low warning signal sounded and Davar's voice interrupted the discussion. "They've cut off all their ship to ship communications except for one tight beam link." There was a pause. "It's coded."

"Put it straight into the computer," said Ersand quickly.

"I've done that," Davar replied. "It'll take... Damn... they're jamming us."

Taithur stood up. "Battle suits, battle posts," he said, quietly but urgently.

Struggling with the fastenings on his helmet, he ran after Ersand along the corridor leading to the control centre. As the visor and direct cortex displays clicked on abruptly, he nearly missed the doorway and walked into a wall. Swearing softly he focussed for normal vision and made for his seat at the main console.

"What are they up to, Ers?" he said breathlessly. "They can't surely be thinking of attacking us?"

Ersand shrugged as he opened all the communication circuits.

"Commander Vronic. Please re-establish all normal ship to ship communication."

There was no reply.

"No change, Captain," said Davar after a moment's delay.

"Locate the ships using the coded beam and those doing the jamming," Ersand said. "Feed the information direct to the shuttles and to our guns."

"It's done Captain, but they're full of passengers."

Ersand grimaced. "Commander Vronic. Coded transmissions and jamming are both illegal activities. Open all your communication circuits immediately."

Taithur could feel the silence hanging dark in the control centre. "What ship is Vronic on," he asked.

"He's on the schooner," said Davar. "But it's like all the others, it's full of passengers and I lost him shortly after he boarded. And there's a dead spot near the centre."

Taithur heard the hiss of Ersand's breath. "The bastard. He's got himself a shielded battle room. If we fire on him we might kill all the passengers and still not get him."

Taithur turned away.

"How vulnerable are we?" he asked.

"It depends what they want to do," said Ersand. "We came out to fight a short holding action at the most, not mount a blockade. They haven't got the firepower to do much damage, but if they scatter there's not much we can do. It could be he only came over to reconnoitre."

"Taithur." Hester's voice was urgent and strained.

"Go ahead Hester."

There was an awkward pause. "If they scatter, you're going to have no alternative but to fire on them."

"What?" Taithur's mind refused to register the remark.

Hester repeated it. "Ersand's first judgement was right. There're too many of them. If they get any ships in orbit and even try establishing bases it'll jeopardize everyone, ourselves and the natives."

"Be specific," said Taithur.

There was a strange note in Hester's voice. Taithur recognised it as a struggle between her need to present objective information clearly, and horror at it what it meant.

"I've only managed to do some quick calculations, but they're accurate enough. The factors involved are massive, no refinement would make any difference. These people simply haven't got enough resources to bootstrap themselves. That, plus the fact that they're already on a downward path means they'll have to incur a huge resource debt, probably irrecoverable, if they try to establish surface bases."

She paused, as though checking something. "They'll not be able to avoid contact with the natives."

Vronic's chilling remark returned to Taithur. "You'll have to exterminate them sooner or later." They won't even try to avoid contact, he thought.

"You know how carefully balanced everything was for us. The high risk of major conflict if contact was premature, and all the consequences of that."

It was a long time since Taithur had considered the problem, but the consequences of the natives obtaining their technology were permanently etched on his mind. They would spread into the galaxy like a plague. That could not be allowed at any cost. A faint hope fluttered that Vronic and his people would accurately assess the conditions on the planet and would not make any attempt at open colonization, but it faded almost immediately. The very phrase, open colonization, displayed vividly to Taithur what Vronic would inevitably do. A man who had allowed such conditions to arise in his own domain would not pause to make the careful detailed assessments that the travellers had made. He had seen enough to know that the locals were primitives who were living completely out of cycle. He'd march in with his superior technology and attempt to sweep them aside if they stood in his way.

A vision of the fighting capacity of the natives rose in front of him. It was primitive certainly, but also massive and terrible. Their numbers alone made them formidable, but the missiles and bombs they had made and cherished were capable of the most appalling destruction. There were sufficient to destroy the entire population several times over and render the planet uninhabitable for generations. Even now, the travellers would be hard pressed to cope with such an onslaught, and they were well established and battle ready. As for rehabilitating the planet after such a war...

"He'll do it, won't he?" he said, speaking his thoughts out loud. "He'll blunder down there and start a worldwide conflict. He's no idea what those people are capable of."

"Yes," came Hester's simple reply. Taithur glanced up and caught Jion's eye. He nodded a pained confirmation. His quick calculations would be even better than Hester's, Taithur thought, and he saw no escape. And we'll probably have to intervene, taking the conflict to its likely outcome before the natives reached the point of damaging the planet so badly that even we won't be able to repair it. He could not suppress a twinge of bitterness. It was the very capacity of the natives to annihilate themselves more than once and to render their planet so uninhabitable that formed the ironically elegant and beautiful core of the mathematical analysis of this grotesque society.

Both his head and his heart told Taithur that Hester's analysis would be correct in all major particulars and that he must accept the fact that these new arrivals must be kept from colonizing the planet at any price. But could he bring himself to levy such a price? Could he bring himself to fire on these almost unprotected ships?

He tried to cling to the simplicity of Hester's analysis and the consequences of failure on his part to stop the convoy, but other thoughts intruded. If indeed Vronic were a criminal, how did he come to be in command of this motley array? And all these people, who were they? And what did they want? Vronic had referred to his passengers searching after him, Taithur, following the holy man to his new world. A lie? Possibly. But why so many people, and why women and children, families?

"Taithur?" It was Hester, concerned at Taithur's silence.

"I'm thinking, Hester," he replied. "I accept what you've said, but I need to think. There has to be some other way than shooting these people down indiscriminately."

Hester did not reply.

Taithur looked around the control centre. Such members of the crew who were there were busy with their allotted tasks, monitoring the stationary convoy intently. But his conversation with Hester had been on an open circuit and Taithur knew that just as in the Council Meetings, he had become the focus of all attentions. Everyone could see his dilemma, but none could help. They had come out armed to fight against overwhelming odds—a heroic gesture for a heroic cause. It had been an act of considered courage. Now they were faced with using their arms to slaughter people who might have looked to them for succour. That needed courage of an entirely different order.

Taithur looked bleakly at the visor and cortex arrays detailing the dispositions of his forces and those of the convoy. These flickered and shifted as the scanners collected more data and the computers assessed its implications. Clear, factual, accurate, insofar as the jamming allowed—everything he should need to make a judgement; but battle oriented for facing the Fleet—decisions necessary for victory in combat, not for achieving peaceful settlements.

Step by step. Taithur gave himself the answer as he felt the old question forming. He knew it was pointless to pursue the thought, but equally he knew it would come, and often it marked some subtle change in his thinking.

How did I come to this? There it was, then came a slight feeling of release.

What was it Davar had said about the intership communications immediately after the convoy arrived? They were alarmed and frightened. That was an initial response, and thus probably an honest one. And the man who had first contacted them.

"Is that the Rithid?" And "We're looking for the Rithid. Taithur's expedition."

Nothing in his manner had given the impression of insincerity or deception.

I must reach the people, Taithur thought. Bypass this Vronic.

"Jion," he said. "Give Davar the primary analysis of the consequences of premature contact with the natives. Davar, prepare to transmit it on my command. Tight beam to each ship and maximum power on every frequency. Maximum," he emphasized. "If they won't open the door then we'll have to try kicking it down."

"It'll take a few minutes to set up," said Davar.

Taithur nodded, "As quick as you can," he said. Then he lowered the intensity of the security screens to his own command circuits. Just sufficient, he hoped, to give the impression of a power drop. Somebody over there must surely be listening. Somebody in control. Let them hear this order to his crew.

"All weapon crews stand ready. The convoy appears to be preparing to scatter with a view to establishing random bases on the planet. You all know the likely consequences of premature contact with the natives. They affect far more than us here and they can't be allowed to happen." He paused. "We face a harsh choice, but there can be only one decision and we can't turn away from it. This is a dark and lonely part of the Way, but we must walk it. As your leader, both by our Charter and by your choice, I formally absolve you from all legal responsibility for what I must ask of you." His voice was sad and grim and he paused again before continuing. "If any ship moves, the disruptors and all other weapons will fire for maximum destructive effect on that schooner. They will then fire for maximum destructive effect on the moving ship. I repeat, maximum destructive effect. No ships must be allowed to escape." Then, in a resigned tone. "Ersand. Have the perimeter defence shuttles move up. With luck there might be one or two survivors we can pick up."

There was a flicker of activity on his visor display, but the computers could not interpret it through the jamming. Taithur felt very cold.

"Call again, Ers," he said.

Ersand nodded in acknowledgement. "Commander Vronic. I must

ask you again to cease coded transmissions and to cease jamming our transmissions to your convoy. Apart from being illegal, your action is preventing us from finding out what your people need."

Silence.

"Davar," said Taithur. "I can't interpret the scanner signals I'm getting. What do you make of them?"

"I'm working on it," came the reply. "But it's difficult. They're just blanketing everything with that jamming signal, but it sounds as if there's some kind of disturbance going on."

"Disturbance?"

Davar shrugged and bent over his console. "Their signal is erratic. Every now and then I get clear contact, but then everything seems to be noise and movement."

Taithur pondered the absence of information. Should he remain stationary, listening and trying to communicate, or should he act, and if so how? He could order low level fire against the tug which was the source of the jamming signal. That might throw up the automatic debris screens and cause a brief drop in the power to the transmitter, and then enable him to broadcast to all the ships simultaneously. On the other hand, such an act might be seen as a signal for the convoy to scatter and then his last order would be implemented and hundreds of probably innocent people, people who travelled half the galaxy to seek him out, would be killed. And still some ships might reach the planet and land on it.

The dilemma clarified itself almost immediately. Having to fire on these ships if they scattered was a repellent decision, leavened only by its dreadful necessity. To fire on them because they were fleeing in panic and disorder as a result of his own actions was unthinkable. He would have to wait.

"Have the coded transmissions been broken down yet?" he asked, clutching at a faint hope.

"No," replied Davar. "It's all random double protection. Probably some reconditioned Fleet machine. We'd need the key to even begin to make anything of it, then..." Abruptly he leaned forward, his hand moving up to his ear. "Listen," he said urgently, and flicked the scanner signal onto the ship's communication circuit.

The hissing roar of the jamming signal filled the control room, varying uncertainly in intensity. As it wavered, Taithur was able to pick out faint sounds that could be human voices, faint, distant, voices. He gestured to Davar to turn the signal off.

"What are they doing?" he said softly to himself. "What's happening?" He stood up and walked over to the viewport. "What ship was that from?" he said, gazing out at the waiting convoy.

"The schooner," Davar said. Taithur picked out the ship with its characteristic sweeping lines. Old fashioned and battered, like the Rithid, but still beautiful, and fast. He stared at it intently, leaning forward slightly as if he were trying to hear those distant sounds across the cold emptiness of space, but the ship hung silent and still against the backdrop of the wilderness sky with its sparse scattering of stars.

Then recognition dawned, and the sounds became clear to him. "They're fighting," he cried, vainly trying to snap his gloved fingers. "They're fighting. My God, that's what it is. There's some kind of a mutiny going on. Davar, send that signal now, maximum power. And send my last order with it. Quickly."

There was a flickering light outside and Taithur started.

"It's the other shuttles," said Ersand. "Newin's hopped them through on automatic." He sounded a little surprised, but his tone indicated approval of his protege's action.

Taithur had the feeling he was being carried along by circumstances not of his making.

The perimeter defence shuttles carried pioneers who had been training for what might have been suicide attacks on any Fleet ships closing on the planet. Taithur spoke to them urgently.

"You've all heard what's been going on. I'm working on the assumption that Vronic is having more than a little difficulty with his passengers. Move out to that schooner and punch your way through to that battle room. Take rescue sacks with you and do what you can for any injured, but get to the heart of that ship or we'll have a real massacre on our hands."

Before he had finished speaking the shuttles were moving forward like a pack of predators closing in on a dying animal.

"Davar," said Taithur. "Stop that last message and tell them what we're doing. Tell them we want to help, and we will help, but we can't let them land indiscriminately on the planet. With a little luck someone might

172

hear it and there'll be a little less panic. All guns transfer to that tug with the jammer on board. If it moves, destroy it. If any of the others move do your best to put them out of commission."

He moved away from the viewport and returned to his seat at the main console. Now he must conduct this battle away from the distraction of the visual reality. He tried to drive from his mind the seared memory of the death of Konrad and the knowledge that even now this could be happening to people on board the schooner as the pioneers blasted their way through the hull. He stared ruthlessly at his visor displays and tried not to hear again the terrible noise of the air shrieking out into space carrying with it the choking screams of the dying.

"They're through." Ersand's voice reached him at the same time his displays recorded the fact. "No external resistance." The remark was superfluous. Only the largest Fleet ships carried external weaponry to deal with direct assault by small groups.

"At least that one won't be hopping out now," Ersand added.

Taithur watched the idealized schema in front of him. It was unspectacular and uncomplicated, unlike his own reactions. He could not keep his mind from the tormented interior of the schooner. It would be too late for some but the emergency screens would be automatically sealing off the evacuating sections of the ship... or should be. But a group so far deteriorated as this was would be unlikely to show any special regard for basic maintenance. On the other hand, Captains were Captains. It was unlikely that they would countenance such neglect, and Captains had special powers of coercion when necessary, simply by dint of their unique attributes. Then again...

Taithur dragged his attention back to the displays, and increased the volume of the direct transmission from the pioneer leader. Much of it was meaningless, being orders and acknowledgements given in the specialized jargon that the pioneers used amongst themselves. Occasionally a brief summary of progress was transmitted back to the Rithid in more intelligible language. These plus his displays told Taithur that they were now well inside, but his displays told him also that the pioneers were moving through high buffeting winds and falling air pressures. There was also evidence of lifeforms and activity outside the ship.

The other ships were motionless, waiting, like placid grazing animals

173

watching one of their fellows being brought down by carnivores, and knowing that they were now safe for the time being.

"Davar," he said. "See if you can use the spare circuits on the pioneer's suits to relay transmissions directly into the ship."

Davar acknowledged and within seconds confirmed the link.

Taithur connected into it. "My name is Taithur. I beg of you all, please keep as far away as possible from our attack force. They're proceeding in a straight line from your port docking area to Commander Vronic's battle room, and the damage will be extensive. We mean you no harm but greater harm will come to all of us if you do not listen to us. Your Commander is preventing this. Please do what you can to open transmission to us so that we can speak to you. We want only to help you."

There was no response, and Taithur saw the pioneers moving inexorably towards the heart of the ship. A shuttle was returning to the Rithid. Taithur reached out to alert the medical section, but it had already been done. The casualties would not be pioneers, that he knew. They could only be people unfortunate enough to be in the vicinity of the pioneer's entry point. The memory of the dead native returned to him—his friends killed by the traveller's technology and he himself killed by a trivial disease.

How can it be that in our search for peace and freedom we bring death to those we meet? he thought.

Abruptly there was a flurry of activity on his visor and the Rithid shook with the unfamiliar vibration of its disruptors and improvised gunnery.

The tug carrying the jamming transmitter had cut in its engines and attempted to break out of the silent formation. It had been a sudden and unexpected manoeuvre, but not fast enough for the Rithid's nervous gunners.

Taithur knew there would be no point sending rescuers to the ship. The Rithid's disruptors would have left precious little of a far bigger ship than a tug. There was a sudden blankness in his display that seemed darker and deeper than anything he had ever known.

"Oh my God," he said. "What have we done?"

Then, the jamming gone, the air was full of a thousand screaming voices.

# Chapter 23

It was Taithur's heartfelt cry of horror that in the end did more to heal the dreadful hurt of the encounter between the travellers and the newcomers than any of the harsh logical reasoning that had made it so tragically necessary.

It had been carried at maximum power to every open receiver in the tired convoy, and the pain in it had spoken to the hearts of all who heard it, telling them of his great love and of the agony of his great burden.

Taithur too felt the cry of the people rise through the countless clamouring voices that filled the Rithid's receivers. It was the eternal cry of those caught impotently in the consequences of the acts of others more powerful.

Immediately he ordered the pioneers to halt their attack and, leaving sufficient to lay siege to Vronic's battle room, to move back out and assist with rescue and repair work.

At the time, this instruction had been instinctive and based on concern for the people on the schooner, but looking back later he realized that it had also been both tactically and politically sound. Vronic may have had most of the ship's controls, but the damage that had been done precluded D-h flight and in any event the pioneers held the actual engines. It would have been wasteful and potentially dangerous for the pioneers to smash into the heavily armoured battle room, and the time spent would have meant more deaths among the passengers as the schooner leaked its precious air into the voracious vacuum of space.

Over the next few hours varying degrees of pandemonium reigned. A small group of pioneers established a tight siege around the battle room, while the others worked frantically to seal the gaping wound in the schooner's side. They had suffered no losses, nor even injuries, but their actions had caused an explosive evacuation that left the Rithid's medical team overloaded with casualties. There were also several casualties from the fighting between passengers on the convoy, but these in general were less severely injured than those caught in the evacuation. Taithur and the rest of the crew were occupied in calming the occupants of the other ships and trying to attend to their immediate needs.

It was a monumental task. The end of their journey, the unexpected violence, the bitter paradox of the planet they had at last reached, and the hope and care in Taithur's voice seemed to have opened floodgates which had restrained years of almost unbearable fear and frustration. Taithur found himself being submerged in the clamour, and in the end it was Hester who reached out from her polar base and pulled him to safer ground.

"You're shocked and exhausted, Taithur, as are all these people," she said. "You must rest now." Her voice was concerned but purposeful. Taithur demurred, making a gesture towards the convoy and muttering about, "All these people."

"Listen to yourself, Taith," had come back the stern reply. "You can hardly talk let alone think. You're going to start making mistakes. Get to your quarters and rest or I'll have Medical come and collect you. Your crew will secure the convoy and look after everything that needs to be looked after immediately. The rest will have to wait. A lot of these people are just telling you their life stories anyway."

Taithur was still sufficiently alert to note the tone of Hester's remark and he was reluctantly obliged to agree with her. Successive decisions were becoming progressively less urgent and he was indisputably drained; his thoughts were beginning to repeat themselves. The crisis was over. They had not fought the battle they had expected to lose, and they had won the battle they had not expected to fight. New routes into the future had been irrevocably laid down and nothing would be materially changed by any false urgency. He must let go.

Twelve hours later he woke slowly from a remarkably relaxed sleep.

"I'm not sure I care for the way you sleep so well when I'm not with you."

The voice was Malva's. Taithur mumbled unintelligibly and rolled onto his back. His brow furrowed. Through his closed eyelids he sensed an unaccustomed brightness in his room. Opening his eyes, he had to close them almost immediately as it flooded in painfully. Malva laughed, "Come on, sleepy head, prop them open and look at this."

Cautiously Taithur peered through narrowed eyes, using one hand as a shield against the powerful light. Gradually a picture came into focus: brilliant sunshine and blinding whiteness, and a bulky black figure in the middle of it. It was the communication viewer back to planet.

"Good morning," Malva's voice rang out with alarming cheerfulness.

"Malva, is that you?" Taithur said, still screwing his eyes up against the brightness, and staring in disbelief at the strange figure. It waved in acknowledgement. "I thought you'd like to see this," said Malva, and the figure threw both arms wide in an all-encompassing gesture before disappearing to one side as the viewer moved slowly round the horizon to reveal a white landscape brilliant under a clear blue sky. Grey and white mountains guarded the distance like massive teeth.

"It's beautiful," Taithur said. The figure reappeared.

"Malva, is that you? Where the devil are you, and what are you wearing?"

"I'm outside the base," said Malva, the whiteness of her smile appearing through the shadowy gloom of her hood, but dimmed by the intense glare of the icefield.

Taithur sat bolt upright, wide awake. "Outside?" he shouted. "Malva, what are you thinking? Get back inside."

"Oh nonsense," Malva replied. "It's unbelievably cold but it's wonderful, providing you're properly dressed, and providing you watch the weather. It's so still and quiet. It's like a place of great spiritual learning."

Taithur shook his head and smiled. "You're just an old-fashioned romantic," he said. "But I suppose I'll end up coming with you when I get back." He swung out of the bed and started changing. His mind began a parade of the happenings of the previous day.

"What's happened while I've been asleep?" he said, looking at his watch.

"Hester will tell you," said Malva. "I just thought you'd like to wake up to something different from your ship's quarters after yesterday."

"You were right," he replied. Then thoughtfully he looked past his wife, incongruous in her bulky protective clothing, and out across the vast ice plain towards the mountains. This was indeed a rare and beautiful place. The need for its preservation and that of all the other beautiful places on this planet had been the cause of the previous day's agony, and the sight of it reminded Taithur of the rightness of his actions.

"It was a happy thought," he said. "Thank you. I love you."

Malva waved. "And I you," she said. "Take care. Here's Hester." And abruptly the brightness was gone.

It took a moment or two for Taithur's eyes to adjust to the new level of illumination, but gradually Hester's familiar form emerged from the gloom. She looked tired.

"You've been busy I see," he said. "I think it might be my turn to tell you to go to bed Hester."

She smiled. "That won't be necessary," she said. "I need no telling. I've just been waiting for you to wake up. Everything that's happened overnight is in the computers, but I just wanted to summarize it for you briefly before I get some rest."

Taithur nodded. "Carry on while I finish changing," he said.

The situation that Hester described was at once better and worse than the one he had left twelve hours earlier. The pioneers had secured all the ships to prevent any of them leaving unexpectedly and had actually joined four of the smaller ones together to form a single dormitory unit. "The work's a bit rough, but it's safe enough and it'll do the job until we can work out a better arrangement," was the pioneer leader's conclusion.

Taithur was impressed and surprised. It was a considerable achievement, but why? Hester gesticulated vaguely. "Oh, several reasons," she said. "There were some severe cases of claustrophobia in the smaller ships. There were families that had been split up…" There was a flash of anger in her face that cut through the fatigue, and which Taithur felt across all the miles of space that separated them.

"That Vronic has got some questions to answer when he comes out," she said with that quiet menace that Taithur had seen quell many an obstreperous opponent in the days when they were touring the inner systems preparing for their journey. But she did not elaborate, choosing instead to continue with her report.

Even jury-rigged, the whole life support system of the combined unit was far more efficient than those of the individual ships, and this would help the people start their way back towards balance again. It had also proved necessary to separate different factions within the convoy.

"There seems to be all shades of opinion for and against Vronic.

We're going to have to do some thorough investigations to get to the bottom of what's been happening. I suppose we might have expected that if we'd had time to think, but I doubt it would have made any difference to what happened."

"What's the position with Vronic,?" Taithur interrupted.

Hester glanced at a nearby console. "Still in his little citadel, with a handful of cronies. It's a clever piece of work for an improvisation. He's very nearly autonomous, but he's going nowhere. We're eavesdropping as far as we can, and we've established formal communications, but he's not talking much at the moment."

Taithur nodded. "Let him wait. If he's self-sufficient he's not costing us anything, and when he starts to run short he'll be more amenable to discussion. Just make sure he can't communicate with anyone else. Factions or no, he'll be the heart of whatever problems those people have and the sooner they realize they're going to be without him for some time, the sooner we'll find out what's been happening."

Hester smiled to herself. "You'd have done well in Education, Taith," she said.

"That's not funny, Hester," Taithur replied defensively. Hester raised her hands in apology.

"Sorry," she said insincerely. Taithur nodded and motioned her to continue. All the Captains had been brought aboard the Rithid, thereby further immobilizing the convoy.

Marvellous, thought Taithur. Extra Captains will be very useful, and there shouldn't be much trouble explaining the realities of the situation to them. That boded well. But his rising optimism faltered as Hester gave him the casualty figures.

"About 137 dead and 76 injured from the schooner, about 214 dead from the tug."

"About?" Taithur queried.

Hester looked up, her face sad. "Disruptors, Taith," she said, in pained surprised. "That tug disintegrated instantly. There was hardly any recoverable metal left, let alone people."

Taithur nodded and grimaced. In addition to his personal sense of responsibility, he knew these deaths would hang between the two communities like a bloodstained curtain.

"What about the casualties?" he asked.

179

"Medical was inundated," Hester replied. "They had to resort to simple field surgery and first aid to patch people up well enough to get them back to the planet."

"Where are they all now?" Taithur asked.

"Scattered about the four bases."

"Make sure they're all properly quarantined," Taithur said, the thought springing unexpectedly to mind. "We've been getting pretty careless since we found out the natives offered no problem, but these people are our own kind, they could be carrying anything living in such bad conditions. The last thing we need is an epidemic amongst our medical staff."

This time it was Hester who grimaced with self-reproach. It was a measure of her worth that she shouldered the responsibility for this omission immediately and made no attempt to plead in mitigation. She turned away from Taithur and spoke briefly on her IFT.

"It's done, Taith," she said, turning back. "I'm sorry."

Taithur waved the deed aside. "What else have you got for me from your night's endeavours?" he said.

"Not much," Hester said. "And it's mixed, like the rest of it. We've started a full-scale Resource Audit of course, and I've started making arrangements for individual questioning. It's going to be a hell of a job with so many, but I don't see any alternative. We've got to find out everything about them if we're going to find niches for them. Subject to your approval I've given it top priority."

Damn, thought Taithur. She's fretting about that quarantine business. "Don't go formal on me, Hester," he said. "Since when did you need my approval for doing what was blatantly obvious? Is that everything?"

"Nearly," Hester answered. She looked a little awkward. "I'm afraid we may have a spot of trouble with the natives."

Taithur gazed at her in disbelief. "What?" he said, frowning.

"It'll probably fade away, but we'll keep an eye on it," said Hester with rather affected casualness.

"What's happened, Hester?" he said slowly and purposefully.

"One of the shuttles bringing back the wounded flew near one of their passenger aircraft," Hester replied hurriedly.

"And?"

"And it's all over their news media—television, press, radio."

Taithur sat down. "Did they get any hard evidence? Radar plots, photographs, anything like that?" he said after a moment's silence.

"Not as far as we can tell. The shuttle's D-h surface stopped the radar, and he was travelling very fast. None of the news items we've intercepted indicate anyone managed to take any photographs."

Taithur swore softly to himself. "Have Ersand give that pilot a good kicking," he said angrily. "Just remind him we only survived our encounter with the Fleet because it wasn't the Fleet. We've got all our old problems, plus an indeterminate mass more from this lot." He flicked his thumb in the general direction of the convoy. "And the last thing we can afford now, or in the foreseeable future, is trouble with the locals." His voice became quieter and Hester's face became impassive as she recognized the signs of his real anger mounting.

"Make that totally clear to everyone, Hester," he said, his jawline tight. "We've just killed 351 of our own people and maimed 76 to prevent that happening. Tell everyone to remember that, whenever they get the urge to be careless in their monitoring work or their travelling. We're going to need more discipline than ever, not less."

"Ersand's attended to the pilot," Hester said. "And I'll have general security tightened up. We've become so occupied with facing what might have been our end that we've all become careless."

Taithur's anger faded at Hester's tone. "Go and get some sleep," he said. "You've done well as usual. Time's a little bit more on our side than it was. As you told me, we mustn't drive ourselves into making mistakes. This isn't what we'd have chosen, but we'll come through it eventually. We must take the strengths of these new people and develop them, and protect ourselves against their weaknesses."

When the viewer had gone blank, Taithur played back his wife's greeting. He stared out across the dazzling landscape. Stark but beautiful, cruel but pure. The images relaxed him, and the tasks ahead of him gradually turned from being onerous to being exciting. These new people way well present many problems, but in the end he was sure they would be a source of new strength to the travellers.

He stood up and smoothed the creases out of his tunic. And, the thought occurred to him for the first time, they would have news from home. No, he corrected himself. This is home. They would have news from the inner systems.

# Chapter 24

As envisaged, the work involved in dealing with the newcomers proved to be considerable, and many a nostalgic glance was cast back to the time when the travellers were struggling to establish their first bases on the planet.

Taithur had been correct in his estimation of the effects of the deaths. Women and children had perished in the shrieking turmoil of the evacuation when the pioneers had smashed through the hull of the schooner, and no amount of reasoned justification could reach down to the roots of the pain in their loved ones.

"All these years. Travelling. Hoping. Looking for you, Taithur. Your words, your vision, carrying them through endless deprivation and hardship. Such courage. They offered no harm. And to end like that. And you did it. Why?"

The question came in many forms and Taithur could offer nothing but his own pain. "They have to say it all," he said to Malva. "They have to. It's for the best. Grief's an unbearable burden, they must speak it, for their own sakes. And they may as well shed it onto me."

But Malva doubted that. "Who's going to carry your burden, my love?" she said, trying not to let her own distress at his pain add further to it.

He put his arms around her and said, "There aren't any burdens except those that I choose to carry, and I don't accept any, any more than the flower in the field does. What we did was inevitable, unavoidable, like a surgeon destroying healthy tissue in order to destroy diseased."

"That's your head talking, Taith," Malva said. "What about your heart?"

Taithur looked at his wife and knew that he too must speak his grief. To avoid her question would put a distance between them crueller than infidelity and would leave them both weaker and more isolated than any amount of shared pain could. He took her face in his hands and looked into her eyes. His voice was soft and strained.

"When I think about those people, I think about you, trapped and screaming, like Konrad, and beyond any help I can bring except to wish that you'd die as soon as possible to end your pain. I think of you being there because of my actions. I want to turn away from the thought, but I know I have to look at it because of who I am and where I am. I didn't wish this, but now I'm here I can't walk away. I, above all, must face the worst that's to be faced. When I've done that I can accept other people's burdens and let them fall away from me into nothingness." He put a finger on her lips to stop her speaking. "I know," he said. "That's my head not my heart, but I have to use the one to sustain the other. My mind on its own is cold and distant and limited, like a machine. My heart on its own is too soon bruised and helpless. But together, the one guides and protects the other, one sees and one feels."

Malva threw her arms around him tightly. "I don't understand you at times, my love, but I do know you're a liar, and I do love you."

Taithur kissed her forehead. "It's not a lie," he said. "I just don't have the words for it. Perhaps they don't exist. Perhaps I'm deceiving myself. Perhaps it's only you that sustains me." He pulled away from her gently, and moved over to the viewport. "But it doesn't matter," he said. "Whatever happens, I can't walk away. Every step forward is always an act of faith. If I'm crushed, I'm crushed. Someone somewhere will learn from it and perhaps do better. One thing's for certain, the problems will continue whether I live or die."

And continue they did.

Time and harsh necessity eased the grief of the friends and relatives of the dead, but the action of the travellers in assaulting the convoy provided a fertile breeding ground for the dissension that already existed amongst the newcomers. A sizeable group grew up who wanted nothing to do with the travellers and who began to demand the right to establish their own bases on the planet. They found sympathizers amongst the travellers themselves, as the removal of the threat of the Fleet, the increasing prosperity and strength of the bases, now virtually cities, and the growing population reduced the need for the sense of community that had bound them so tightly in the past.

It surprised several of the Council members that Taithur was so relaxed about this development.

"The plant's growing," he said. "It can't be confined in one pot forever. Providing we maintain goodwill towards one another no great harm will come of it."

"But some are talking about removing you as leader," Proktor said.

Taithur smiled. "My leadership, as you call it, was only ever intended to be temporary. It could only work with a small number of people facing a common problem. I don't want the task of ruling a planet, it's a ridiculous idea. When the time's right I'll step aside, and the different communities can try their own ideas about government."

Proktor scowled. "But it's not right for them to talk like that after what you've done," he said.

"Proktor," Taithur replied. "Even these uncivilized natives we've landed among know enough to keep a shrewd eye on their tribal leaders. At least most of them do. Just because they're primitive doesn't mean they don't understand human nature. In fact I'm beginning to think it's just the opposite."

Similar sentiments were expressed in Hester's first reports to the Council on the new arrivals.

"They're such a mixed bunch," she said. "They don't have the same commonality of purpose that we have and I can't see any way in which we could bring it about. My staff have had quite a lot of opposition to contend with, even obstructiveness at times. Sooner or later I'd say they're going to have to go their separate ways, or we'll have some real problems on our hands."

In the early stages, however, the deeper divisions were hidden by the need to improve the physical conditions in which the newcomers were housed. That they could not move down onto the planet was accepted by most of them fairly quickly, albeit with an ill grace. The Resource Audit figures were irrefutable and made it abundantly clear that the newcomers would not be able to undertake any major establishment work themselves. Taithur then showed them the narrowness of the traveller's own margins to demonstrate that only a few of the newcomers could be accommodated in the cities.

Some of the newcomers disputed the need for the expensive defence precautions that were being taken against discovery by the natives, but here, Jion and Hester's calculations painted an even more vivid picture.

"It's unbelievable," said Gared, the chairman of the large and quarrelsome committee that the newcomers elected to represent them. "Are you sure they're human?"

Jion nodded. "Oh, without a doubt. Any reservations we might have had disappeared when we accidently killed a couple of them. We had a really good look at them I can assure you. We've no idea how they came to be here, but they're human all right. Not as robust as we are. Their immune systems are not as well developed as ours and so they're much more prone to disease than us. And to radiation damage. I think that's probably because they live out here in the wilderness with so few stars. It's ironic really when you consider they actually use fission devices for weapons and power generation."

Gared's eyes widened in disbelief, but Jion's gaze was sombre. He displayed a set of contingency calculations outlining the probable effects of premature contact with the natives. Gared bent forward and squinted at them earnestly. "It's a long time since I did this kind of projection calculation," he said. But when he straightened up, he was noticeably paler.

"And this," continued Jion. Another set of calculations appeared. "If they push their pollution to... this level. Or start any major conflict involving those fission devices, then independent of the risk, we'll have to intervene directly to stop them for our own sakes. You can see that, can't you?"

Gared nodded.

"Please explain all this to your people," Jion said. "It's the main reason we had to take such strong steps to make sure you didn't land. Tell them what these people are like, it's all here." He indicated the calculations. "I'll have copies done for you. If these people find out about us, there's a very high risk they'll turn on us and there's a fair chance they'll defeat us and take our technology. It's less of a chance than it was, much less, but it's still too high to risk those consequences." He pointed to the hovering calculations again. "We'll all be dead, and they'll be loose in the galaxy with technology far beyond their moral understanding."

While not everyone could understand Jion's calculations, those who could had to admit they were sound, and their conclusions accurate and alarming. Coupled with the generally open and generous behaviour of the travellers, the calculations did much to ease the tension between the two peoples and slowly the moderate core of the newcomers began to recover from the degradation of their journey and to assert itself.

The newcomers had a few pioneers with them, and like the Captains, they readily accepted the realities of the situation and cooperated fully with the travellers to work out a future for their community. The major priority was for improved living conditions generally, and this was achieved through considerable effort, by further utilizing the older ships to make a large self-contained station.

The making of the station presented many difficult technical problems and the solution of these brought pioneers and engineers and other specialists together in common endeavour. Taithur became optimistic.

"We're over the worst, I think. Look how everyone's cooperating."

Jion and Proktor were less sanguine.

"I doubt it," said Jion. "That's just the camaraderie of shared disciplines. They're professionals doing their jobs. It's patently necessary work, and technically interesting, so they're content to get on with it, leaving the subtler political problems to others. I think you'll find we'll be back where we started when the job's finished and everyone's rehoused."

Proktor was blunter, but to the same effect. "I wouldn't trust that lot as far as I could throw them. They're too wishy-washy, too easily led. They let that thug Vronic take charge, didn't they? And followed him right out of cycle like so many daft sheep. They're going to give us trouble sooner or later."

Taithur chased them both away.

Sadly, however, both were correct. The new station was more comfortable, more spacious and more efficient than anything the newcomers had known for several years, and they soon settled down to running their own affairs and planning for the future.

"That is a good sign," Jion conceded. "Getting back into cycle so quickly. Old habits reasserting themselves."

But as the immediate problems were dealt with, the unease between the two communities began to manifest itself again. The station may well have been a considerable improvement, but familiarity soon dimmed the memories of the past and resentment began to grow about the respective conditions of the station dwellers and the surface dwellers. Straightforward envy began to weigh heavily against the logical reasoning that kept them effectively captive in 'this poky tin box.' In time-honoured fashion, a substantial number of the newcomers prepared to bite the hand that had fed them.

While countless petty squabbles came and went, each leaving its small scar, the main focus for contention became the treatment of the erstwhile commander, Vronic. With four others he remained in voluntary confinement in the schooner's battle room for several months. After one or two futile attempts at communication, the Council decided to leave him alone and to content themselves with sealing him off from all external information. They reasoned that whatever influence he exerted must almost certainly be pernicious and that the newcomers as a community should be nursed back to some form of social health before they were exposed to it.

Vronic, however, became leader in his absence of the group that wished to part company with the travellers and establish their own colony on the planet. They accepted the Council's refusal to allow this rather as an act of superior force than as an act of reasoned necessity, and turned their attention to a clamour for the release of Vronic.

It was with some relief that Taithur was able to tell the Committee that Vronic was his own jailer and apparently had no desire to be released at the moment. But he refused to allow anyone to contact him.

"We've some covert contact with him so you can listen to and watch him if you're concerned for his safety. But no-one is to speak to him."

There was a modest uproar at that confirmation of the gossip, but Taithur stood silent until it died away.

"I need hardly remind you that it was his actions that led to so many tragic deaths. If he'd kept open all communications and negotiated properly none of that need have happened. Now he's locked himself in that battle room and with the damage he can do from there he's effectively barred anyone the use of the schooner. That's a very considerable resource he's negating. He just takes things from you all the time. Why do you defend him?"

The Committee fell into a rather surly silence with different factions glowering at one another and all declining to talk. It gradually became apparent that while Vronic was actively supported by a minority of the newcomers, and actively disliked by a similar group, all seemed to feel an obligation to him that precluded them from condemning him outright for what he had done.

"The man's part in their journey is a mystery," he told the Council. "It's certainly more complex than we first thought judging by the support he has, or rather by the comparative lack of any active opposition to him."

"The whole venture's a mystery," Hester added. "Everyone is so reticent about who started it and why. I don't know whether you've realized it but virtually no-one has told us anything about what's happened in the inner systems since we left. We're having to use some very elaborate interrogation techniques to piece it all together."

She smiled as she caught the brief look of suspicion on Taithur's face.

"We're having to do a lot of it by specially profiled re-questioning. We just pretend to be a little inefficient. It makes us look very un-Service, makes them feel at once superior and helpful, and gives us what we want to know. Well, some of it anyway. We're also getting something from the analysis of omissions. That should pay off dividends later but it's a slow process."

Taithur was ambivalent about Hester's remarks. He could not avoid some resentment at the reluctance of the newcomers to discuss their voyage and its reasons, and Hester's wry enjoyment of her surreptitious wheedling was infectious. However, it was pure Service technique, with its layered and interlinked deceptions, and he was saddened by the need for its use. Ever since the travellers had started to develop their bases into proper communities where people could begin to live ordinary lives, he had been haunted by a small spectre that he and the Council were forming the nucleus of another Service.

"Well," he replied to Hester. "Time's on our side there. The story's bound to leak out eventually. But we have to decide what we're going to do about Vronic fairly soon. As we get further from the deaths, people are forgetting his part in it and the feeling that he's being persecuted is going to grow. The last thing we need is for him to have a political power base when he comes out. The discussion's open, let's have your suggestions."

Several people wished to speak, but Taithur selected Proktor first. Let's get the wilder notions out of the way, he thought, then we can discuss the matter properly.

"Go ahead, Proktor," he said. Proktor nodded a gracious acknowledgement and paused theatrically. Taithur and Hester exchanged glances.

"I've been thinking about this a great deal," Proktor began carefully. "At first, when I saw the conditions on some of those ships, and the general negligence that pervaded the whole community, I thought like a lot of others that we ought to cut our way in there, drag him out and Return him immediately. But that was just the heat of the moment. It was never really a practical alternative. What we're faced with now is the fact that while Vronic was in some way responsible for the appalling state of the convoy, he was also apparently responsible for them surviving and reaching us." He sat back and looked round the table. "As Hester and Taithur said, for all the squabbling these people do, there's a peculiar unity among them when it comes to avoiding questions about how they started their journey, and what part Vronic played in it. I think that unity's going to be very dangerous. It's going to push the moderate opinion among them the wrong way if we force the issue. In fact I think it would be the height of folly for us to decide Vronic's fate without his own people having a very substantial say in it."

Taithur had to admit to himself that he was surprised. He had not expected either the content of Proktor's comments or the measured tones of its delivery. He was learning how to make people listen to him at last.

"We can discuss that, Proktor," Taithur said. "But I presume you've some idea as to how we should allow them that say, haven't you?"

"Yes, Taith," said Proktor. "It's quite simple. I think we should ask Gared to attend a special Council meeting to discuss the problem and to bring as many of his Committee with him as want to come."

Taithur raised his hand to stop any interruptions before they started. Although almost absolute power was vested in him through the Battle Alert, Taithur took great pains never to use it if possible. He was anxious that the real power should remain in the hands of the Council, which was chosen by a combination of appointment and election to represent all the bases. Having been created at the very beginning of their plans to journey off into the galaxy in search of a new home, it was an institution precious to the travellers and the idea of allowing the newcomers representation on it had never even been considered. They were, after all, refugees from something, uninvited and to a degree unwelcome, but above all...

"They contribute nothing, Proktor," Matten said, ignoring Taithur's injunction. "That's the very essence of Government. Anyone who doesn't contribute can't expect to have representation. We've given them every conceivable practical help to get them started again, and we'll continue to do that. We let them govern themselves, and we take note of what their Committee says, but letting them have a say in Council proceedings..." He concluded his speech with a pursing of his lips and a substantial shake of his head.

"Proktor?" said Taithur.

Surprisingly, Proktor did not argue. "I agree with you, Matten," he said. "I wouldn't suggest formal representation. As you say, with the kind of imbalance there is between the two communities, there's no practical way it can be done." He chuckled slightly. "Unless of course we go native and adopt the tribal method of letting everyone have a say regardless." But except for basic security procedures, few of the travellers took any serious interest in the social habits of the natives, and apart from a brief smile by Jian and Hester, Proktor's joke fell flat. He coughed awkwardly.

"But we do have to face realities. To a lesser degree, our relationship with the newcomers is similar to that we have with the natives, in that they outnumber us considerably and could make themselves a considerable nuisance, or worse, simply by dint of that."

This brought some immediate interruptions together with much reproving head shaking and scowling. The natives were, after all, wild and appallingly destructive, while the newcomers were simply their own kind fallen on hard times. A flash of impatience shone in Proktor's eyes briefly and he waved the comments aside.

"I won't labour the point," he said. "It's not all that relevant but it's a contingency we can't afford to neglect. I know it's in bad taste to do that kind of calculation for a civilized human community, but let's be honest, these people slipped very badly in the not too distant past, and having done it once, they might do it again." He prodded his finger into the table for emphasis.

"Make your point, Proktor," Taithur said. Proktor nodded. He was beginning to lose the statesmanlike demeanour he had been affecting. Keep going, Proktor, thought Taithur. You're talking sense. He gave him an encouraging look. Proktor seized on it and took heart.

"What I'm trying to say is that we have an exceptional circumstance here. We have two communities that are unbalanced in many ways, but who must learn to live together. In the middle we have this… Vronic… whatever he is. To us he's the possible source of a great many ills, quite conceivably a criminal by his recent actions and perhaps his past ones. To them he's some kind of a… hero… a leader certainly. If we handle him wrongly, then we're going to lay down seeds of dissension and trouble that will plague us for years to come. Whatever is to be done with him must fully involve the newcomers. Their representatives must be allowed to contribute to any decisions that are made about him."

Quite subtly his manner had become purposeful and serious again, and his words faded into a listening silence.

Liefer spoke eventually. "I agree," he said.

"But non-contributors, Liefer?" said Hester. "It strikes at the roots of Government."

Liefer nodded. "Indeed it does," he said. "Indeed it does. But the fate of Vronic's a matter of legitimate concern to both communities, so both communities must judge him. And what Proktor says is true. Eventually those people will be contributors themselves and we must help them towards it, not aggravate our differences by some crass insensitivity. We've learnt a great deal over the years by discarding old rigid ways of thinking. We'll have to be flexible here too."

Hester looked doubtful. "That's true," she conceded reluctantly. "But we still can't have non-contributors determining policy. That's not being flexible, that's collapsing. It's totally wrong. It's immoral."

The discussion moved to and fro across the table for some time until Alachev suggested that Gared and his committee be invited as fully participating observers, but not be allowed to vote.

Liefer threw up his hands in an uncharacteristically flamboyant gesture. "Babes and sucklings," he said. "I apologize, Taith, for not seeing the blindingly obvious half an hour ago. That's an almost ideal solution."

Even Hester conceded the point. "It's probably the best we can do," she said. Then, thoughtfully: "We might even be able to get the best of both worlds by talking the meeting into an obvious consensus and avoiding the need for vote. And then there's the things these people might let slip…"

# Chapter 25

Taithur sat in the relaxing old-fashioned simplicity of Liefer's quarters on the Rithid. Unusually, Liefer had a large viewport open and the room was dominated by the bright curving bulk of the planet. Both men were staring at it absently.

"What can we do with him anyway?" Taithur asked.

Liefer shrugged. "Technically, anything you like," he said. "We're still at Battle Alert, and you still have absolute authority."

Taithur scowled. "Come on Liefer," he said. "I know that, and you know what I mean. We've stayed at Battle Alert as much by accident as by design since the newcomers arrived. There's no real justification for it now, and to use my own personal whim to deal with Vronic will do more harm than good no matter what I do."

Liefer smiled at Taithur's impatience. "I'm sorry," he said, insincerely. "It's just an old lawyer's habit. Laying out the groundwork first." Taithur grunted.

"Still," continued Liefer. "It's a valid point. It could be argued that Battle Alert forms the only legitimate basis for our disciplinary procedures. It's an emergency status and a strong case could still be made for it." He placed his hands together and tapped the edge of his fingers against his mouth thoughtfully.

Taithur looked at him narrowly and then smiled. "You're not pleading now, Lawyer," he said. "Don't start going technical on me. We've got to come up with practical solutions to this problem, not elegant points of law."

Liefer's face lightened. "Ah, you won't be needing me then?" he said cheerfully. Taithur opened his mouth to say something, and then thought better of it. Occasionally Liefer had expressed regret that he could offer so little practical help to the community, and while Taithur had reassured him that his many contributions were indeed most important, he knew that it was an area of debate on which Liefer was sensitive.

Liefer looked at him, eyebrows raised. Taithur raised a warning finger. "None of that, Liefer," he said. "I'm no match for you when you're in a provocative mood. This is serious. I know this… committee cum council will discuss what to do, but we… I've got to have some framework within which to work or we might go on for ever rambling round, and I don't want us to split into warring camps."

"Groundwork," said Liefer, with the air of a man pleased that his point has been agreed.

"Groundwork," Taithur conceded with resignation, leaning back in his chair and staring again at the planet ahead of them.

"Right," said Liefer in a businesslike tone. "Interesting this. I'd be inclined to say that we're completely adrift legally. By colonizing this planet—a palpable health hazard—we're in breach of a substantial number of very stringent, and quite clear, statutes. It could be argued—well argued, I think—that this planet is beyond the writ of the Law. But we certainly aren't. Briefly, what we've done is declare ourselves independent of the government of the inner systems. We're rebels."

Taithur looked uncomfortable, but nodded.

Liefer continued. "We might just be able to argue that we acted within our Charter by invoking Battle Alert regulations, these representing a very ancient principle established probably during early colonizing days. But even that's weak." He turned his hands palms upwards and moved them up and down slightly, as if weighing his arguments.

"On the one hand, if we'd obeyed the Law and not colonized this planet, then emergency regulations would not have been needed. But… I think we could argue that our condition did not allow this. Then again it could be argued that we should have contacted the Service when we saw the state of this place."

Taithur turned to him to speak, but Liefer raised his hand. "It's all right," he said. "Just teasing you a little. I know this is old ground. And it's irrelevant now, the die is well cast. The simple fact is that we're in rebellion and any legal novice could prove it. Our only argument, if argue we have to, will be, I fear, violence." He paused and stared reflectively out at the planet for a moment. Then, with a nod, he continued. "However, that's a separate matter and may never happen. The immediate problem on the other hand is decidedly pressing, and it's useful in that it brings us to a matter we'd have had to face sooner or later anyway."

Taithur waited.

"Being rebels, we're outside the Law. Equally, the Law is outside us. By our choice it no longer applies to us." Liefer smiled mischievously. "We have no law, Taith. We have no formal basis for anything we do."

Taithur looked at him studiously. "You're serious aren't you?" he said eventually. Liefer's smile did not flicker as he nodded.

"You seem to be very calm about it," Taithur said.

Liefer shrugged. "I find it rather amusing," he said. "All that incredible mass of statutes and case law, rules and regulations, procedures and precedents. All gone. Just like that, poof!"

In spite of himself, Taithur laughed. "I never thought I'd ever have to describe you as impish, Liefer, but I think I must today. Can't you muster any regret for the demise of what you've spent your life studying?"

Liefer's face became suddenly quite serious. "No Taith," he said. "Virtually no regrets at all. I've been travelling to this point all my life. All the study when I was young, all the work I did for the Service, all the work I did later for ordinary people against the Service. All of it was necessary so that I could arrive here."

Taithur felt concerned. "But a life's work. You can't just dismiss it," he said. A brief flash of irritation crossed Liefer's face but it changed almost immediately to a look of self-reproach and he leaned across to Taithur and put a hand on his arm.

"I'm sorry, Taith," he said. "I'm afraid old age is making me more impatient." He gave Taithur's arm a reassuring shake. "I don't dismiss anything," he said. "It was all very necessary. I feel more strongly about the principles of justice that the Law is supposed to enshrine than I ever did before. But the dross that goes with it; the accumulated years of deadwood and dust, fusty ramblings by fusty intellects. Bright edges dulled and rusted. No. No regrets at all."

He became quite animated. "This is a new start, Taith, a new start in so many ways. We can carry on for the immediate future just using the momentum of our old ways, but fairly soon we're going to need a codified framework within which to deal with the more complicated problems that will arise as we grow."

He reached forward and dimmed the viewport. "I've started," he said. "Look."

Writing appeared over the table in front of them. Taithur peered at it closely. It was headed "Constitution (Draft)". He began to read it intently, but Liefer turned it off. Taithur let out an exclamation of disappointment. Liefer was dismissive.

"It's only a start. An outline draft. It'll take a lot of work yet, but I can do it, Taith, I can do it. All my years of experience will go into this. Set us on the right track. Bring justice and the law closer together again. Establish principles by which we can govern ourselves and still enable each to pursue his individual destiny. Freedom under law. We can even build procedures into our law that'll prevent the development of an organization such as the Service."

The thought chimed with Taithur's own concerns.

"That'll be important," he said. "That, we must do. It's so easy for us to revert to our old ways without realizing it."

Liefer raised a finger. "Trust me," he said. "Trust me." Then he increased the transparency of the viewport, and the light of the blue green planet washed back into the room. Taithur turned his gaze away until his eyes adjusted to the increased brightness.

"You're making me ramble," said Liefer. "Let's get back to the matter in hand." Then before Taithur could protest his innocence. "I think all we can do about Vronic is talk. As Hester said, talk ourselves into a consensus and avoid any need for a vote." He struck the arm of his chair with the flat of his hand to emphasise his remarks. "We must use the method which was presumably used before the Law was actually written down. It's all we've got."

"All?" Taithur queried.

"All," Liefer answered. "Any form we impose on the meeting will be purely arbitrary and, if questioned, quite indefensible. Could well cause more trouble than it avoids." The mischievous look returned. "Our sole guide is that awesome commodity—common sense."

Taithur sighed, and Liefer chuckled

* * *

Although the Council invited the Committee to send as many representatives as they chose, Gared brought only five others to the meeting in the Rithid's Council chamber. They looked ill-at-ease when they arrived and Taithur threw a concerned glance at Hester. Was there the slightest chance that this meeting would turn into a reasoned debate, or would it simply deteriorate into a sour stalemate in which the Council, or worse, himself, would be obliged to make a decision that must inevitably prove divisive. Hester looked puzzled and then, adjusting the monitor by her side, watched a recording of the six men being escorted from the landing bay to the Council Chamber. After a moment she nodded.

By prior arrangement, the Committee members were spread out among the Council members. Not so far apart as to feel isolated, and threatened, but enough to let them feel part of the whole Council. To emphasize the point, Taithur greeted each one individually in his opening remarks, and the tension eased slightly.

As Taithur completed his brief welcome speech and prepared to begin his main summary of the problem of Vronic, Hester caught his eye, asking permission to speak. Taithur hesitated. They had discussed extensively how to structure the opening of the meeting to ensure the maximum co-operation from the newcomers and now Hester wanted to change it. However, she would not deviate from a plan that she had been largely instrumental in preparing, without good reason. He nodded.

She began. "My friends. As you know, we've called this meeting to decide the fate of the man Vronic—insofar as we've any control of it since he's made the schooner's Battle Room his own." She used a light, slightly deferential delivery which, from such a powerful personality, made listening compulsive. "It's an odd, not to say unique situation and as we may well be talking for some considerable time, we've agreed to use informal procedure. That being so I'd like to get one small, technical point dealt with straight away before we start the meat of our discussion." She glanced round, as if inviting objection, but none came.

"This concerns the schooner itself. This is in remarkably good condition and is one of the biggest ships in the newcomer's convoy." She made an expansive gesture with both arms. "While Vronic has been occupying its Battle Room, his access to the destruct mechanism of that Room has obliged us to evacuate the ship, leaving only enough on board to guard it and to prevent him leaving. Similarly, we daren't incorporate any of its substantial resources into the newcomer's station. That could prove disastrous. In effect, Vronic's self-imposed isolation has forced us to place the ship, and all these resources, into strict quarantine." As she spoke, she leaned forward and slowly brought the palms of her hands together as if pushing against an increasing pressure. Taithur's brow furrowed slightly. What was she doing? Hester didn't normally wave her arms about when she talked. He followed her gaze. She was talking directly, in fact perhaps only, to the six newcomers.

"So I'd just like to suggest that when we get involved in discussing the many aspects of Vronic's conduct and his future treatment, we give a high priority to removing him from that ship as soon as possible. We must remember that after years of hardship these people are struggling to become contributors again. They need, and are entitled to, the resources that this ship can offer, resources that would greatly aid their recovery and reduce, perhaps by years, the time to the establishment of their own bases on the planet. And we must also remember that they are numerous. They need, and are entitled to, the space this ship can give them." She emphasized the word space. "Space to move, space to breathe, space to grow. It would be criminal of us to forget these matters in our concern for the fate of just one man." As she spoke she gestured expansively again, and raised her voice to project powerfully across the room. Then she sat back and seemed almost to shrink. "That's all I wanted to say. I felt it was important. Sorry for going out of order, Taith."

There was a general murmur of approval from the gathered representatives and while acknowledging Hester's comments, Taithur watched the six Committee members carefully. With a couple of exceptions, they were almost glowing. He could not forbear asking on the IFT: "What was all that about, Hester?"

"Just a touch of the obvious, Taith," was the brief reply. "Just watch your monitor. I'll switch it through."

Taithur turned and looked at the scene unfolding in the frame by his side. It showed the six committee members arriving and walking through the Rithid on their way to the Council chamber. They moved through ante-rooms, along wide corridors, public areas and finally along one of the balconies overlooking the massive leisure area. Hester slowed down the movement occasionally and brought their faces into close-up. The men were gazing to left and right, craning their necks back to look at the ceilings of the high chambers. They actually stopped to look out over the leisure area. Hester gave Taithur the sound of part of their conversation.

"It's enormous," said one, almost awed. There were some general grunts of agreement, then another said, "And it's empty."

"We might think the Rithid's claustrophobic," Hester said, "but it's far bigger and more luxurious than anything they've got. You don't need a vivid imagination to realize how they must feel when they come into this kind of space, especially when we've only a skeleton crew on board. If we can concentrate on what they're going to gain from having access to that schooner, I think it's going to be very useful. Whatever Vronic's done for them in the past, he's standing in the way of their future now. It'll help divide loyalties."

Taithur nodded agreement. It was a well-judged decision on Hester's part and could indeed affect the whole course of the proceedings. However, he had to admit that he was always a little ambivalent about Hester's ability to manipulate people and events. It was a trait left from her days in the Education Department, and it was a measure of her true inner worth that she used it so sparingly and to such good effect. But it still made him feel uncomfortable. He dismissed the thought as ungracious. You do it yourself often enough, he thought. Maybe you're just jealous because you're not as good at it.

Gared spoke a few words of thanks. It was obvious that his own prepared response had been thrown into some disarray by Hester's unexpected remarks, and he was visibly moved by this substantial public confirmation of the concern felt by the travellers for the well-being of his people. It was true, he said, that his people were struggling to return their community back to balance after their appalling journey, and that the schooner would indeed make a substantial contribution to this and to their personal comforts. But, "Unlike you, we're not a united community. There are factions among us that hold very different views about what our future on this planet should be and how we should treat the natives."

"You're out of order, Gared." The interjection hissed out from a committee member sitting to Gared's left. "It was agreed that unity should…"

Gared turned on him angrily before he could finish. "Damn you Edduan, be quiet. Nothing was agreed. Your group shouted a lot about unity for fear of being exposed for what you are, but nothing was agreed except to tell the truth. As far as I'm concerned, you're only here on sufferance, so shut up unless you've something worthwhile to say." The two men glared at one another with a viciousness that Taithur could feel even though he was some distance away. Eventually Edduan yielded, with a contemptuous sneer.

"Gentlemen," Taithur said. "There'll be plenty of time for everyone to say his piece. We might be informal, but we're not going to forget why we're here."

Edduan sneered again and turned away. Gared shook his head in distress and anger, as much at his own outburst as at Edduan's conduct.

"You don't understand," he said.

"None of us understand." Hester spoke gently and reassuringly. "We know about your physical conditions and needs, but how you came to be in such conditions and with such needs, we know nothing except what we've deduced from our ordinary contact with you."

She leaned forward, almost pleading. "We came here for freedom, following our faith. To impose our will on others is the very antithesis of what we believe in. You know we haven't interfered with your people, except to help..."

"And kill," said Edduan.

Hester bowed her head. "Yes, that's true," she said. "We did kill some of you. That'll be a matter for lasting sorrow, but it's also part of what we need to know now. Vronic's future is linked totally with your past. Without knowledge or understanding of the one we can make no just decisions about the other. You just said your Committee had agreed to nothing except to tell the truth. Well, let there be truth between us always. And let it start now."

Hester's words hung in the air. Gared turned from her to look at Taithur.

"What else do we have, Gared?" Taithur said.

"These people aren't to be trusted," said Edduan angrily. The sudden sound of Edduan's harsh voice made Gared start, and seemed to bring him to a decision.

You'd have served your own ends better by staying silent, young man, Taithur thought, as he saw the reaction. Edduan was like a caricature of the Proktor of many years ago, who also demonstrated an almost infallible gift for helping the side he was opposing during debate. Proktor, however, for all his faults, had never exuded such viciousness.

Gared looked around at his colleagues. Taithur thought he could feel the Rithid moving on its endless journey around the planet.

"You're right," said Gared finally. "Sitting here, I can't imagine why we ever behaved otherwise."

"Fear and shame," said Hester. Gared looked at her in surprise. "That's what I've deduced so far," she said.

"A shrewd deduction," Gared conceded. "You see more clearly from the outside than we do from the inside." Hester nodded her head in acknowledgement. "Shame at the way we let slip the ordinary everyday standards of civilized conduct. They should have been our mainstay when things became difficult, but…" He seemed suddenly preoccupied, and unable to finish his comment.

Unexpectedly, Malva spoke. "We all falter from time to time, Gared. There's no shame in that. The shame lies in doing nothing about it once you realize what's happened. We nearly came to grief ourselves several years ago, and for less reason than you had. It's like any pain. You can let it turn your knowledge into wisdom or you can carry it like a great, profitless, draining weight."

Gared listened intently to Malva's soft voice, but still did not seem fully to have recovered his composure.

"The fear, Gared. What was that?" Taithur tried to catch the mood his wife had set. Gared made a vague gesture, but did not reply.

"Truth, Gared." Hester's voice had a purposeful edge to it. "It's the simplest way." She paused and leaned towards him significantly. "And the biggest cause of it has been gone from you for some time, hasn't it?"

Gared's eyes rose to meet hers, then he turned and looked at Edduan. The animosity between the two men was electric. This time it was Gared who snarled. He continued staring at Edduan as he replied. "Yes, it has," he said. "And we intend to see it stays away."

"You'll regret this," Edduan growled, his tone full of many meanings.

"I already regret a lot of things," Gared replied. "One more won't make any difference. And in any case, to be frank, I doubt I will."

"Oh, you will," said Edduan, his tone containing only one meaning. "I guarantee it."

Taithur glanced at Hester. She was sitting back in her chair, very still. Her eyes moving between the antagonists. He whispered her name on the IFT. She gave a barely perceptible nod.

"You'll guarantee nothing, Edduan," she said quietly, but with a force that made the man turn to face her. "We might be in the back of beyond, but the Law is still the Law, and you and Vronic and your other 'friends' are outside it and wanted by it. You're in no position to guarantee anything." There was an audible gasp from at least two of the committee members. Edduan remained impassive. Hester's voice became even quieter. "I, on the other hand, am. And I guarantee you'll be punished for your offences when we have all the details." She leaned forward, and the menace in her voice seemed to chill the air. "You may even be punished under Battle Alert regulations. It'll be quicker and simpler for all of us."

The expression on Edduan's face did not change, but he went a little paler, and then, in spite of himself, he licked his lips. He started to speak, his voice husky. "Now, there's no need to…"

Hester flicked her hand towards him dismissively as she turned back to Gared. The rest of his sentence died on his lips.

"How did you know?" Gared asked, his eyes wide in disbelief. "How did you find out about them?"

Hester smiled, radiant with charm. "Everything in its time, Gared. Tell us your tale first, then we can all decide what to do about Vronic and his fellow convicts."

# Chapter 26

Proktor put his hands to his temples and massaged them gently. Lying back on his bunk, he closed his eyes and felt the stress relievers gently seeking out tense and tired muscles. Within minutes he felt completely relaxed and, opening his eyes, he looked around at the temporary quarters he had chosen for his stay on the Rithid.

The ship as a whole felt very strange. Occupied only by its skeleton crew it was so empty. Even the presence of all the Council members seemed to add nothing to it. He found himself wondering if the spirits of those who had died on the journey wandered here, walking through the miles of echoing corridors, still travelling in hope.

Perhaps that was why he had chosen his old room. The room he had spent so many years in as the Rithid had wandered out of the civilized universe and into the wilderness. It was as small as he remembered—it had not taken long for him to get used to the larger more conventional rooms that became available as the Rainforest City was built—but it still retained an oddly comforting, reassuring atmosphere.

He patted the wall and smiled to himself. I'm beginning to think like an old man, he mused. It won't be long before there are young people running about down below to whom this ship, this voyage even, will mean little or nothing. Just an old folk's tale. "Old Proktor going on about the 'old days' again."

He smiled to himself, then sat up and swung his legs round so he was sitting on the edge of the bunk. Some of the stress relievers whirred crossly at their allotted task being left unfinished.

Then he frowned a little.

It was going to be important to keep the memory of this voyage alive for future generations without it becoming boring or inducing envy, although, offhand, he could see no way in which this could be done—he squashed the suspicion that it might well be impossible in principle. Still, future generations would probably have enough problems of their own to stop them feeling jealous of the antics of their forbears. He looked at the time. Quarter of an hour, then he would have to do his duty stint.

Some things don't change, he thought. No idle hands on the Rithid while Captain Ersand was aboard. "There's plenty of work to be done," Ersand had said to him. "You're all getting too used to soft living down there. For one thing, we can run a full series of spot checks on our monitoring. There's one due shortly, we may as well bring it forward and upgrade it as well."

Proktor had confined his opposition to pulling a wry face. The humour of the continuing folly of the natives had long since palled, and listening to them now was distasteful at best and downright distressing at worst. They were so stupid. And they did such appalling things to one another. However, an extensive calibrating check would not go amiss. These people still posed a major threat and, as the Cities and the Community as a whole had developed and grown more complex, the time available for monitoring had become less and less. Most of it was now reduced to a keyword alarm system. Not perhaps the wisest arrangement, he reflected.

He lay back again, determined to make the most of the brief rest he had been allowed. He opened the viewport and stared out at the distant stars. That was one thing about being here. There was a restfulness in those points of light that could not be found anywhere except in space. Even this sparsely populated region had a certain austere beauty.

As he relaxed further, Proktor let the day's proceedings drift back into his mind. The meeting with Gared and the other newcomers seemed to have left them with more questions than they started with, though it had confirmed that the move away from the inner systems and the Service had been wise beyond their knowing.

Turmoil—that was the word Gared had used. The word seemed to explode from him, as if some long-suffering restraint had collapsed under a mounting pressure.

"Turmoil after you left," he said. "Affecting almost every system."

Then, following the trail left by this guiding word came a rambling and rapid telling that soon verged on the incoherent.

"Gared, Gared." Taithur said. "Slowly please. We've seen children grow into adults since we last saw new faces or heard anything from our old homes, we can stand the strain of a slow telling."

For a moment Gared looked lost, then he shook his head as if to rearrange his thoughts, and sat down.

"I'm sorry," he said. "It's difficult to know where to start."

"Tell us about this… turmoil," Hester said, looking at Gared's flushed face intently. "I find it difficult to imagine such a word being used for any activity involving every system."

Gared nodded. "It's difficult for me to explain it. None of us can really say what was happening, even though we were involved in it. There just seemed to be a general… breaking apart… a fragmenting of everything. It was so big. I can't imagine anyone being able to understand what was really happening."

"That's nothing new," Proktor interposed. "The Service's speciality was making sure no-one had an overall picture."

Hester shot him an angry glance.

Gared turned and looked at him in surprise. "Service? It wasn't the Service, it…" His voice faded and he looked perplexed for a moment.

"Just tell us how you came to set off on such a voyage Gared, and so ill-equipped," Taithur said. "The whys and the wherefores can wait."

"Yes, yes," Gared said absently. "Of course." He looked at Proktor again, and then seemed to come out of his preoccupation.

"Yes. How we came to be here?" he said. "It's quite simple really. We were following you. After you left, your following dwindled for a while, then suddenly started to grow again. It was as if everyone had been holding their breath until you were safely away, then your ideas went through the systems like fire through a summer heath."

Taithur frowned. Such an expansion must surely have provoked a response from the Service.

"Things like that don't happen spontaneously, Gared," he said. "Who was involved?"

Gared shook his head. "It was spontaneous, Taithur. Granted, Alfrad preached like you…"

Taithur sat up abruptly. Alfrad? Preaching?

"Konrad's brother?" he said out loud with a sharpness he had not intended.

Gared started and then nodded. "Yes" he said, in a tone of some surprise. "He was a most inspired preacher."

Taithur looked across at Hester who shrugged a disclaimer.

"Konrad's brother? Inspired?" He repeated to himself slowly.

"Yes," Gared replied emphatically.

"But Alfrad couldn't string three words together," said Taithur, looking around at his friends who were nodding in agreement. "He worked for us tirelessly, he was very capable, but he was unbearably shy. The very opposite of his brother. He could no more stand up and address a meeting than fly."

"Well, he did," was Gared's simple answer.

Taithur sat back. "I'm sorry for interrupting you, Gared, but that was quite a surprise. We'll try to restrain ourselves if you've any more such."

"Alfrad was a complex and clever man," Hester said thoughtfully. "I always thought his Service Grading was far lower than it should have been." But her tone gave no encouragement to further enquiry. Then, almost to herself, "I've often wondered why he decided not to come with us. It upset Konrad terribly."

Gared looked around to see if anyone was going to pursue this observation, but as none offered, he continued, still apparently surprised at this outburst at the mention of Alfrad's name.

"Alfrad just talked and travelled. He didn't seem to organize anything, but organizations sprang up behind him. System after system. Countless people flocked to hear him. Even high graded Service Officials."

Taithur nodded. The pattern was the one that had followed his own progress.

He anticipated. "And the opposition?" he asked.

Gared's face looked pained. "It was bad," he said. "It just... sprang up... in places as well. I was caught up in some of it. Such hatred." He looked at Taithur as if pleading before his judge. "We neither advocated nor did anything discreditable. Alfrad followed your teachings faithfully. Why should people turn on us, Taithur? Why should we be persecuted?"

After a long silence, Taithur said, "I don't know, Gared. I suppose if we're honest we can find feelings in ourselves towards our persecutors which are just as bad as theirs. I think in some respects we've more in common with these natives than we care to admit."

Out of the corner of his eye he saw the look of contempt that spread over Edduan's face.

Gared returned to his tale. "Anyway, we coped with that, just as you had done. On the whole, the persecution seemed to strengthen us more than it weakened, and Alfrad just carried on, teaching and preaching. Then I don't know what happened." He faltered. "Quite suddenly everything was in... turmoil... as I said. On some systems, for no apparent reason, emergency regulations were enacted. Education department officials took over local administrations. Resource caches were confiscated. People were regraded—moved about to new jobs, often quite inappropriate ones. Almost as if someone was actually trying to bring about local economic collapse." He shook his head. "It was horrible. Like a nightmare. It came from nowhere. There were all these announcements from the Service. 'Don't panic. We're doing everything we can'—that sort of thing, but never giving reasons for what was happening, or worse, giving reasons that were patently wrong."

"How widespread was this disruption?" Hester asked.

"Very," Gared replied. "At least as far as we could tell. It was almost impossible to find out what was happening because even the inter system communication networks began to break down."

This comment caused quite a stir in the Council Hall.

"What do you mean?" Hester asked urgently, leaning forward and extending a hand for silence.

"What I said," replied Gared. "The networks broke down. Visual and even sound transmissions became erratic and unreliable in content. Rumours became the main source of information. Then all the great shipping lines seemed to fall into disarray. Resource cargoes weren't delivered. Some of the major systems even started slipping towards the edge of their cycles."

"If this was the case, how did you have any knowledge about what was happening galaxywide?" Hester's tone was severe, but Gared responded unexpectedly. His voice became confidential. "None of this seemed to have anything to do with us, but Alfrad told us to go underground. I don't know whether he knew something, or sensed it, but we did as he said. We already knew how convenient we were as scapegoats." He paused for a moment, caught on some forgotten memory, then, "We kept our own inter-system network going for a long time using mobile transmitters on inter-planetary ships. They picked us off one at a time of course, but we usually managed to find more volunteers. As far as I know it may still be operating."

"They?" queried Hester.

"The Adjustment Squads," Gared replied. "They were everywhere, and making up their own rules as far as I could see. Bastards."

Taithur glanced round the hall. Gared's words had affected the Council deeply. The atmosphere was brooding and fearful, as members thought impotently about old homes and old friends.

Hester sat back, her face impassive. She nodded to Gared to continue.

"Eventually we developed a sort of sub-culture. One underneath the real one of everyday life. None of us could make any sense of what was happening, even though we were better informed than most. Some systems seemed to be unaffected. Others were worse than we were. There were even rumours that whole systems had been destroyed."

There were murmurs of disbelief.

Gared looked around. "I'm sorry," he said. "We did our best to separate truth and rumour, but it wasn't easy. We know for a fact that the Education Department took over some of our transmitters and used them for their own ends." He became suddenly angry. "You've no idea what it was like. No idea how different everything was from the society you left. And it all came from nowhere. There was nothing tangible to hold on to, or blame. Just Service officials saying there were subversive elements among us, part of some huge plot. That they had to be rooted out. That they were doing their best and everything would be all right eventually. Then they'd be gone and there'd be another lot in. We got substantial rumours that some systems had rebelled or declared independence and had been radically Adjusted by the Fleet—destroyed in other words. That's all we got. None of us actually saw it happening, obviously, but we had information from more than one source, and we believed it. You can give it what credence you like."

"I think we deserved that, Gared," Taithur said apologetically. "But all this takes a lot of believing. Carry on. We'll listen as patiently as we can."

Slightly mollified, Gared nodded. "Things got worse and worse and eventually the idea began to circulate that we should follow you. The early part of your route was public knowledge and the Captains we had with us agreed it should be possible to follow your trail through D-h space once we reached the edge of the wilderness."

Taithur could not help himself. "But how could you even think that? We set off with the Service's blessing, more or less, and with a great deal of careful preparation, but most considered opinion gave us little chance of survival. You must have known that as well."

Gared looked at him grimly. "You asked how we came to set out on such a voyage so badly prepared. Well I'm telling you. I've told you, you can't imagine what it was like. Personal freedom was just brushed to one side. Many of the ancient rights under the Law were overruled by the emergency regulations, and over everything there was this terrible fear, this insecurity. What was going to happen next?" He leaned forward and spoke passionately. "I'll tell you this. The journey here was as awful a thing as I could have imagined, but it was only towards the very end that I began to have any serious regrets. All the problems we had, the discomforts, the illness, the physical fear, even..." He glanced at Edduan. "Everything was preferable to the way we had been. We might all have been going to our deaths but we were going with some semblance of honesty and purpose." He sat back, his face defiant. Then he relaxed and became almost offhand.

"As for gathering our convoy together, we just begged, borrowed and stole. Even with all the difficulties everyone was facing, ordinary life seemed to have a momentum all its own. People have a knack of carrying on as usual no matter what happens—they get by. So we hid underneath this false normality. Oddly enough, any peculiar behaviour could usually be attributed to social conditions generally, so to that end all the changes and confusion helped us. We moved to systems where we'd a lot of support and threw everything we'd got into the idea. I never knew Konrad, but from what I've heard, Alfrad seems to have been a very similar character. All manner of strange contacts—inside and outside the Service, and we were never short of wealthy supporters and people with special skills." Gared waved his arms in a vague gesture. "To be honest, it'd take a week to tell you everything I know, and that's not the whole story by any means. We just struggled on and built up our resources bit by bit—generally two steps forward and one back—but we got there."

"How did you get away without being detected?" Taithur asked.

Gared frowned slightly. "We used all sorts of tricks for that," he said. "Leaving separately over several months and from different systems, filing false flight plans, faking accidents, setting up diversions, using friendly flight controllers, all manner of things, until finally we gathered at a rendezvous point near where you left the official lanes, picked up your trail and hopped off."

"You're frowning," Taithur said.

Gared's frown became a grimace. "It all went... perhaps too easily. I couldn't avoid the feeling that if we'd flown out in formation with all circuits blaring, no-one would've stopped us."

He fell silent. Taithur looked at Hester and then at Ersand. Both shook their heads.

"This is all very... odd," Hester said. "It makes no sense. All this talk of massive social upheaval, inter-systems breakdowns..." She turned hastily to Gared. "I'm not doubting what you say, Gared. It agrees with what we've managed to piece together talking to your people. In fact, what you've said makes a lot of things much clearer. But as to what's been happening, that doesn't make any sense at all." She looked thoughtful. "I think perhaps it would be better to work through everything in detail in private session. Your story's intriguing and complicated, but it's raising more questions than it's answering and we're never going to get round to dealing with Vronic if we try to sort everything out at once. Has anyone any objection to that?"

There was a general, if somewhat reluctant, shaking of heads. As Hester had said, everyone was anxious to ask a great many questions, and the session could have drifted on interminably.

"Gared, I presume you'd prefer that too?" she said.

Gared nodded. "Yes," he replied. "It's proving harder than I thought it would. There's such a lot to tell."

"Good," said Hester. "Now can you tell us how you came to be involved with Vronic and his friends, and what happened to Alfrad?"

She slid the last question in quite casually as she was apparently preoccupied making some adjustments to her monitor, but Taithur recognised the signs. She considered the absence of Alfrad from the convoy to be somewhere near the heart of the newcomer's plight and also directly involved in their concerns about Vronic. Too much pressure might push Gared away.

As if in confirmation of Taithur's thoughts, Gared rubbed his hands together uneasily and looked round nervously, though more to avoid looking at anyone than to seek aid from his companions.

"Vronic's an escaped criminal," he said suddenly. "So are the others in the Battle Room."

There was a contemptuous snort from Edduan. "Finish it, Gared," he said viciously.

"So's Edduan," Gared said. "And six others back on the convoy."

A buzz of surprise and enquiry filled the room. Taithur raised his hand for silence, but Hester forestalled him.

"Be specific," she said simply, her voice firm but not harsh.

Over his initial reluctance Gared seemed to gather strength as he unburdened his tale. Six months out from the edge of the inner systems, the newcomers picked up an automatic distress signal. After some initial fear that it could be a trap laid by the Service they decided to search for the injured ship.

Gared smiled sadly. "'What've we got to lose?' Alfrad said. 'The Service has no need to lay subtle traps for us has it? We can't just sail past. There could be someone alive. Or we might be able to salvage a useful ship.' Anyway we did the 'right' thing."

A few scans soon located the transmitting vessel, and a small hop brought the convoy to it.

"It was a transport from one of the Adjustment systems," Gared continued. "A prison ship." The reliving of old regrets was manifestly distressing to him. No-one spoke. "Even Alfrad went a bit pale when he saw what it was."

But the ship was silent except for its automatic distress signal, and after further debate the newcomers sent an armed boarding party to investigate.

"It was horrible," said Gared. I was one of the boarding party. There'd been some kind of a riot. There were bodies everywhere. And it had been almost completely exhausted." He put his hand to his mouth and squeezed his face in a nervous gesture. "I've never seen anything like it. I still dream about it sometimes even now. Blasted, blown corpses… eyes…" He dropped his head into both hands and did not move for some time. The terrible empty silence of the doomed ship seeped into the Council Hall.

"Eventually we reached the control centre of the ship. That still had atmosphere but the Captain had been murdered, and there were crew members, as we thought, lying about. All held in hypnotic suspension. It looked as if the Captain had just managed to activate the emergency manual override before he died. We revived the others and took them back to the convoy." Gared closed his eyes and shook his head as if he were trying to deny an old folly. "We were so stunned, you see," he said in mitigation. "Staggering through all those appalling bodies and finally finding someone alive. We just didn't think. It was an instinctive response." His voice faded. "Anyway, when they did recover they all seemed peculiarly vague about what had happened on their ship. We thought it was just the emergency sus. It's not much fun—can do queer things to your memory. But all they were doing was finding out about us. It's unbelievable, but we didn't realize what they were even when they said they didn't want to go back. Said they wanted to come with us, find Taithur, find a new world away from the Service and all the disruption." He shook his head again. "We took them at face value. Told them they were welcome. Stripped out some useful stuff from the prison ship and hopped out."

Gradually, however, the true nature of the men became apparent. Careless to the point of negligence in even the simplest duties, they regularly found themselves facing disciplinary charges. This, coupled with continuing vagueness and inconsistencies about what had happened on the prison ship finally brought the truth home to the newcomers.

"You haven't got the discipline of a junior cadet pack," Alfrad burst out at the end of yet another disciplinary hearing. "You're no more prison staff than we are." Then, with mounting realization. "You're the convicts. That Captain must have just been able to throw you into emergency sus before he died. Ye gods, and we woke you up instead of just turning you round and sending you back."

Vronic had taken the revelation with an insolent calm.

"Well that took you long enough, didn't it?" he said. "At least we won't have to pretend to be officers and gentlemen anymore. Let's see if you can be a little bit quicker about deciding what you're going to do about it? You can't send us back. You've neither the men nor the ships. And you'd give yourselves away."

Then the real rot had started. Vronic's frank admission and his accurate summary of their position had been followed by a direct appeal both to Alfrad's openness and his pragmatism. "It's true we're all convicted men. But that riot wasn't our doing. There were some really violent men on that ship. They started it. Not that they didn't have provocation. That Captain… well, you can decide for yourself what he was like. What kind of a person is it that exhausts his ship and kills most of his own crew to stop a riot?"

"A desperate one," said Alfrad grimly. Vronic looked at him half pityingly. "Yes. Well you weren't there were you? There's a lot of things happen in the Adjustment Department that you civilians would prefer not to know about. When we managed to reach him to try and reason with him, he tried to exhaust the actual control centre. The rest you can guess."

Alfrad said nothing. Correctly interpreting the silence, Vronic continued. "Let's look at this realistically. We have to come with you. That's unavoidable, but we're none of us in for violence. We'd all welcome a new start and we've some unusual skills between us. Things that'll come in handy on a long voyage, or setting up a colony."

"And that's how it started," Gared said. "Vronic could talk anyone into anything given time. I'm only surprised he was so foolish with you, Taithur. I suppose he'd become careless over the years. But he was violent. They were all violent when need arose. They wheedled their way in, corrupted others with their indiscipline and their shortcut solutions to some of the problems that arose with being almost under-resourced. Then they wouldn't hesitate to terrorize anyone who tried to stop them. Always quietly and secretly though."

"And Alfrad?" Hester asked.

"They killed him." Gared's blunt reply came without hesitation.

"You liar," shouted Edduan, jumping to his feet.

"Shut up," thundered Taithur. "And sit down."

Edduan tried to protest, but Taithur's gaze pressed him into his seat.

"Explain," Taithur said to Gared.

"They killed him," Gared repeated. "Killed him with their negligence at best, but I think they killed him deliberately."

Edduan clenched the arms of his seat, but did not speak.

Gared continued. "Alfrad went on a routine maintenance check, and his suit failed."

"Failed?" said Taithur.

"It was an old one, most of our suits are. A badly mended seam blew. One that one of their 'experts' was supposed to have mended. Opened as if it had been wet paper. Just like that. That's no way for any man to die, let alone a man like that."

Taithur bowed his head and rested his forehead in his hand. Konrad and Alfrad, both dying the same terrible way. It was not easily faced. And so many questions out of all this new information.

After Alfrad's death, Vronic and his men had consolidated their hold on the stunned and shocked convoy. It had not been difficult. Vronic was a powerful personality and cruelly perceptive in reading the weaknesses of others. Within weeks he had assumed the title "commander" and together with his companions and a growing following from the weaker elements among the newcomers, he had, in effect, absolute control over the whole convoy.

"And how long would you have survived if he hadn't taken charge," Edduan said angrily as Gared neared the end of his tale. "Do you think you'd have got this far?"

Gared hesitated, his jawline stiff as he clenched his teeth. He avoided Taithur's gaze.

"Well?" Edduan pressed.

With considerable reluctance Gared conceded that, for all his faults, Vronic had shown both leadership and courage on many occasions during the journey, without which the convoy could well have foundered.

Slightly mollified, Edduan spoke to Taithur. "There's another side to this tale, Taithur. Will you listen to that so enthusiastically?"

Irritated by the man's manner, Taithur waved him to silence angrily. "That's what this meeting's for, Edduan. To listen, to find out what's been happening. We're all stuck out here, we've got to find some way of living together. Everyone's going to be listened to." He paused thoughtfully for a moment. The news of the death of Konrad's brother had, he realized, upset him more than he had first appreciated. He needed time to think, to order his thoughts.

"Friends," he said. "All this is so much more than we expected. I think we'd all benefit from a break. I propose we recess now and meet again in the morning."

* * *

A warning signal scattered Proktor's clamouring memories of the meeting and brought him upright. Two minutes later he presented himself in the control centre.

"You look frightful, Proktor," was Ersand's greeting. "Still, it's been a bad day for us all in many ways. I'm putting you on long-range scan. We haven't used it at full range for years, but we may as well run a quick check while we have the bodies here to do it."

Proktor nodded. Not a bad duty. A bit boring, but perhaps it would give him chance to think once he'd remembered how the thing worked.

As the duty period passed, the control centre settled into a familiar quietness. Proktor sat at his console re-familiarizing himself with the sophisticated apparatus. Slowly he edged the sweep back to its design limits, then gently beyond. Nothing there. Everything blank and still, just as it should be.

Then, with terrifying suddenness, a blaring warning filled the control room, abnormally loud in the restful silence. Proktor jumped up and stepped back from the console looking in confusion at the flashing lights in front of him.

He became aware of Ersand by his side.

"Oh God," he heard. "We're being scanned. Someone's locked onto our beam."

There was a fear in Ersand's voice that Proktor had never heard before.

"They'll break cover in a moment, now they've found us."

Ersand pointed at the display frame as if he were giving a lecture to cadets. Abruptly, a signal appeared, bright and strong.

Ersand took a deep breath. "There it is," he said softly. "No mistake this time. That's the Fleet. And look at the speed it's moving."

# Chapter 27

The next day's Council meeting was of an entirely different tenor to the previous one. Following Taithur's announcement of the detection of the approaching Fleet there was a stunned silence, then uproar.

When it subsided, a faint voice asked, "Are you sure this time?"

Despite the gravity of the situation, Ersand could not help smiling a little at this plaintive rebuke, but he crushed the faint flicker of hope with a ruthless gentleness.

"Yes," he said. "There's not the slightest question. They were screened from our scanners, routinely I suppose, but when they locked onto our beam, which took only seconds incidentally, they dropped their screening and effectively announced themselves. God knows what kind of equipment they've got, but only the Fleet could have it. I'm afraid they know exactly where we are and judging from their speed I'd say they're doing quite a lot of crash-hopping. They're very anxious to reach us."

"How long, Ers?" asked Hester.

"At their present rate… less than twelve months," he replied.

Hester's face remained impassive.

"Gared," said Taithur. "How do you want to tell your people. We can put the whole of this meeting on open circuit."

Gared shook his head. "No," he said. "It's not a way we're used to working. There might be a panic. They'll expect us, the Committee that is, to come up with a few answers for them to choose from, and a recommendation."

"I think we'll have to do the same, Taith," said Proktor. "I see no point in broadcasting all this until we've worked out some of the implications and alternatives. It's only going to disturb a lot of people who aren't in a position to do anything."

Taithur grimaced. "I'm not happy about this kind of secrecy," he said. "People are entitled to know what's going on, however unpleasant. We're not the Service. But I suppose you're right. It should be all right providing we make the full transcript available as soon as possible."

He glanced around the Hall, looking for dissent, but found none. All eyes were watching for his decision. Edduan indicated he wanted to speak.

"I think you should route all this through to Vronic," he said. "He's at least as much to lose as anyone else here, and he's had some experience dealing with the Fleet."

Taithur looked at Gared, who nodded reluctantly. Within seconds the figure of Vronic appeared in the monitor frames. Davar signalled to Taithur.

"Vronic," Taithur said. "Your friend Edduan said you might be interested in this. Here's a summary of long-range scan signals we received last night. They're self-explanatory. I'm opening this meeting to you. If you want to speak, do so."

The figure inclined its head slightly, but gave no other sign that it was listening. Taithur ignored the affectation and turned his attention to the people in the Hall.

With an effort he forced from his mind the dark images that had been tormenting him all night, and hoped that his fear would not find its way into his voice.

"Friends," he said. "We find ourselves back where we were several years ago, although with more certainty and less time. We'd all hoped that that threat had passed from us when the newcomers arrived, but apparently it wasn't to be. It's a sad and frightening change to our plans and I wish that it could be otherwise. But having faced this once I don't feel inclined to spend too much time either bemoaning our fate or debating our response. We don't, of course, know why the Fleet is coming, but I doubt it's to look after our welfare. In addition to colonizing a major health hazard, we're now sheltering both known criminals and illegal refugees. We're way beyond the pale now. No amount of pleading in mitigation will save us. Also, if Gared's to be believed, and I think he is, the Fleet's coming from a society very much changed from the one we knew." He stood up and held out his two clenched fists. "But we've committed no real crime. Against all the odds we've established happy prosperous communities here. Soon these newcomers will be able to do the same and by then we'll be in a position to start educating the natives. Then we'll be able to spread ourselves over the whole planet. We've carved ourselves a home amid savages and desolation. Each of us must make his own choice, but I for one don't intend to have all our achievements smashed and discarded just because there's no Service Regulation to cover this case. I propose that we spend the time we have as we've spent the last years. Preparing to defend ourselves against the Fleet."

It was not Taithur's normal habit to declaim. Rather he would encourage comment and argument, guiding the debate in the direction he preferred by occasional interjections. Thus his audience sat silent and metaphorically open-mouthed when he finished so abruptly and sat down.

Then Proktor clapped his hands together violently and shouted, "Bravo," in a tone combining both surprise and agreement. As if shaken by the vibration, the rest of the Council followed suit like an avalanche of stones down a hillside.

Taithur looked both pleased and embarrassed. He raised his hands for silence. "It would appear that we're all of the same mind. Still, we've faced this before, and this is no more than the renewal of an old decision, but the newcomers…" He looked at Gared and the other Committee members. "You must make up your own minds. Those who aren't prepared to fight will be set on a safe base on the moon and the Fleet will be notified of their decision when it arrives. It'll only be a subsistence base, but they'll get by. Those who are prepared to fight must accept my leadership under the Battle Alert." Gared opened his mouth to speak, but Taithur stopped him. "Don't speak until you've spoken to your own people. Go back to them now, and tell them everything that's happened." Gared hesitated and then nodded. As he rose, there was the characteristic hiss of a communication circuit opening.

"My men and I will fight with you, Taithur." It was Vronic. "Edduan, what about the others?"

Edduan smiled, showing his teeth like a predator that has brought down its prey. "They'll fight, commander. We've nowhere to run.

219

And the Fleet'll give us short shrift. Besides…" He cast a grin towards Taithur. "These people are tougher than they look."

Taithur met the grin with a stony stare. "Vronic," he said. "You've questions to answer before we decide what you're going to do."

Vronic narrowed his eyes slightly, peering into the body of the Hall. "Ah," he said eventually. "I can believe it. I see you've got Gared and some of the other weepers with you. I suppose…"

"Suppose nothing, Vronic," Taithur interrupted sharply. "You'd have had your say in due course. Now we've got more urgent things to attend to. What happened on that Prison Transport?"

Vronic started, as did several people in the Hall, so sudden was the question and so grim the voice. For a moment Vronic stared intently at Taithur, his mouth moving as if he were chewing the words he had to speak. Then he shrugged like a man discarding a last faint hope.

"Whatever you've been told," he said, with a sneer. "Gared's nothing if not honest. But that Captain was unhinged." A look of genuine horror replaced the sneer. "There are some bad bastards in the Adjustment Department. Riots aren't all that rare, I've been in a few. A bit of mayhem, a shot of knockout gas, and it's off to the punishment cells. But no gas for that one. He had to exhaust damn near the whole ship. Taithur, he was an old cock, D-h crazy. He killed half his own crew without a thought. We only just made it to the control centre. I make no bones about what we are, but that slaughterhouse was none of our making."

"And Alfrad?" Neither Taithur's face nor his voice gave any indication of his thoughts.

Vronic stared at him intently again. "He got killed out on maintenance, when his suit blew."

"A suit you rigged."

A look of genuine indignation flashed momentarily across Vronic's face, but he hid it almost immediately as if ashamed. "That's a damned lie," he said angrily. "What had I got to gain from killing him? Anyway I could've done it much more quietly. I dealt with the man who was responsible for the suit."

Taithur glanced at Gared who avoided his look.

"What you gained was control over the whole convoy," Taithur said. "Removed all chance of your being sent back."

Vronic shook his head in impatience. "For God's sake," he said.

"What would I want control for. There's damned near ten thousand of them, and most of them useless without Alfrad. I was more than happy to let him do the work. And there was never the slightest chance he'd send us back."

Taithur remained silent. Vronic breathed out noisily. "I had to take over, Taithur." His eyes narrowed slightly. "There were women and children to be looked after. I couldn't leave them."

Taithur raised an eyebrow and Vronic coughed uncomfortably. "All right," he said after a moment. "I had to take over to make sure we'd got some chance of survival. No-one else could've done it."

Taithur turned from Vronic and looked at Gared questioningly,

"It's complicated," Gared said eventually. "He's telling the truth and lying at the same time."

Taithur nodded. He sensed layer upon layer of interwoven complexity in the relationships that existed among the newcomers. Tangled shifting knots that it would be pointless to even try to untangle. We haven't time, he thought. I must seize what there is and use it for what it is.

"Vronic," he said. "We need that schooner. Get out of it now. The guards will bring you and the others to the Rithid. Make sure you come out unarmed and quietly or the guards will kill you."

"Taithur, I want some guarantees before…" Vronic began.

Taithur turned on him. "I've no doubt," he said fiercely. "Well you've got my word you'll not be killed if you do as you're told. And like Gared," he mimicked Vronic's sneer, "I'm nothing if not honest. I'm not going to waste time dealing with your past misdeeds. They'll keep for a few months I'm sure, and will probably be irrelevant by then anyway. You above all have no alternative but to join with us if you're looking to survive. Now get out of that schooner and get over here." He cut the reply circuit without further comment, and turned to Gared.

"Go back to your people and tell them what's happened," he said. "Give your waverers one chance and one chance only. We haven't time for endless breast-beating and half-hearted commitment. Pick out your most capable people to serve on the War Council."

The sighting of the Fleet was a devastating blow to the travellers, particularly after the elation that had followed the appearance of the newcomers in lieu of the Fleet. For a brief period morale dropped to a low that it had not reached since the very darkest moments of their long voyage. However, under the urgent influence of Taithur and the other Council members, the mood slowly passed and within days it was almost as if the past months, where the only problem had been how to deal with the newcomers, had never happened.

Ersand and Hester resurrected their battle plans. Matthew and the pioneers set about with relish, arming and streamlining the remaining convoy ships. The newcomers responded to Taithur's call far more quickly and effectively than he had imagined they would, though whether it was his leadership or their fear of the Fleet he did not care to think.

He was relieved that none had opted for living in a subsistence base on the moon. That would have been a resource consumer they could well have done without.

Any doubts about the intention of the Fleet were dispelled about one week after the release of Vronic from the schooner. With almost malevolently accurate timing, a high speed emergency probe crashed out of D-h space midway between the Rithid and the convoy in the middle of a War Council meeting.

On all frequencies it blasted out a simple and noisy message.

"Taithur, your Charter is cancelled. Sentence of Adjustment has been passed on you and all in contact with you. All personnel and ships are to remain in that system pending our arrival for execution of sentence. Lynnart, Commander, Fleet Adjustment Squad, Sector 198."

Delivered to the meeting by a nervous cadet orderly, the message provoked several different responses.

Liefer chuckled. "Even the Courts can only suspend our Charter, Commander," he said. "And then only after due process. It's we who've cancelled it. And we've no intention of going anywhere."

Hester scowled. "Sector 198? There's no such place. And who's this Commander Lynnart. Ers?"

Ersand shook his head sadly. "Never heard of him," he said. "And there is no such place as sector 198 unless they've started zoning the rim of the galaxy. It's insane. I can't imagine what's happening back there."

Taithur however, smiled a grim smile. "Well, whoever he is, Commander Lynnart has simplified a lot of our decisions. He's either spoiling for a fight, or he's grossly incompetent. His little missive will harden resolves more effectively than any rhetoric I can muster. We'll…"

He was interrupted by an oath from Jion, who jumped to his feet, sending his chair spinning. Taithur misunderstood the action.

"Jion," he said half-consolingly, half-reproachfully. "There's no need for that. This is frightening, but it's no more than we expected…"

"No no, Taith," Jion said hurriedly, waving his hand as if for silence. "That message. It's been blasted all over the system, on all frequencies."

Taithur looked at him blankly.

"All frequencies," Jion repeated with emphasis. "With that power it'll have been picked up on every radio and television receiver on the planet."

Taithur put his hands to his temples and closed his eyes. After a long moment he spoke on his IFT to the Watch Officer. "How long was that thing broadcasting for before you shut it up?"

"About half an hour, Taithur. And we didn't shut it up. We blew it up. It was homing on the Rithid, and judging by the way it went up it was mined."

Vronic puffed his cheeks out and blew a long breath. "And that'll harden resolves even more than the message."

Taithur nodded slightly. "We'll consider that in a minute. Jion, Hester, what are the implications of the natives receiving that message?"

"They won't be able to understand it," Hester said. "But they'll work out it was a coherent signal. They'll have it recorded and they'll be working on it."

Jion rubbed his forehead. "Coming from space it'll have frightened them badly… and there's a risk that each of the two major tribes will think the other has established an orbital war station. If memory serves me right, that's in breach of all manner of their major treaties." He paused and gazed absently at his hands. "They don't normally take much notice of their treaties but this would be very serious. With their paranoia, I've got to say there's a possibility of a major conflict."

"With their fission devices?" said Taithur, his eyes widening.

"Without a doubt," Jion replied

Taithur swore softly. "What else?" he said.

"I'll tell you what else," said Ersand, anticipating Jion's response. "They'll be looking for us. They'll divert all manner of scanners to search for the source of a radio blast like that. Optical, radio, heat—everything. Excuse me." He spoke on his IFT. "Davar, put out a general announcement. All emergency and stand-by monitoring crews to report for duty immediately, repeat immediately. When you've done that, get all the navigators to the control centre, and get all the Captains linked up."

He stood up. "Go on, Ers," Taithur said. "Attend to it. The last thing we need now is the natives spotting one of our ships. They'll be all over us."

As he was leaving, Vronic called to him. "Ersand. Have your monitoring teams look out for silent probes as well. If that Lynnart mined a probe, he'll mine others for sure. And not all of them will be broadcasting."

Ersand paused to assimilate Vronic's comments, then, with a nod, he left.

Taithur put his hands to his temples again. "If those creatures spot us, or start a war we have to interfere with, our efforts towards dealing with the Fleet will be halved, or worse."

"Well there's no point fretting about it," said Hester. "Ersand's the only one who can keep us out of sight, and he'll be doing that right now."

As she spoke, the Rithid lurched slightly and the image of the planet in the viewport moved rapidly to one side, Instinctively, Hester put her hands on the table to steady herself. She smiled. "Quite literally, right now. And fast too, by the feel of it. As for their starting a war, all we can do is watch and hope. They've managed to avoid one so far. Perhaps even they realize how dangerous it'd be. We'll just have to watch and pray."

Taithur nodded. "Maybe," he said.

"You're going to have to do something about those natives sooner or later, Taithur." Vronic's voice had the tone of a helpful friend breaking bad news.

Taithur frowned and turned to him. "Do something?" he said. "What do you mean?"

"They're always going to be a problem," Vronic said. "Right now they could actually wreck everything we've got and leave us defenceless when the Fleet arrives."

"I'm well aware of that," said Taithur. "They've always been a problem. And always posed a threat. But what can we 'do about them'?"

Vronic looked down awkwardly for a moment. "You could take charge of them," he said. "Get down there. Sort them out. They'd scatter like mice against our technology."

Hester snorted impatiently. "Vronic," she said. "We studied these people for ages before we landed. Did a great deal of work on them. And we've kept an eye on them since. There are millions of them. They're vicious and unstable, they have an inordinately complicated tribal system, and they have weaponry that could do a great deal of long term damage. The risks involved in dealing with them are enormous. We have to wait."

"I disagree," Vronic said. Hester's jawline tightened and her mouth became a razor slash.

"Well, all right, all right," Vronic said hastily, anxious to avoid Hester's response. "Perhaps we couldn't take control over them just yet, but we might be able to use them."

"There's no question of us ever taking control over them, Vronic," said Taithur. "For all their faults, they're human beings, not livestock. Given time we'll educate them, and expand our own community here in harmony with them."

Hester interrupted as Vronic was about to reply. "How could we use them?" she said softly, her expression unchanged.

"Vronic leaned forward, his eyes cunning and his hands flickering as he made his points. "Make a deal with one of their tribal chiefs—give him a few trinkets—perhaps something to beef up his own defence systems. It'll be easy enough to impress someone so backward and we needn't give anything precious away. Tell him we need his help." He gave a knowing grin. "You could even tell him the truth. After all, we are in pretty desperate straits." The pleasantry withered under Hester's icy glare.

"Get to your point," she said.

"Tell him we'll give him all manner of advanced technology if he'll give us land for a base, and protection from his own kind."

"And the benefits of this?" Taithur said.

"We could cut down on a lot of our monitoring. And we could avoid the considerable expense of defending the buffer zones around our bases." Hester answered the question. Taithur looked at her.

"All important resources, Taithur," Vronic said, sensing a movement in his favour. "And we could use some of their people to do menial jobs. Release valuable equipment."

Taithur continued looking at Hester. A brief spasm of pain crossed her eyes. "It's too risky," she said, softly, though without the menace she had shown before. "And not very practical. It's also illegal and immoral, as you know full well."

Vronic sagged a little. "I could make it work," he said. But there was no response.

"Anything that improves those creatures has got to be moral," he offered finally.

Taithur shook his head. His limited knowledge of Vronic had given him extremely mixed feelings about the man. He was capable, indisputably, forthright and original in many ways, even amusing, but...?

He contented himself with being polite. "That's an arguable point, admittedly," he replied. "But we reached our conclusions over a long period and we must stay with them. Jion will show you the original work if you're interested. We really can't risk facing the Fleet with these people scrabbling at our backs. As for using them to do the work of machines, you know we couldn't do that."

Vronic gave Taithur a long look then shrugged. "Those people, as you call them, are on their way out, and we're the ones who will be the prime cause. You know that deep inside—all of you—sooner or later we'll have to bring them to heel." His voice had lost the rough edge it normally bore, and his tone was measured and thoughtful.

There was a long silence around the table.

A silent paean to the birth of a dark idea, Taithur thought. How long have you been gestating?

Another lurch of the Rithid broke his reverie.

Ersand's voice came through on open IFT. "We're clear. I've put us behind the moon pending detailed analysis of the situation. The other big ships are too far out for detection. Monitoring crews are scrambling, but initial inspection shows there's mayhem down there. They'll be looking for something with everything they've got. We're really going to have to be very careful."

Taithur thanked him and then rested his chin on his hands.

"Send an emergency probe back to this Commander Lynnart, Ers. Tell him our Charter cannot be cancelled except by due process of Law, etcetera. Tell him his probe was faulty. It struck the Rithid and exploded doing considerable damage."

Vronic looked at him again, his eyes narrowed and uncertain.

# Chapter 28

Ironically it was the need to avoid the prying eyes of the natives that brought both newcomers and travellers into a more cohesive whole. The speed with which the natives rose to a pitch of paranoia, and mobilized for a war which would mean global suicide, made a vivid impression on the newcomers. It was not lessened by the fumbling manner in which the natives subsequently avoided the war. As a result they acceded happily to the traveller's insistence on avoiding all forms of contact.

When the initial uproar and antagonism had died away, the natives began to co-operate with equal enthusiasm on efforts to find the source of this massive and mysterious broadcast, prompting Gared to remark that he wasn't sure when these people were the more dangerous: when they were quarrelling or when they were co-operating.

Even after many months, the unifying effect of the natives on the community as a whole still prompted occasional comment.

"How strange," Hester said. "Logically the natives are a far lesser threat to us than the Fleet. Yet we hide from them, almost desperately, while we blatantly announce our presence to the Fleet."

"Paradox," Ersand said, with a smile. "It's the nature of the Way."

"Tactics you mean," said Hester returning the smile.

Ersand leaned back in his chair. "I don't think I've seen you smile in months, Hester," he said. "Come to think of it I don't think I've smiled much myself recently."

Hester rubbed her face as if the smiling had indeed stretched long unused muscles. "No," she said. "It's not really a smiling time is it? Even Taith's showing the strain."

Ersand nodded. "Yes, but only to us. It's a peculiar kind of privilege I suppose. Knowing that he can trust us with his doubts."

"Yes," said Hester, standing up and moving to another console. "His very simplicity makes him complex. He's honest enough to know he mustn't show his honest doubts to the people."

"So honesty leads to deceit?" Ersand asked. Hester looked up from the console and smiled again. "Paradox, Ers," she said. "The nature of the Way."

Ersand made a brief gesture of surrender and returned to his work.

A companionable silence lay warm between them for some time, until almost simultaneously the two of them turned off their consoles and stood up.

"It's no good," Hester said. "We're wasting our time. Everything that could be done has been done. We'd be better off relaxing."

The door to the small workroom hummed open and they stepped out side by side into a long corridor awash with light from the planet. Its garishness did little for the strained appearance of either, but both were oblivious to such superficial irritations. All lighting together with every other resource had been strictly rationed since the Fleet had been sighted. However, as with the fear of the natives, the minor deprivations caused by this brought people together rather than divided them.

"The ship has a haunted feel to it when it's so empty," said Hester, folding her arms and hugging herself slightly.

"Not to me," replied Ersand. "Rather, it usually feels crowded."

Hester turned and looked at him curiously. Odd breed, Captains, she thought. Even in the strange reflected sunlight she saw that distant look hovering behind Ersand's eyes. The look that characterized Captains wherever they were found. She could even see flashes of it in Newin's eyes from time to time. Then again, I suppose we're all odd really, Taithur not least. Why did we give up everything and follow this man who's led us out into the wilderness and set us among these unspeakable savages, to be saddled with these newcomers and pursued by the Fleet? Why do we still follow him?

She knew she could never fully answer these questions. Taithur had shown her the Way, as he had others, and she could do no more than follow it. Wherever it led she knew that not to follow it would be to lead her life into endless doubt and futility.

But to face the Fleet? The great enforcing arm of the Education Department, that most pervasive and powerful of all the Service's many sub-divisions? That was surely insane. Yet although it was only hours away now, she found she was apprehensive, not terrified as she should have been. A snatch of conversation buzzed in her mind. A declamation of the essence of war.

"Why do we fight? Why us?" asked the question.

"Because we're here," came the reply.

The thought had come unbidden and she had no idea where she had heard it, but she found it oddly comforting. Of the many answers to that particular question, only that one could serve the fighter when his need was greatest.

Ersand, too, was preoccupied with his thoughts as they strolled along the silent corridor towards the control centre. He understood Hester's unease at the stillness of the empty ship but to him it was strength and a comfort. In this silence he could feel his ship resting on the sweeping gravity contours that made the vastness of space so small. To have the sight of a Captain was a privilege given only to the very few, to be a Captain and to follow such as Taithur gave him an almost unbearable sense of gratitude.

He stopped involuntarily. Hester looked at him. "What's the matter?" she said. "You're looking very pleased with yourself."

He shook his head and started walking again. "Nothing," he said, putting an arm around her shoulders. "Nothing I could explain. But I know why I'm here and why I'll fight tooth and nail to stay alive even though I'm not afraid of dying."

Hester reached across herself and laid her hand on his. "It's the extremity of the moment," she said. "It clears the vision. You see things the way they are. It's a good way to be. Not comfortable, mind you, but good."

When they entered the control centre they found a similar silence. Taithur and Jion, alien in their battle suits, were sitting at their consoles quietly working through check routines.

Turning at the sound of the door, Taithur said, "Time to go, Hester?"

Hester nodded. "I'm afraid so," she said. "Newin will hop me back. It'll only take a few minutes. Is everything ready?"

"Yes," said Taithur simply.

There was an awkward silence. Taithur stood up and peered through his visor at Hester. Then he opened his arms to her and they embraced one another. It was an ungainly business, and both of them laughed nervously. "They're not meant for this are they? Battle suits," Taithur said. Hester shook her head. "No," she said, softly. Then she took his gloved hands and held them tightly. "We've no more words for one another, Taith. Take care." And she turned and left.

Without realizing what he was doing, Taithur followed her progress on his visor display. Watched the signs which told him of Newin hopping into D-h space and out again almost immediately, by the planet. Then the cortex displays showing Newin's careful avoidance checks before dropping down to the polar base.

He became aware of a flickering light in the control centre.

"Foreshadows, Taith," said Ersand's voice somewhere. "They're minutes away."

Then he heard his own voice on open circuit to all personnel.

"Enemy imminent. Prepare for engagement."

A throbbing light on his visor told him his heartbeat was increasing, and for a moment it started to race, until he took stern control of his breathing.

From the foreshadows it looked as if their estimation of the Fleet's arrival point was correct. But what would they be facing when it materialized? There were strange aspects to the approaching force. They made no attempt to hide their position from the traveller's scanners, and these soon revealed that there was only one ship. A large one, but unaccompanied.

Ersand made regular backsweeps with the scanners to look for following ships, but there was nothing. He was puzzled.

"It makes no tactical sense," he had mused. "How do they expect to prosecute a war with lines of supply so long?"

"Perhaps they're not anticipating a war," was Taithur's reply. "We're a civilian expedition, and a religious one. As far as they're concerned, we're unarmed. They don't seem to have made any detailed scans. Perhaps they're expecting a routine and orderly embarkation."

Ersand was less sanguine. "I wouldn't think so. They must be expecting some trouble from us surely. And if that's the case then they must be very confident of being able to deal with us very quickly and without difficulty. They must have some new ship with a new drive. The speed they're travelling at is unbelievable. If that's a conventional drive, they're going to have dead Captains on their hands." The thought seemed to startle him and sent him into a deep reverie. He muttered to himself. "They'll go into one hop and not..."

He left the sentence unfinished, and retreated into a dark silence.

Taithur's attitude was that new ship or no, it would do no harm to state their case and also foster an impression of their weakness. To these ends he had endeavoured to inaugurate an exchange of views with Commander Lynnart using emergency probes. The Commander, however, had declined to enter into any debate concerning the legality of his mission, contenting himself with various reiterations of his original message. Taithur had thus contented himself with making a great many legal points, knowing that they would be automatically entered in the log of the approaching ship, and with repeatedly describing their general defencelessness and peaceful inclinations.

Such blatant deception was uncharacteristic, and surprised and even saddened some of his friends, though he redeemed himself to some extent by admitting his own ambivalence about using such a technique.

"I know it's wrong," he said bluntly in reply to an unexpected look of reproach from Hester. She had stepped back, pained, reproaching herself for having let her doubts show.

"All I can do is plead in mitigation," Taithur said. Hester had reached out to him to apologize. She understood the reasons better than anyone. She wanted to apologize for inadvertently letting part of her burden fall on him, but he pushed her hand away gently. "That's why violence is wrong Hester, it corrupts everyone it touches. It sends us crashing back through our ethics and morals into an older darker place. A place of chaos and pain where the sole ethic is survival, that makes us ask the question, 'What's the point of love and caring if it gets you killed?' or worse, 'What's the point of love and caring if it gets thousands of others killed in your name?' I may be failing in some duty I don't understand, Hester, laying down a path of consequences to some unspeakable destination, but I can't stand in front of that juggernaut and do nothing. I have to be like Konrad. I have to fight for what I see and know now, and take the consequences of the corruption."

It is the right thing to do, Taithur thought as he looked at his console, the memory running again through his mind. Life is a balance between corruption and growth. The one begets the other. To lie down passively before this approaching ship and all the horror it could work was as wrong an action as that which had launched it towards them.

A brilliant flash crashed in through the viewport as though a great thunderstorm had suddenly broken outside. For an instant the control centre became a dazzling white, streaked with harsh black shadows, then the light was normal again. Taithur heard Ersand whistle to himself.

"Bad, Ers?" he ventured.

Ersand nodded slightly. "Fast," he said, then, "Seconds now."

Taithur looked out of the viewport, excitement vying with fear. When the newcomers had arrived, their convoy had appeared clear and solid in the blink of an eye. A Fleet battleship appearing similarly would be quite a sight.

But instead there was an uncertain haziness, as if his visor had misted over. Taithur reached up reflexively to wipe it before he realized that the haziness was indeed there. And it was indicated on the visor display as well.

Suddenly he heard Ersand giving orders. He was speaking quickly and urgently, and though his voice was level and calm, Taithur sensed an unusual tension in it. On his visor he watched their small battle group move and turn until it surrounded the shifting haze.

"Pioneers, get those mines in now. Right now. Full speed. Before she stabilizes. Move, move, move."

Stabilizes? thought Taithur. Then he watched the symbols on his display. They converged on the haze and began building a lattice of red-blinking dots around it. Their progress was painfully slow and Taithur heard Ersand muttering under his breath, "Come on, come on!"

Abruptly the haze disappeared and was replaced by a large clear signal.

"Get out or stick," shouted Ersand, but ahead of his call the symbols on Taithur's visor had started to scatter. For a moment there was a milling confusion then three of them disappeared. Taithur checked the symbols—suits only—thank God.

"Ers?" he said urgently. "What's happening?"

"First move's ours, Taith," Ersand said. "We've got a useful number of mines in, and four of the pioneer suits have landed on the ship. We've lost three suits." But the elation in his voice was tempered with a quality that Taithur could not identify.

"So much for your peaceful intentions, Taithur. How fortunate I took it for granted you'd be lying." The voice was assured, cultured and arrogant, and sent a chill through Taithur. The frame on his console clicked into life and the image of a battle suited figure formed. Taithur peered at it intently but could see little of the features of its occupant. He looked at Ersand.

"Commander Lynnart, I presume," he said. The figure nodded. "I apologize for my little deception. I had hoped that together with my legal observations it might have persuaded you to turn about and return home."

Taithur detected the white slash of a smile from within the helmet, and the voice betrayed a bored amusement.

"No, Taithur," it said. "You hoped we'd come hopping in with all screens down and a token crew on watch so that you could launch whatever futile effort it is you've been preparing."

Taithur did not reply.

"Taithur. I'm a professional. There's not a tale one of you maladjusts can tell me that I haven't heard twenty times before. Believe me, it'll make everything much simpler for all of us, and far less painful for you," he emphasized, "if you deactivate your little mines, cut out your decoys and advise your people to prepare for Adjustment."

"I'm sorry, Commander," Taithur replied. "That won't be possible. There are considerable questions about the legality of your mission which prevent my surrendering to you. If you can show me the correct Orders of the Court then obviously I'll obey them, but the terms of our Charter are clear. Any action for suspension of the Charter would involve our presence to submit evidence, and that has not happened. I've no alternative but to consider your visit here as illegal and if you take action against us emergency probes will be sent back to announce this fact."

The figure looked up and stared directly at Taithur. Its tone was harsher. "The legality of my mission is beyond your competence to test. Many things have changed since you left. You'll obey the order of an Adjustment Officer of the Education Department first and your superiors will perhaps consider any legal arguments second. Arguing with me is an offence in itself. Resistance will have the direst consequences."

While Taithur was speaking, Ersand turned round and looked out through the viewport at the battleship, its ungainly form massive even in the distance. Its surface was streaked and discoloured and parts of it shimmered occasionally.

There was a sudden flash of light in the far distance, followed rapidly by another. Taithur cut his communication link.

"They've knocked out two of the decoy transmitters. He's talking just to give himself time to track through the chain. I'd dearly like to know why he's here, but it's not to negotiate, that's for sure."

He opened the link again. "We may be amateurs, Commander," he said. "But we're not so foolish. If you fire on anything again, we'll begin detonating the mines."

The figure chuckled. "Taithur, I don't know why I'm wasting my time talking to you now. We'll have plenty of time on the return journey." It stopped talking and inclined its helmeted head a little as if listening to something. "I see your mines are primitive fission devices. That's rather naughty of you." Its tone was patronizing and sarcastic. "But didn't your Captain explain to you about screens?"

Ersand cut in. "I did, Commander. I explained how you'd have to lower them to release any fighters or use any of your heavier weaponry. We took the idea from the local natives. It may only be rather crude rock throwing, but I think you'll find it effective if we have to use it."

The figure continued looking at Taithur. "Is it your habit to allow crew members to be so insolent, Taithur?" it said.

Before Taithur could answer, Ersand spoke again. "Where's your Captain, Commander? Still in medical? How many have you killed on this voyage?"

Taithur recognised the tone he had heard before. It was anger, but an anger from some deep pain that would not spend itself idly in words. Taithur looked at him. Superficially he was unchanged, but Taithur could almost feel the inner force that was rising within him.

The figure started. "How...?" it began involuntarily.

Ersand leaned forward, his eyes glaring. "Or is Medical too full to take any more?" Then, with a ferocity that made Taithur start, Ersand burst out. "You madman. I don't know who you are or why you're here, but I do know that I'll act as retribution for what you've done, whatever the cost, Lynnart. Make your peace with whatever God you know because I'm going to send you to him. Captain's Oath."

The figure disappeared from the frame.

There was a terrified silence in the control centre. Taithur looked at him thunderstruck. "Ers," he said desperately on IFT. "What are you doing? We have to talk. Try to avoid a battle. We might do some damage but we're no match for a battleship." His voice was a mixture of bewilderment and rage.

Ersand turned towards him and Taithur found himself staring into such certainty and power that he could not hold the gaze.

"What are you doing?" he whispered.

"That's no new ship, Taith." Ersand said. "No new drive. That's a conventional Service 3 battleship. And it's been crash hopped solidly all the way here." He strode over to the viewport, and gestured violently. "Look at that surface."

Taithur followed the pointing arm to the sinister bulk of the battleship but the significance of the streaked surface eluded him, and he shrugged. "Ers, I'm not a Captain," he said. "I don't understand. What do you mean?"

Ersand seemed to recollect himself. "I'm sorry Taith," he said. "It's just so…" He shook his head and moved awkwardly. Taithur saw the agitation register on his visor at the same time he felt it emanating from his friend. "Crash hopping's an emergency manoeuvre," he said eventually. "A battle tactic. It imposes a strain on everything. Ship, Captain, passengers, everything."

He moved back to his console. "That surface, Taith, measures the very soul of that man. I can almost hear it screaming even here, in ordinary space. It's unbelievable." He fell silent for a moment. Then he turned to Taithur again.

"Captains are precious, aren't they, Taith?" he said. "Rare creatures with a strange vision that enables them to make the galaxy small and navigable. People sought after and cherished and who give thanks for their gift by their service." Taithur nodded hesitantly, uncertain where the conversation was going. Ersand leaned forward towards him. "Taith, they call the Service 3s the death ships." He pointed. "But that's a ship of the dead. Aside from injuries to that surface which you can't begin

235

to understand, most of whatever crew he's got left will be down with distortion fever, and if he's killed one Captain, he's killed a dozen to get here the way he has."

Ersand's agitation had vanished and his voice was calm and steady, but there was a grim resolution about him that made Taithur's body prickle with fear. With an effort he pulled himself together.

"I note your assessment, Ersand," he said coldly. "Now give me your opinion of their battle readiness."

Taithur's tone seemed to bring a little humanity back to Ersand. "Still more than a match for us," he said. "But we have to defeat him, Taith. No matter what the cost. He has to be defeated."

"We might still be able to negotiate," Taithur said. "We can't just sentence all our people to death by launching an attack on that thing."

"You haven't been listening," Ersand said. "We've no choice. He's slaughtered his own to get here. God alone knows why he didn't slaughter us as soon as he stabilized. Either his crew position is even more serious than I thought or he's a plain old-fashioned sadist. But whatever the reason, slaughter us he will, given time, and then he'll snuff out that planet and everything on it."

Taithur made to speak, but his protestation faded in the light of Ersand's certainty. For a moment he felt very alone and vulnerable, acutely aware of the burdens he was carrying. He looked at Ersand, strange and distant. The man who had guided them faithfully across the galaxy to their new borne. The man who had trained Newin to make the D-h surfaces which lessened their isolation and opened an entirely new future for them, and alone gave them some chance against the might of this Fleet ship and its eerie commander.

Trust, he thought. Trust him. It was all he had.

"Take over," he said.

# Chapter 29

Even as Taithur spoke, events made the order unnecessary. The great battleship fired its engines and started to move forward. On his visor, Taithur watched the lattice of gravity linked mines pause and then move after it.

"A mistake, Lynnart," Ersand said softly. "You should've stood your ground and picked us off at your leisure." He opened a circuit back to the planet. Taithur winced but said nothing.

"Hester," said Ersand. "Follow my strategy and take over if anything happens to us. I'll feed my assessment to you. Study it while you watch."

"Yes, Ers," came the reply.

"Pioneers, prepare to detonate all the starboard mines except those by the exit ports, on my order. One third at a time, two seconds apart. Newin, prepare to take your men in on the port side and attack the leading ends of those streaks. Use open formation..." Ersand paused "...there's a lot of surface defence weaponry on those things Newin, take care. Maximum evasive action."

"Understood," Newin replied. "Please confirm target."

"Leading ends of the streaks. It'll disrupt their surface. Listen." He flipped the circuit out of code and onto open transmission. "Lynnart. Your D-h surface is unstable and I'm going to peel it off like a fruit skin. If your Captain was fit I'm sure he'd tell you what that means. You'll not only not be able to hop, the disruption will cause shield feedback. You'll be crippled and stuck here forever. We've no repair facilities for that kind of a job. If you'd care to make a run for it while you can we're prepared to let you go."

The battle-suited figure of Lynnart appeared again. "Taithur, your

237

Captain has a turn for the poetic." His voice sounded bored, though how much was genuine and how much affectation, Taithur could not guess. "His conjectures about the state of our crew and our condition generally are ingenious but naive. I'm sure he'll advise you that even if they were accurate they'd make no difference to your situation. One of our lighters could deal with any assault you could offer."

Taithur glanced at Ersand, who nodded slightly. Lynnart continued. "As you've been so kind as to let me know your immediate intention, let me tell you mine. We're heading now directly for your adopted planet. I see from preliminary scans that it's a positive sink hole, well beyond redemption. So we'll stand off and use our disruptors on it until it's been fully sterilized. As a gesture of goodwill we'll then provide you with accommodation back to the inner systems for trial."

The figure disappeared. "Ers?" Taithur whispered urgently. Ersand waved him to silence. "He's bluffing," he said. "His Captain's down or he'd have hopped by now."

"But…"

"But if he gets within disruptor range of the planet we'll have a real problem. Newin, attack now. Good luck."

Taithur watched as the tiny dots on his visor display started to move. Many of them were decoys, both dummy ships and false signal transmitters, but one by one they flickered out as the Battleship's local defences swung into action. The control centre was filled with the noise of the shuttle pilots' radio exchanges as they closed with the great ship. Taithur felt very alone again, listening to the excitement and terror—and the deaths.

After what seemed an interminable interval Ersand ordered the pioneers to detonate the starboard mines. Instantly, the battleship disappeared in a blinding blaze of light which washed through the viewport into the control centre.

The mines had been intended to prevent the battleship lowering its shields to allow its fighters to scramble or to use its heavier weaponry. There was no possibility that they could have any material effect on the ship while its shields were activated. Nonetheless, the detonations were sufficiently heavy to result in an automatic shift of power to the starboard shields and a corresponding reduction in the strength of the remainder.

The tone of the voices filling the control centre turned to exultation. The port shields had weakened enough to let the shuttles through. Even Taithur felt a tremor—battle madness. His mind shied away from it, but a darker voice spoke inside him. Rights and wrongs are no more. Reason and compromise are no more. There is only survival. You must be more savage than your opponent if you are to survive.

"Look at those kids fly." The voice was Jion's, standing by the viewport. Taithur turned to look. He screwed up his eyes. The battleship was so big it distorted his sense of scale, then he made out the shuttles, tiny against the huge bulk, twisting and turning like insects persecuting some great animal. The surface of the ship flickered with threads of light as its defenders fought back against these stinging flies.

Reluctantly he turned away from the reality before his eyes to the harsher reality of his battle visor. The cries of exultation were mingling now with pain and terror as the battleship's awesome defenses took their toll. The visor display starkly confirmed this. Look at them die, he thought.

Taithur cast a glance at Ersand. His hands were clenched in one another as if in prayer, and his mouth was moving silently. Taithur reproached himself briefly. You're lonelier than I am Ers, he thought. Everything I've got is yours.

"The shields are firming up again," said Ersand. "Get out Newin, now."

"No. We'll never get back in," came a breathless reply. "Parts of the surface are going Ers, I'm sure."

"Newin," Ersand shouted. For a long moment there was no reply. Just the sound of Newin struggling to control his breathing as he executed an elaborate twisting manoeuvre to avoid the blasts of one of the surface defence guns.

Then there was the characteristic splutter of the shuttle's guns firing.

"It's gone." Newin's voice was cracked with disbelief. "My God, it's gone. Get out, get out."

As he watched the remaining handful of dots on his visor display converge and then scatter wildly away from the battleship, Taithur turned to look through the viewport. His view was obstructed by Ersand who had pushed Jion to one side and was pressing his helmeted head against the port as if every inch nearer the battleship were vital.

One of the dark streaks running along the battleship was glistening silver, as if wet. "It's gone," Ersand said excitedly. "The surface has disrupted. Not as much as I'd hoped, but they're stuck here now and their shields have taken a beating from the feedback."

Taithur was at a loss. "What now, Ers? We can't bring them to their knees using the remains of our shuttles, and ourselves and the schooner."

"They'll surrender," Ersand said. "They must. They've got a crippled ship full of sick people. We've hurt them far more than they thought possible and they don't know what else we can do. We'll have destroyed whatever morale they had left. They'll have to yield, it's the only logical alternative." His voice faltered slightly.

Taithur looked at his visor again. The battleship was accelerating. Ersand's face contorted as he tried to reach into his opponent's mind. Finally it froze in horror. "It can't be," he said.

As he spoke, the figure of Lynnart appeared in the monitor frame again. It was unsteady and the background was confused, but the voice was clear.

"A valiant attempt, Taithur," it said. "But, I suspect, at the cost of almost your every resource. You may take satisfaction in knowing that you've fulfilled at least part of your declared intention; we'll have a great deal of difficulty returning home. However, I'm about to fulfil all my declared intention and, that done, you'll have no home to return to." The figure disappeared.

As it vanished, the figure seemed to take with it all life and movement from the control centre.

"An illogical alternative," Taithur said eventually into the eerie stillness. "He is a madman after all. What can we do Ers?"

Ersand closed his eyes.

"Can we detonate the rest of the mines?" Taithur asked.

Ersand shook his head. "It'll do no good," he said. "It'll only cause a temporary realigning of his shield power. And what would be the point. We've precious little left to attack him with even if an attack were likely to be of any use. And we'd have nothing left to keep his fighters pinned in."

"He'll have to lower what's left of his shields to fire the disruptors," Taithur said hopefully. "We can hit him with ours."

Ersand shook his head. "He's attacking a planet, Taith. A large stationary object. He can fire short duration bursts on a broad spread, his shields will be down for barely a second at a time. There's no way we could time it. And just one burst getting through would do enormous damage."

The silence closed around them. Ersand moved back to his console and sat down, resting his head on his hands. Taithur's mind clattered to and fro in its distress. All the images that came to him bounced helplessly off the bulk of the battleship into nothingness. Self-pity, reproach, regret, rage, all clamoured to be heard. God help me, he thought. Let my mind be clear. But rage broke through. Dark and horrible. Rage that seemed to rise from the very beginning of his life and beyond. Rage against the malign forces that had driven them there. Rage against the demented natives that had so despoiled this planet and hampered their progress. Rage against the forces that had sent the floundering newcomers and pitched this mad warlord after them. Rage that he should have to bear this burden.

Abruptly the tumultuous darkness of his vision was shot through with red, like a menacing twilight. He turned to Ersand.

"He has to be stopped or everything's lost. No matter what the cost," he said. "The responsibility's mine. We'll ram them. Their shields are precious little use now. We'll set all our destruct devices, and hit them at full speed. You can abandon ship and I'll take her straight towards their control centre."

Ersand looked up but did not turn towards him. After a moment he said. "They'll destroy us as soon as we get anywhere near them, Taith, even at full speed. It'd be a futile gesture." Then, although he did not seem to move, his manner changed. Slowly he turned to Taithur, his eyes alight with that strange aloofness which was the distinctive mark of a Captain.

"We can hop right in," he said. "They can't stop that. We'll attack their control centre at point blank range with our disruptors and hop out."

Taithur returned the gaze, and drew on his limited knowledge of flying technique. "Hop! We're too close to such a mass, and using our disruptors at close range could do as much damage to us as it will to them." But his own words rang false even as he spoke them.

Ersand, staring at him with those disconcerting, distant eyes, set aside the doubts without speaking. Yes, he seemed to say, in our normal lives, but now we're at the very end of our cycle, the time for Return has come. The journey of our whole lives has brought us to this special place, where all our knowledge will be used in one simple act.

Taithur closed his eyes and nodded slowly.

"Disruptors, are you ready to fire?" he asked simply, turning back to his console.

"Yes. Have you a target?" came the reply.

"No," said Ersand. "Just set them to fire…" He leaned back and looked out through the viewport. "Vertically downwards. Firing will be from here."

There was a momentary pause then the order was acknowledged.

Ersand touched a switch on his console. "Everyone's in sus now Taith, except us. I can fly the ship but I can't fire the disruptors." He hesitated. "You'll have to come through D-h with me unprotected."

The two men looked at one another. Both knew what was being asked.

"I understand," Taithur said quietly after a brief silence. Ersand lowered his gaze. "Don't be afraid, old friend," he said. "Your hand's on the trigger. Listen for my voice and my voice only. When you hear 'Now'—fire!" Taithur nodded again. All the rage and fury had gone—vanished at the touch of Ersand's voice. No other way existed.

Abruptly he felt as though he had been exploded into countless twittering shards of light, spread thin across the whole universe and through every time. He was indistinguishable from the very stars themselves. Only a faint thread winding into the unknown connected him to one place, one time—told him he was Taithur. But who was that? Sights and sounds swirled around and through him, though he could not tell which was which. The thread stretched further and further.

Then everything was gone. A strange harsh vision appeared. A hand? The word was familiar, but the solidity of this body—this crib—was stifling. Who…?

"Now!"

The song of the Way filled the universe. The hand moved forward. It had no other task. That was its destiny.

Next was darkness.

Ersand crashed backwards from his console and rolled across the floor, his hands to his head. Struggling to his feet he dropped back into his chair and old reflexes brought his crew out of sus and steadied the

Rithid. Then he became aware of noises, good noises. All the circuits were wide open and full of cheering voices.

Hester's voice came through on IFT, penetrating the babbling rapture that was filling the control centre. But even she sounded like an excited schoolgirl. "He's down, Ers, he's down. You tore the heart out of him. Incredible, incredible!"

Ersand shook his head, there was something important to be done, but it eluded him. He clicked on the main display frame. The battleship came into focus, a great gash across its ugly brow. Its engines were dead, and a glance at his monitors showed its shields were destroyed utterly. Above all it was transmitting a distress signal. He gazed at the sight almost hypnotized. They'd done it.

"Ers." Jion's voice cut through him and brought the forgotten deed into awful clarity. He turned to stare into Jion's face, wide-eyed with fear. He had his arms around the figure of Taithur slumped across his console.

With a cry Ersand ran across and helped Jion lift the dead weight upright into its chair. He fumbled awkwardly with the fastenings of the battlesuit's helmet. Glancing up, he caught sight of the battleship through the viewport. For an instant, the gash looked like a malevolent wink.

"Newin," he said. "Get Hester up here fast to take charge of mop-up, and get Andreas at the same time."

The fastening finally yielded, and Ersand gently lifted off the helmet, supporting Taithur's head as he did so.

As he tilted the head back, Taithur's eyes opened wide, and Ersand found himself gazing down into madness.

# Chapter 30

Taithur lay for a long time fighting the terrible D-h distortion fever that the brief unprotected hop had released in him.

All the care that could be lavished on him, was. But on his arrival on the Rithid that sad and glorious day, Andreas spoke the truth they all knew.

"There's nothing can be done. There's nothing can ever be done for distortion fever, you know that, except cope with the more obvious symptoms and hope that the spirit of the inner man will be strong enough to see him through."

At a gloomy and subdued meeting, the Council appointed Hester as leader under the Battle Alert, until Taithur recovered, or...

Almost as great a casualty as Taithur was Ersand. Wracked with guilt about the effects of his action, he seemed to age visibly, finding solace only in work.

His immediate friends supported him resolutely, Malva above all, but the community as a whole was as divided and confused as he was.

Had there been an alternative? Many were conjectured but none stood serious examination, although that did not prevent some holding to them passionately.

Could Ersand have handled the disruptors as well as fly the ship? Even the most incensed accepted that that would not have been possible. Ersand's crash hop to the battleship and his brief flight in normal space across its bow before hopping out again, was of a quality destined to place it in the great legends of space fighting,

Could Taithur have been put into sus? Here again there was no strong disagreement. The brief interval required for recovery after waking would have been disastrous. The Battleship's surface defences would have destroyed the Rithid effortlessly.

Could another Captain have taken Taithur's place? Unlikely. The manoeuvres of the transfer would have identified the Rithid among the decoys, and its shields would have been lowered to allow embarkation.

But...?

The doubt hovered. The action had won the battle, but had cost the community its great leader, perhaps forever. The grief of the people had little or nowhere to go and festered sullenly.

"It was all that could be done," Ersand said. Half statement in mitigation, half question. "And he was the only person who could possibly have done it. I gave him what protection I could, but it had to be done."

Subsequent events proved him correct. The battleship surrendered without further resistance but the Council found themselves taking charge of what was tantamount to a plague ship, and the evidence they gathered clearly pointed to Lynnart's insanity.

Despite the surrender pledge, Hester sent in several heavily armed platoons, equipped if need be to take the ship corridor by corridor, room by room. She reasoned that from what she had seen of Lynnart, treachery was very probable and any lesser response would have been foolish in the extreme. However, on entering, the troops found dead and dying everywhere. Of those who were alive, a large number were ill and the remainder exhausted.

Lynnart had been killed in the Rithid's attack, along with many of his officers and crewmen, though the sole remaining Captain had escaped because, as Ersand had conjectured, he was in Medical, an area traditionally situated near the heart of the ship, and independently shielded. He was, however, too ill to act as representative for the survivors, and that task fell to Terson, an official of the Adjustment Department, and the highest graded civilian on board.

His rank was substantially higher than any other member of the colony, but he made no attempt to impose the legal authority that this gave him. Like the colonists, he had come, over time, to see his cherished ranking as comparatively worthless, though for a different reason.

He was weary and his eyes bore the haunted look of someone just recovered from distortion fever, but Hester, dazed from the news of Taithur's fate, was blunt to the point of harshness.

"A thorough and honest accounting of this business is essential, Terson. You've flown half across the galaxy in a manner that verged on the insane, on a mission that didn't have a vestige of legality, and you concluded with an attempt at genocide. Genocide not only of a colony of your own people, but on an aboriginal civilisation who are totally outside your jurisdiction. Only an act of unprecedented courage saved us all, and the cost to our community of that act has been appalling." She leaned forward and almost spat the words at him. "If I smell the least hint of prevarication or deceit, I'll have you Returned on the spot."

Despite the deadness left by the fever, Terson winced at Hester's onslaught. It was, after all, unnecessary. Like everyone else on the battleship who had survived the last twelve months, Terson was older and wiser by far than when he had embarked.

"I won't lie," he said. "All I want to do is get back home. Get out of this wilderness and this insanity. I don't know everything you've been told, there were several more senior officials than me on board. What do you want to know?"

Hester, angered by his lifeless tone, ignored the question and lashed out at him again. "Well you've been promoted now, and as a senior member of your party you'll doubtless be relieved to know we'll be giving your sick all the care we can. We too are anxious to see you back home." Liefer laid a hand on her arm, and for a moment she dropped her head into her hand. When she looked up, however, her face was a hard mask.

"Tell us who you are and why you came."

Terson answered the questions he was asked without hesitation and without attempting any excuses for what had happened. This, and his obvious weakness, gradually moderated Hester's manner, but she could not keep the hostility from her eyes.

The question "who?" he could answer only in vague terms. He himself had been seconded to the ship, along with several others. Who had made the decision to send the ship he did not know. That surprised no-one. It was not Service practice to question orders, especially in the Education Department.

"Speculate then," said Hester.

Terson shook his head and shrugged. "So much has changed since you left. The Rift…"

"What?" Hester interrupted.

"The Rift," Terson repeated, a slight tinge of surprise in his dead voice. "The split between the Education Department and the rest of the Service, or rather between the Adjustment department and the rest."

There was a buzz of interest around the table.

"Explain," said Hester tersely.

Terson looked openly surprised. "It's been coming for years," he said. "You must…" Then he looked thoughtful as the truth dawned on him. "Of course," he said, without any satisfaction. "You wouldn't know. Even at my level it was only informed gossip." He rested his forehead on his hand wearily, as if he had been given yet another burden to bear.

"There've always been disputes between departments at every level of the Service. Most of it looked like petty rivalry, but at the higher levels, where the real power lay, they were said to be genuinely savage. Over the years, power inevitably gravitated towards the Adjustment Department, with its special emergency dispensations and its squads of armed forces and of course, the Fleet. Shortly after you left, something serious happened—right at the top, rumour has it."

His audience were mesmerised.

"Whether it was some major change in policy that Adjustment wanted—greater legal powers, greater efficiency, less personal freedom—something along those lines—or whether it was some attempt by the other departments to curtail their power, I don't know. But all of a sudden all inter-departmental co-operation with Adjustment stopped. Just like that. Stopped dead. And we started getting all manner of new regulations to implement." For a moment alarm showed on his face. "You must understand. We just obeyed orders, like always. Adjustment's a disciplined service, you don't argue."

"What was the effect of these Regulations?" Hester asked.

"Chaos," said Terson. "Adjustment has enormous power, enormous resources. Transport and communications seemed to be the main targets. It seemed to me they… we… were almost trying to bring the galaxy to its knees."

"And nobody did anything about this?" Hester asked. Terson did not reply, but looked at her knowingly. She nodded.

"Besides," Terson continued. "There began to be talk about infiltration of the department by spies from other departments." He hesitated. "It was very difficult."

Further questioning soon exhausted Terson's knowledge of the topic.

"I never realised the Service had such appalling potential," Hester said later to Liefer. "There's Terson, an intelligent, capable person. Graded far above either of us. Yet he was helpless. He knew he was part of something massively wrong, but he couldn't speak out because he didn't have the accurate information and he was surrounded by the mistrust and paranoia that that self-same secrecy bred. Great God, we protect ourselves constantly against damaging our environments, we pride ourselves on resource economy and efficiency, but we let the Service squander the resources of the human spirit more..." She searched for a word. "More wantonly, more indiscriminately than even these natives here." She shuddered. "We're well out of it." Then, passionately: "It mustn't happen here, Liefer. It mustn't. Taithur mentioned your Constitution. We've been given a second chance. We have to learn, Liefer, or sure as fate we'll make the same mistakes ourselves."

The matter of why the battleship had been sent fell neatly into place against the haunted background that Terson had painted.

"Scapegoats," he said. "There'd always been a lot of opposition to your religion within the department, but Taithur was a charismatic leader and it was difficult for anyone to move directly against him. There was quite a lot of celebrating when he decided to go off on his exploration."

"Were you involved in that?" asked Liefer.

Terson shook his head. "No, no. I imagine that was engineered at the highest level. Although..." He paused, a faint puzzlement showing in his eyes. "We were told to oppose it. I suppose, looking back, either faction would've had an interest in his staying. Our department to use him as an excuse for greater powers, the other to use him as front line defence against our expansion." He paused again. "Then again, either faction could benefit from his leaving." His face contorted momentarily as if he were in pain. "We'll never know. We were all being used."

There was a sadness and an awareness in his voice that made even Hester lower her eyes, and the room fell silent

Eventually Terson picked up his tale unbidden. "Your religion fizzled out after Taithur left. But then Alfrad came out of the blue and the whole thing started all over again."

"Was that the cause of this... rift?" Hester asked.

Terson shrugged. "I've told you, I've no idea. I've no doubt it would have been a contributing factor. All I know is that we were supposed to come and collect the lot of you to be returned for trial and adjustment—reason unspecified." He leaned forward and smacked his chest. "I didn't need to know, therefore I wasn't told. But I can't think of any reason why Commander Lynnart did what he did. Everyone knew he was ambitious, but what he did was insane, crash-hopping through distances like that. I know for a fact there were some blazing rows with the Captains. But a Commander's a Commander, and that's that. He never went down with the fever but it takes people different ways. Looking back I think he was probably deteriorating mentally from hop one." He sat back, the deadness returning to his eyes.

"Perhaps this will help." The voice was Ersand's. Hester started in surprise, not realizing he was there. It was part of Ersand's pain that even entering crowded rooms was an ordeal.

"I see such confusion in every gaze," he had told her. "They turn and look at me and there it is, a huge silent court. Trying me over and over again. Even my friends." She had not been able to reply.

"What is it, Ers?" she said, gently. Ersand activated the main display.

"We found these in the battleship's automatic log a few hours ago." he said. "I was going to discuss them with you later, but I heard the way the meeting was going, and these are relevant. They're messages sent by emergency probes."

Hester peered at them intently. "Good God," she said after a while. "They're recall orders. Dozens of them. Whatever the reasons for his setting out, they changed damn soon after he'd started, but he just thundered on." The symbols hovering over the table changed rapidly as she skimmed through them. "Terson. What did you know about these?"

Terson's eyes were alive now with dancing pain. "Nothing," he said. "I knew probes had arrived, obviously, but not what was in them. Everyone presumed they were just routine. This is horrible. All those people dying at that man's whim. My friends—all killed—for his—what?" His eyes rolled back and he lifted his clenched fists and smashed them into the table. The room juddered with the impact and Hester grimaced as she heard bones breaking. Before Terson could move again, Andreas had anaesthetised him.

He shook his head as he looked at him. "There'll be no more out of him for some time. I'm afraid he's relapsed."

"Well, that tells us more about his involvement than any amount of words," Hester said, as Terson was carried out. "He's told us the truth and we're only a little the wiser." She slashed through the mounting hubbub. "We can speculate and ponder, but the simple fact is we'll never find out what's happened back there; who's using who and for what reason." She paused and began tapping her hands on the table in front of her, her face growing grimmer and grimmer as the noise grew. Finally, she stopped, and the echo of the last slap seemed to hang in the room. No-one dared to breathe.

"Another simple fact we must face is that we can only go forward. Taithur showed each of us our way and led us here, through the wilderness and to this beautiful tainted planet. His spirit built us our bases–our cities–and our communities, and he paid a terrible price to ensure our future here. We belong here now. We can't look backwards. It would be a betrayal of both ourselves and him. I propose we offer the survivors of this battleship an opportunity to stay with us. Those who do not wish to will be given adequate resources to return to the inner systems—our old homes—and they'll carry a message with them." She looked round at the watching faces, and like Taithur before her, felt that awesome isolation of the burden that cannot be shared. You'd have done it eventually, Taith, she thought. "They'll tell them that this star and its planets now constitute an independent system under our jurisdiction. We'll make our own laws, suitable for our own needs, and while we'll offer friendship and hospitality to all people of goodwill, we'll defend ourselves to the death if we have to."

She turned to Liefer, who was nodding slowly to the rhythm of her words.

"Liefer, finish your Constitution."

# Chapter 31

Hester herself was probably as surprised as anyone else at her uncharacteristically impulsive proposal that the colony formally declare independence.

It caused a considerable stir throughout the community, but the dominant emotion it generated was one of relief. On reflection, though admittedly in a mood of some self-congratulation, Hester assessed the move as having been unusually perceptive.

It chimed with the mood of the majority of the people, severing as it did the last lingering emotional links with their old life. From then on, the community would go forward unfettered by the past; looking back only to learn from the mistakes of others.

Despite the illness of Taithur, morale was good. They had met and defeated their greatest fears, and even though the cost had been high, they had survived. And the effort of cooperating to meet this common enemy had pushed the colony far further forward into self-sufficiency than could have been expected under less difficult circumstances.

In addition, the capture of the battleship had added dramatically to their fighting capabilities. It provided them with substantial quantities of advanced weaponry, a large number of small and medium ships, extensive repair facilities and many other technological improvements which would help them in colonizing the planet, and give them access to other nearby systems.

Perhaps above all, however, was their perception of their new logistical position. Their own highly sophisticated scanners complemented by those of the battleship gave them an even greater range of observation, and the ability to cut through standard Fleet screening. It would be many months before sufficient of the battleship's crew were fit to undertake the return journey, and necessarily it would take them some years to reach home. Hester's carefully drafted message would not only tell of the colony's declaration of independence and offer peace and goodwill to their erstwhile masters, it would also say "leave us alone" in a manner that could be read as either plea or threat, but which carried the spectre of a great Fleet ship defeated by an ostensibly impoverished but determined people.

Whatever the political situation when this arrived, it would be as many years again before an attack force could possibly reach the colony, if it was not to be in the same debilitated condition as the first one. And when it did arrive, it would find itself expected and facing a foe that would be stronger by far than that which defeated the first expedition.

"If we maintain our watchfulness and our strength, we're guaranteed many years of peaceful development," she told the Council. "But we've learned enough from the newcomers and Terson to know that great forces for evil can grow unseen in even the most civilized of worlds. It would be naive to imagine that such forces can be forever defeated. Looking at the natives here, I fear they may be inherent in human nature itself. They merely slumber while they recover, and if we neglect our watchfulness, or allow ourselves to become weak, then we could find ourselves swept effortlessly from the skies or wake one day to find ourselves enslaved."

It was not however, from the Service and their old ties that the colony's next agony came. It came from both within and without.

"Someone's been dealing with the natives." Davar's statement cut into Hester like an assassin's knife. She squashed a flurry of alarm and looked up at him carefully.

He had been fretful for some time, but now she saw a man clutching for help. The chill inside her deepened, and afraid her voice might betray her fear she nodded to him to continue.

"One of the tribes has been putting up a lot of satellites recently," he said. "We picked it up during routine avoidance procedures."

Hester nodded.

"Jion got curious," Davar continued. "You know he's made a bit of a hobby studying these people. Anyway, he started doing some more detailed calculations in off-duty hours and he estimated that these satellites represented a highly improbable technological leap."

"How improbable?" Hester asked.

"This improbable," Davar replied, flicking on a display. Hester looked at the hovering symbols for a moment, then her eyes narrowed slightly and, without speaking, she nodded to him to continue.

"He told me what he'd found and we've been looking at it together. We kept it quiet of course. Didn't want to cause any undue alarm. It could just have been coincidence."

"Just," said Hester in cautious agreement.

"Well, it wasn't," Davar continued. "We decided to do some close surveillance and…" He hesitated.

"And?" Hester prompted.

"And we found they're developing weapons down there which are unmistakably crude versions of some of our own. They've no idea how to power them fully yet, thank God, but it still puts them centuries ahead of the other tribes."

Hester closed her eyes. "Anything else?" she said.

"Not really," Davar said. "We've only just confirmed this. I've come straight to you with it."

"Good," she said, standing up and walking over to the window. Down below her she could see the broad traffic ways of the City and in the distance the hazy blue buffer zone that kept the great ocean at bay. She rested her hand against the wall as if for balance. The Sea City had never been one of her favourites among the original bases. She knew it was imagination, but she always seemed to feel the sway of the surging ocean that carried it.

"We're too vulnerable here," she said abruptly, without turning round. "Not a word to anyone, but get up to the Rithid immediately, and take Jion with you. Contact Ersand and Newin and tell them to be there. I'll join you shortly with Proktor."

Hester heard Davar's acknowledgement, but did not move even when she heard the door humming shut as he left. For a moment she stood paralysed, until a childish thought formed itself and released her. My God, it isn't fair, it just isn't fair. Not after everything we've been through."

She smiled at it and mentally noted that that was to be the extent of her self-indulgence.

Fear of the potential within the natives had loomed large in her life for years. Costly procedures had been adopted and maintained to minimize all forms of contact with them other than those necessary for security, and even the watchers had had to be watched to avoid the risk of contamination. Now someone had wilfully contacted them and given them access to a technology they weren't remotely ready for. It was a uniquely horrible act, the outcome of which must surely be more death and destruction. There was even the possibility that the natives might succeed in doing what a Fleet battleship had failed to do, namely, destroy them.

Back on the Rithid she summarized Jion and Davar's finding briefly for the benefit of the others. There was a stunned silence.

She continued before any of them could speak.

"Finding out the extent of the interference with this tribe will be fairly easy. But we need to know who's doing it and why. And very urgently."

There seemed to be little need to debate. Proktor and Ersand spoke simultaneously. Opposites in every way, young and old, rash and thoughtful, they not infrequently agreed with each other these days.

"It's Vronic," they said. Jion and Davar nodded, Hester raised her eyebrows at this unanimous verdict, even though she agreed with it.

"Why?" she said coldly. "Granted, he didn't start out too auspiciously, but he's pulled his weight since and so have his people. Newin, he actually flew with you against that battleship, didn't he? And he made some very worthwhile contributions to our tactical plans for dealing with the Fleet. A touch of proof wouldn't go amiss before we condemn him."

Proktor scowled. "Just because he's neither cowardly nor stupid doesn't mean he's one of us. I'll concede that what you say is right. He's a considerable leader; look at the way he pulled that convoy together. But at what a cost. And he's a convicted criminal who joined that convoy under the most suspicious of circumstances, and may have had some part in Alfrad's death. Once the Fleet appeared on the scene, it was in his best interests to co-operate with us. He'd have got even shorter shrift than us if they'd won. As it was, he not only survived, he was rewarded."

"That's still no more than personal prejudice, Proktor," Hester retorted. "It's all circumstantial."

Before Proktor could reply, Jion turned on the display monitor.

256

"That's all we're going to be able to get, Hester," he said. "But here's a list of key personnel currently in Vronic's camp."

Hester examined the display. "So," she said. "These are all his old cronies, and the usual crowd that hang around him."

Jion spoke quietly. "If you remember, Hester, we deliberately broke up his old group. Gave some of them very good positions elsewhere. But they've all gravitated back to him even though they're worse off there."

Hester still refused to be particularly impressed.

"Do a full search of his camp population," she said. "See how many of them are those out of the convoy who've been moaning about the speed at which we're allocating surface space for them."

Jion nodded and set the floating symbols whirling busily.

"Then there's this," he said, activating another part of the display. "I only discovered this on the way up."

It was the current crew manifest for the Rithid.

The first display finished its search, and Hester looked at the two sets of symbols hovering in front of her.

She swore softly. "Everyone at Vronic's camp is a known malcontent or low contributor. And half our current engineering section are as well."

She adjusted the display and waited silently until the symbols steadied. "And at the next major shift change, the whole of our engineering section will be."

"Who's in charge of shift rotas?" Proktor asked. Hester seemed reluctant to answer. "Gared," she said eventually.

Action after that was quiet but swift and determined. It needed no great faculty of analysis to know that whoever controlled the Rithid could control the space around the planet and the information that was passed to it. The ship also had no small offensive capability following the stripping out of the battleship. It carried several fighters and some weaponry that could be used against the surface without the appalling destructiveness of its disruptors.

Within the hour, an engineering crew taken exclusively from the travellers had been shuttled up to the Rithid and discreetly replaced the existing crew, using vague excuses about an unscheduled sun-scour trip.

Having secured the ship, a full crew was taken aboard and a brief debate was held about the best course of action to be taken.

257

"Why's Vronic doing this?" Davar asked. "What's he hoping to achieve?"

"Who cares?" said Proktor. "He wasn't on a prison ship for nothing. He's a criminal. He doesn't think like ordinary people."

"I doubt he thinks at all," interposed Jion. "Doesn't he realize what these natives are like, He'll have no control over them if they go on the rampage, and they may well turn on him before it's all finished. He must surely know they'll start throwing their fission bombs at one another eventually." He stopped. "Unless…"

"Unless what?" Hester asked.

Jion stared into space vacantly for a moment. Proktor shifted impatiently. "Unless he wants to force us out into the open," he said slowly. "He's starting a train of events that'll mean we have to intervene. Perhaps he'll be looking to gain something from the disruption that'll cause to our long-term plans. He's always said we'll have to 'deal' with the natives eventually. He's always thought of them as a potential slave labour force."

Hester looked at him, and then round the table. No-one spoke.

"I think that's as near as we're going to get," she said. "We can think about Vronic's motives later, but what Jion says is true. From what I can remember of these natives, the main tribes keep one another at bay by threat of mutual annihilation. If one thought it could overwhelm the others without triggering that response, then it would. Am I correct, Jion?"

Jion nodded. "Near enough," he said. "And there's always a precarious balance in the leadership of each tribe between those who would risk such a venture, and those who wouldn't."

"And your immediate assessment of the position now, Jion?" Hester said.

Jion hesitated. "I'll really need to look at it much more carefully. This has all happened very suddenly, but offhand I'd say that Vronic's already tipped the balance."

Hester put her head in her hands, and sat motionless for a long time. When she looked up, her face was drawn and her eyes shone with tears.

"If he hasn't tipped it yet, he will soon," she said. "And we can't take any action against him now because our evidence is still circumstantial. If we call him to account, his people will doubtless continue his work while he's wasting our time lying. And if we take vigorous action against him it'll be illegal by our own lights and we'll make ourselves highly visible. It seems to me the question we face is not whether we contact these people, but quite simply when."

Later Hester went to see Taithur sitting alone with Malva in an observation dome high on the ship. He smiled when she entered and held out his hand to take hers. It was warm and gentle and Hester had once again that day to fight down tears. It was a peculiarly harrowing feature of distortion fever that it left the body sound and whole while it damaged the mind.

"Trouble?" he said unexpectedly as he caught her eye. Hester started. "I..." she began, but her voice failed. She sank to her knees, and resting her head in his lap sobbed out the whole tale. He placed his hand on her head and listened patiently.

Eventually her sobbing faded and she lifted up her head to look at him. "Taith, I'm sorry," she said, wiping her eyes incongruously on her sleeve. "I shouldn't bother you. I've let you down. I don't know what to do. Everything's slipping away." She glanced nervously at Malva, fearing the reproach in her eyes for this further burdening of her husband. But Malva was smiling.

"Today's been a good day," she said simply.

Taithur leaned forward and looked into Hester's eyes. "This had to happen, Hester, you know that. It would have been painful at any time. But you do know what to do, don't you? You and Proktor. You know exactly what to do. Don't be afraid."

"I don't understand," Hester said.

Taithur smiled. "Yes you do," he said. "Don't be afraid."

Hester reached forward and embraced him. When she released him, he was gazing fixedly out at the wispy edges of the galaxy.

# Chapter 32

Even as Hester began planning how to deal with Vronic and his supporters, matters were taken from her hands by the natives.

Jion's estimate might have been offhand but it was all too accurate. The technology that Vronic had passed to the natives more than tilted the balance of power that had for decades separated the major tribes.

Armed with it, the hawks amongst the Eastern Bloc leadership emerged to centre stage and stood triumphant over their more moderate comrades.

Using guidance and surveillance systems far beyond their most advanced technology, their troops smashed their way through neighbouring countries in days while the defenders found themselves powerless. They stood by radar equipment that refused to function, and died in tanks and aeroplanes that were being destroyed by an enemy they could not even see.

The leaders of the Western Bloc floundered. Blinded by the new-found technology they were powerless to act and were suddenly desperately fearful for their own safety.

Recriminations thundered to and fro across what passed for an international forum but the Easterners continued consolidating their advance while denying everything and attributing the worldwide loss in communications to sun spots.

Vronic sat nervously in his headquarters. It would not take Hester long to deduce the cause of this conflagration. Thank God the Rithid was away on sun-scour. Those damned savages, why hadn't they waited for his instructions? It beggared belief. Still, the cat was out of the bag with a vengeance, and with a bit of luck he'd be able to do very nicely out of the ensuing chaos. It wouldn't be the first time he'd had to think on his feet.

But the Rithid was not on sun-scour. It was on station watching developments intently.

"Enough," said Hester eventually. "There's more than enough evidence now. Proktor, contact the Chief of these… Easterners. Identify us and tell him to cease hostilities immediately."

"They won't respond to that," Jion said. "They're a hard people. They're almost straight out of the darker reaches of the Adjustment Department, but with fewer redeeming features. They'll respond only to superior force."

Hester looked at him, and then at a summary of the destruction that had been wrought in the last few days. Such patience as she had had for these people had evaporated very quickly at the sight of such wanton devastation. She sighed. "Very well, a lesson it has to be then. Contact this Chief—name one of their cities—tell him he has half an hour to respond and if he doesn't, destroy it. Continue every half hour until they see sense. And see if you can thin their troops out a bit as well."

She looked at her friends. "This is truly appalling, but far less than the Adjustment Department would have done. Whatever Vronic had in mind, I doubt it was this, but we've nowhere to go but forward. From what I understand of these people, it's only a matter of time before the other side starts firing their missiles, and then we'll have a real mess to clean up. As for Vronic and his cronies, enough's enough. I'd welcome your comments, but I intend to use my authority as leader to order the destruction of his base."

She looked at the pale faces around her. No-one argued with the decision. Vronic had brought it on himself. His actions were jeopardizing the whole community.

"Newin," she said. "Vronic's armoured his E C shield so we can't touch him from up here. You and your men are going to have to go in low and fast."

Newin nodded. Hester looked grave. "Take care Newin. That base'll be heavily defended. You'll have one run with surprise on your side and that's all. If Vronic scrambles fighters, you're going to have a real problem, and we won't be able to help you unless you can draw them out into space."

I must be as savage as the savages if we're to win, she thought, as she watched him leave. Damn you, Vronic. Damn you to Hell for making me as foul as you.

"Could have been worse," Hester concluded later. They had had to destroy several cities before the Easterners believed what was happening, and this had led to the discharging of several missiles from their submarines. Two Western Bloc submarines succeeded in discharging theirs in retaliation before Davar was able to jam all their guidance systems.

"Sorry about that, Hester," he said apologetically. But Hester was in a comparatively rosy mood.

"I don't think they're going to be much of a problem, Davar," she said. "We can sweep up any hotspots, although I think it's going to take its toll amongst the natives. They're far more vulnerable to radiation than we are. Sad, that."

Vronic succeeded in making a last stand, escaping just as Newin's fighters hissed in and obliterated his base in a single blazing run. A superb pilot, Vronic skimmed and dodged across the planet's surface for forty minutes, destroying one of Newin's flight before they managed to bring him down. The impact of his crash razed a large portion of a major capital city.

At a Council Meeting, Newin was honoured for his action and Hester was confirmed as Leader with Newin as deputy until such time as Liefer could finish his Constitution. Taithur did not attend. He had recovered greatly from his fever, but did not seem to have the concentration to handle matters of administration. He preferred to stay in his high starry dome gazing out into space, and talking softly to his wife. But he nodded sadly when Hester told him what had happened.

"You had no choice, Hester. None of us did, ever. Sadly, Vronic was right. I'd hoped for a better way, and certainly a better future for these poor souls, but it wasn't to be. Take as much care of them as you can."

At the Council meeting a start was made on determining an entirely new policy for the colonization of the planet. Hester was formal and radiant.

"My friends. This is a new beginning for us. Not the one we would have chosen, but one we must accept. We're as secure from assault by the Fleet as it is possible to be, and with careful husbandry we'll become more so in time. We're no longer threatened by the natives to any great extent, and we've torn out much of the evil that had grown in our midst. But the cost has been born mainly by others, and we owe them a debt of care which we must give as unstintingly as we can.

"With the destruction of so many of the natives we've been relieved of many of the constraints that have made life so hard for us here. We can build our communities where we wish now and begin the task of bringing this tainted world back into balance.

"As for the natives themselves, their plight is indeed tragic. Their tribal societies have been smashed by their conflict, and millions of people were killed. Many of the remainder are suffering badly from radiation sickness and, sadly, from illnesses that we have given them—illnesses trivial to us, but fatal to them. They're also suffering from the terrible shock that must follow such a catastrophic meeting of two cultures. For the most part they're lost and bewildered and well deserving of our compassion.

"Understandably, some of them resent our presence and, with the residue of Vronic's supporters will doubtless take up arms against us. It will be to no avail, of course, but I'm afraid more blood will yet be spilled. That said, we must be as tolerant as we can be of their savagery and Return them only as a last extremity. Our watchwords, I think, must be firmness and fairness. I'm sure they'll respond to that in time.

"As a first step towards the rehabilitation of these people, I shall shortly be meeting their leading Chiefs. I will put to them the proposal that their people be moved from their ruined cities and placed in special reserved areas where they can be properly housed and tended. In time we may be able to offer more, but our own development must come first and we still have much to do. If peaceful resettlement can be achieved, we can start to look after the education of their young, and within a generation or so it may be possible to let them emerge into civilized society, and take up the lives that our great guide Taithur always wished for them."

There was prolonged applause.